A SHOCKING DEBUT

The play was going well. The Guv'nor seemed to have regained most of his stamina and was charming the audience in his usual manner. They were eating out of his hand. I stood behind the prompt and watched from the wings. Scene Three finished and I saw Hamlet, Rosencrantz, and Guildenstern gathered opposite me, with Maurice Withers as Fortineras on my side of the stage waiting to go on. The lights were not dimmed for the brief scene change; it was a simple matter for the backdrop to come rolling down and the scene to start. At a cue from me, Sam Green and his men sent the backdrop rolling down. There was a sudden gasp from the audience, followed by a scream from Edwina Price, the prompt. The scream startled me since Miss Price normally never uttered a word during a performance, unless called upon to prompt.

"Lights! Douse the lights!" Someone responding faster than me shouted the order, but the lights remained steadily burning. I saw the reason for the commotion and leapt forward.

As the scene backdrop unfolded, something that had been rolled up inside it came bouncing out. It was a severed human head!

CURSED
in the ACT

Raymond Buckland

BERKLEY PRIME CRIME, NEW YORK

THE BERKLEY PUBLISHING GROUP
Published by the Penguin Group
Penguin Group (USA) LLC
375 Hudson Street, New York, New York 10014

USA • Canada • UK • Ireland • Australia • New Zealand • India • South Africa • China

penguin.com

A Penguin Random House Company

CURSED IN THE ACT

Berkley Prime Crime Books are published by The Berkley Publishing Group.
BERKLEY® PRIME CRIME and the PRIME CRIME logo are trademarks of
Penguin Group (USA) LLC.

Berkley Prime Crime trade paperback ISBN: 978-0-425-26801-8

An application to register this book for cataloging has been submitted
to the Library of Congress.

PUBLISHING HISTORY
Berkley Prime Crime trade paperback edition / January 2014

PRINTED IN THE UNITED STATES OF AMERICA

10   9   8   7   6   5   4   3   2   1

Cover illustration by Bill Angresano.
Cover design by Diana Kolsky.
Interior text design by Tiffany Estreicher.

To Tara and in loving memory of "Tish"

ACKNOWLEDGMENTS

Many thanks to my wonderful agent, Grace Morgan, for her enthusiasm and tenacity, and to the beautiful and talented Michelle Vega of Berkley Prime Crime for sharing that enthusiasm. Thanks to Marianne Grace for her excellence in copyediting, and to artist Bill Angresano and designer Diana Kolsky for the eye-catching cover. Thanks to all the many people at Berkley Prime Crime who have contributed to the production of this book. I am extremely grateful.

Thanks also to the Killbuck Valley Writers' Guild for listening and critiquing over the years—stalwarts Barb Lang, Denice Rovira Hazlett, Ed Schrock, Michele Brown Skolmuch, Susan Corl, Bruce Stambaugh, Jennifer McCluggage, Leslie Keating, and Nöraa Hazlett. And special thanks to my wife, Tara, for her constant encouragement and always brilliant constructive criticisms.

Chapter One

London, 1881

There was a light dusting of snow, though not enough to hide traces of the filth and detritus that covered street and pavement at all hours of the day and night. There was enough built up in the gutters to camouflage the edge of the curb and make stepping off it a hazard. At that late hour, with the theatre district finally deserted, traffic was no longer heavy in the heart of London. The gaslights outside the Lyceum Theatre had been extinguished, although one solitary mantle still burned over the side entrance. A sign above it read *STAGE DOOR* in faded, weatherworn letters. I held my coat collar up and tight about my ears and pulled my bowler hat down more firmly on my head as I approached the theatre.

Ahead of me a hansom cab pulled in close to the entrance and a tall man in a heavy Inverness coat got out. The cab moved away, its wheels muffled as it passed over the snow-covered cobblestones. The man held on to the brim of his top hat as a gust of wind blew around the corner, stirring his cape and swirling eddies of fresh snow into miniature white whirlwinds. He hurried inside the theatre, the door banging closed behind him.

"Mr. Stoker has got there before me," I muttered to myself. "So much for making a good impression."

Not that I needed to make an impression, good or bad. My position was secure, I knew. I had been Mr. Bram Stoker's stage manager for three years now and we got along well . . . as well as any employer and employee might. I hurried forward and pushed through the stage door.

"Good evening, Bill."

Old Bill Thomas, head buried in a copy of the *Sporting Times*, barely glanced up as I passed his cubicle. I wondered, not for the first time, if the man lived there. It seemed he was always behind his little window no matter what time of the day or night I entered or left the theatre. Bill was the doorman, keeping out the riffraff while acknowledging the cast and crew.

It had been an odd sort of a day, even for a Henry Irving first night. First nights were always full of nervous actors, prima donnas, and unforeseen crises. Actors forgot lines they had repeated innumerable times; props got mysteriously moved from where I—as stage manager—had carefully placed them; scenery that had been securely fastened threatened to fall down. But on this occasion there had been an added distraction . . . Mr. Henry Irving had been poisoned.

I remember the scene—it will be a very long time before I forget it—with Mr. Irving, face like that of a dead man, leaning against the jamb of the door into his dressing room. Miss Ellen Terry was admonishing him to go to bed.

"You cannot go on, Henry. Admit it. Why, you can hardly stand up straight."

"I can stand perfectly well, Ellen."

"The doctor says you have probably been poisoned. Come now! You have an understudy who is able to take over."

The little group in the passageway outside the Guv'nor's dressing room turned briefly to look at Mr. Peter Richland, the understudy in question. He did not inspire confidence. Mr. Irving's voice could fill the theatre, from the pit all the way up to the gods. Mr. Richland's voice reflected more the weaknesses of the Prince of Denmark. All eyes turned back to Mr. Irving.

"It is a first night," he said, a little of his usual fire breaking through. "I have never missed a first night in my life, nor will I."

"It may well become a last night if you do not follow your doctor's advice," said Miss Terry.

I glanced at Mr. Stoker, now helping support Mr. Irving, who was already in costume. Whether or not he had applied makeup I couldn't say; his face was so colorless. I then looked at Dr. Cochran, hovering in the background behind this pale figure of Hamlet. He was fidgeting with items in his bag and was obviously trying not to be drawn into the argument.

"I have made my decision!" The Guv'nor pushed himself away from the doorpost, patted Mr. Stoker on the shoulder, and then lurched back into his dressing room. "Where's that callboy? Must be overture and beginners by now, isn't it?"

The drama offstage was frequently a match for that onstage, I had come to realize. Happily, I was still young enough to adjust. At twenty-two I, Harry Rivers, had been delighted to obtain employment at London's famous Lyceum Theatre, home of England's prominent Shakespearean actor Henry Irving. I had dabbled in stagecraft during my education at the Hounslow Masonic Institution for Boys, which I attended courtesy of the Honorable Gregory Moffatt. I should explain that I am not of that class by any means, but my father, a blacksmith, had done a great deal of work for the Hon. Mr. Moffatt (third son of Baron Runnymede) and that gentleman had looked kindly upon me. There were one hundred and fifty boys at the school, taught by three masters. We were drilled in Greek, Latin, French, German, mathematics, history, and geography. I did not excel in any one of these subjects.

My mother died trying, unsuccessfully, to bring my brother into the world. My father passed soon after that, so, at the age of fourteen, I had been forced to come to London to seek my fortune. After a few rough years as a crossing sweeper, errand boy, and newspaper seller, I began working as a cabdriver and thus met the owner of the small Novelty Theatre on Great Queen Street, Lincoln's Inn Fields. Through this acquaintance, I obtained the job of theatre doorman. When I later heard that Mr. Irving was to take over the running of the Lyceum—a much more prestigious theatre—I applied for a position there. Apparently Mr. Irving had brought over from Ireland a Mr. Abraham Stoker, a theatre critic who had written very favorably of Mr. Irving's performances in that country. Mr. Stoker became the Lyceum's business manager and I became stage manager . . . a job with which I fell in love.

I worked closely with Mr. Stoker and also became his personal assistant. I came to admire him a great deal, although I have to admit, even after three years, that I still could be caught off guard by some of his idiosyncrasies. He was not afraid to display his emotions and, despite a fine business sense, backed by years at the best Irish university, was easily swept up by tales of ancient Irish lore and legend. He openly believed in ghosts, sixth senses, and even "the little people," and spent what little spare time he had writing his own stories. I must admit that I would not change my employment for any other.

But now, Henry Irving had been poisoned. Happily, he had survived, although he was severely incapacitated, and Mr. Stoker and I had vowed to determine who was responsible. After all, if Mr. Irving died, the two of us would be out of a job.

"Sit down, Harry."

I moved across the small office and perched on the edge of a straight-backed chair, close to the theatre manager's old and battered desk. It wasn't really a desk as such; it was an ancient kitchen table. I knew that Mr. Stoker had brought it across from Ireland with him when he came to the Lyceum Theatre three years ago. He called it his "lucky table." It had once been the family table at his home in Clontarf, a suburb of Dublin. Mr. Stoker—known to close associates as Bram, though Mr. Irving always insisted on using the full Abraham—had told me how he had grown up leaning on that table when, for the first seven years of his life, he had been barely able to walk. He had gone on to recover, had entered Trinity College, and had taken the table with him to his study where he advanced to graduate with honors. I knew that the old table was dear to him, full of memories. Right now the top surface was almost completely covered with papers: playbills, programs, call sheets, and innumerable scraps of paper with scribbled notes on them.

"How's the Guv'nor?" I asked. Everyone called Mr. Irving "the Guv'nor."

Stoker fingered his bushy mustache and looked at me with one piercing gray green eye; the other eye scrunched up. I knew that meant he was worried, though he'd never admit it.

"He should never have gone on tonight."

"We all tried to tell him," I said. Not that anyone can tell Mr. Irving anything he does not want to hear. "Peter Richland was beside himself, of course. This is the fourth or fifth time that he's been ready to go on and the Guv'nor has made a comeback."

Stoker nodded his large head. "I feel for him," he said. "Always the understudy and never the star. Must be very frustrating."

"I thought Mr. Irving was going to take ill at the start of Scene Five. He said the line 'Alas, poor ghost!' and then began that terrible retching cough, and I think he actually held on to a flat at one point."

"Mmm." Again Mr. Stoker nodded.

"Doctor Cochran says he doesn't know what poisoned him. At first he thought it might just be food poisoning, but then he decided that it was far more serious than that. He said the Guv'nor's lucky he didn't die."

"You can't kill Henry Irving."

"I agree, sir," I said. "But someone certainly tried."

Because it was opening night Mr. Irving had insisted that the police not be called. The performance should have been postponed, with the star so desperately ill, but there had been a rush to open before the Sadler's Wells Theatre launched their production of *Twelfth Night,* starring Philius Pheebes-Watson as Malvolio and Gladys Stringer as Olivia. There had been a keen rivalry between the two theatres ever since Mrs. Bateman had left as manager of the Lyceum and taken up the same position at Sadler's Wells.

Just ten years ago in 1871, Mr. Hezekiah Linthicum Bateman, an American, had taken over the lease of the Lyceum and assembled a company with Henry Irving heading it. When the Guv'nor did a widely acclaimed performance of Mathias in *The Bells,* he became something of a major player on the London stage. Four years later Bateman died, leaving his widow in charge of the theatre. Mrs. Bateman was capable but not really able to manage such a massive undertaking, and she relinquished the Lyceum in 1878 and moved to Sadler's Wells Theatre. The Guv'nor then took over the Lyceum's lease and, with the extremely capable assistance of Abraham Stoker as theatre manager, built up a formidable reputation for the theatre.

Mrs. Bateman and Mr. Irving did not get along. I should say that they *had not* got along . . . At the beginning of January Mrs. Bateman had gone to join her husband. However, her place had been taken by her eldest daughter Kate. Kate—almost forty years of age—had married the actor George Crowe. The Guv'nor felt no friendlier toward Mrs. Crowe than he had toward her mother.

"Where is the Guv'nor now?" I asked.

"I finally managed to send him off home to bed. Not to stir until tomorrow night's performance."

It was my turn to nod. When the curtain had come down—and after the usual number of curtain calls—the cast had dispersed to their various abodes, and both Mr. Stoker and myself had slipped out for a bite of supper. As usual after an opening, we had come back to the theatre for a quick review before going home ourselves.

"It was a good house," I said.

My employer did not immediately respond. I studied his dark auburn hair—a far cry from my own "ginger" carrot red mop. Funny we should both be redheads, I thought. Perhaps his six feet and two inches compared to my puny five feet and six inches affected hair color in some way? Or his thirty-three years of age to my twenty-two? In the flickering lamplight I saw that Stoker's generous beard and mustache were already highlighted with the slightest touches of silver gray. Bram Stoker was married to his work and carried the burden of the entire Lyceum Theatre, with its more than three hundred employees. He kept a finger on every aspect of the enterprise, from the payroll to the actors and actresses, the scenery builders, the front of house, programs, advertising . . . everything. I don't think he had much time to spend with Mrs. Stoker or even their young son. I had heard rumors that the marriage was not a happy one, though I tried not to listen to gossip.

"I'll be interested to see what the critics have to say," he said, and sighed. "They are never willing to give an inch, no matter the circumstances."

"Not that they would know about the poisoning," I responded.

"Oh, they'll know." His big head nodded once again, slowly, up and down. "Theatre tittle-tattle is the life's blood of critics. Believe me, Harry, they'll know."

It was nearly an hour later that I locked the office door and left the theatre. Mr. Stoker had, reluctantly it seemed to me, dragged himself away ahead of me and asked Bill Thomas to find him a hansom. When Bill would leave, I had no idea. Thoughts of Mr. Henry Irving's poisoner could wait until tomorrow yet could not be disregarded. Someone had tried to poison the Guv'nor and we needed to know who and why. Bill Thomas had suggested that we might consider Herbert Willis.

"He was always trouble," Bill had said.

It was true, though Bill did tend to think the worst of just about everyone. Willis was a stagehand and Mr. Stoker had let him go because he had been inebriated on the job once too often. He left shouting curses at the Lyceum—which I think disturbed Mr. Stoker more than he would admit—but it seemed too early to think of Willis as a would-be murderer.

I set out through the dwindling snow in the direction of Chancery Lane. My gloomy rooms at Mrs. Bell's establishment were never an attraction, but I knew that at least I'd find a cup of cocoa waiting for me and perhaps a scuttle full of coal in my room, to bank up a bright, warm fire.

It was my job to pick up copies of all the major newspapers on the morning following a first night. Although theatre managers, producers, and especially the actors themselves may pooh-pooh the opinions of the critics, those opinions can make or mar a production costing hundreds of pounds. I bought the *Times*, *Morning Herald*, *Daily News*, and *Morning Chronicle*. The more important *Era*, *Stage Directory*, and *Referee*, all of which focus on the theatre, were all weekly publications, so we would have to wait to see what they had to say. With the newsprint under my arm, I hurried into the theatre and made for Mr. Stoker's office. I found the big man already there, a copy of the *Times* spread out across his desk and his gold-rimmed spectacles perched on the bridge of his nose.

"I got that," I said, indicating the *Times*. I couldn't help adding, "As I always do."

He grunted and stabbed a finger at a column near the top of an inside page.

"Did you see what our Mr. Matthew Burgundy has to say?"

"I haven't read anything yet, sir." I was, perhaps, a little testy. "I only just got here."

He ignored my impertinence. "The old fool says that the Guv'nor 'was not up to his usual brisk portrayal, making of the tragedy a veritable dirge.' I ask you!"

"Perhaps he doesn't know of the poisoning," I suggested.

"Oh, he knows, Harry! He knows."

We went through the other reviews. The *Morning Chronicle* critic seemed to think that the Guv'nor's hesitations and clutching at his stomach were all part of a new characterization and applauded it. Obviously that gentleman did *not* know of the poisoning. The rest seemed to share the opinion of the *Times*'s critic.

"Well, not as bad as it might have been." I tried to sound hopeful.

Stoker grunted. He seemed to do a lot of grunting. He stood up, slipped off his spectacles, and consulted his gold pocket watch, which was a treasured gift from Mr. Irving.

"What d'you have to do today, Harry?"

I, too, stood up. The review of the reviews was over and there was work to be done.

"I need to go through the properties after last night's performance—I noticed Arthur Swindon moving things around. Then David wants me to look at the lights for Scene . . ."

"Never mind all that." The big man cleared a patch of space on the top of his desk and pulled down a ledger from the shelf behind his seat. "I want you to get on over to Sadler's Wells and have a dig around, Harry. I've got a suspicion those people know more about poison than they need to for the sake of treading the boards. You're on friendly terms with their doorman, are you not?" He opened the ledger and replaced his spectacles.

I tugged at my wispy red mustache and wished, not for the first time, that I could manage to grow a beard. So much more impressive to pensively tug on a beard than on one's naked chin

"Yes, sir," I said. "Old George Dale has been around for centuries it seems. Everyone knows George. I'll get on over there."

I would much have preferred to stay inside the Lyceum. Drafty as it was, it was still warmer than outdoors in the winter wind. The snow had stopped falling just before dawn and there was even a slight hint of sun, somewhere high up above the ever-present mist that forever blew and drifted off the river. I felt in my pocket for change and, finding a little, decided to take a cab to Rosebery Avenue, Clerkenwell, the home of Sadler's Wells Theatre.

Clerkenwell is on the border of Islington, a neighborhood that is not the most salubrious yet is not bad enough to detract the theatre-goers from attending Sadler's Wells, when their productions are of note. The theatre had, in the distant past, presented such luminaries as Edmund Kean and Joseph Grimaldi, but it had fluctuated between being a legitimate theatre and being a home for pantomime and variety. It had finally been condemned as a dangerous structure in 1878—just three years ago—but it was then refurbished and reopened the following year with Mrs. Bateman, and now Mrs. Crowe, at the helm.

At that hour of the morning the roads were busy with the comings and goings of the gentlemen of the city. Hansoms and growlers were now supplemented by lumbering horse-drawn omnibuses, wagons, drays, delivery carts, and private carriages. The hansom I obtained seemed unable or unwilling to overtake any other vehicle, no matter how slowly it was moving, and I sat behind the leather apron tapping my foot on the floor and inwardly cursing at the time we were wasting. I was sure that Mr. Stoker had good reason to send me on this errand—the poisoning of the Guv'nor was surely cause enough—but I could not clear my head of the one thousand and one little jobs that I knew awaited me back at the theatre.

Eventually my vehicle pulled over to the side of the road and the trapdoor above my head opened.

"'Ere you are, guv. Right as rain!"

Even from where I sat, I felt assaulted by the breath of the cabdriver. Surely he must have breakfasted on beer and garlic—a fearsome combination. I paid him and jumped down to the pavement as he cracked his whip. The elderly nag lurched away back into the line of traffic.

I found George Dale as ever, eyes half closed as he peered through the dirty eyepieces of his pince-nez, looking at me and at the world passing by his little window over the top of the morning newspaper. Unlike our Bill Thomas, George was not especially conscientious as a doorman. He observed those who came and went but did little to verify their authority to be in the theatre.

"'Arry Rivers, as I live and breathe," he said, when his eyes finally focused on me. "Thought you was dead and gorn these many years."

"Oh, come on, George," I said. "Why, I saw you only a month or so back. In fact I bought you a drink, if you recall?"

He squinted his eyes and tugged at an earlobe. "Well, maybe you did and maybe you didn't. I won't let it stop you from buying me another."

"Can you leave your post for long enough to kill a porter?" I asked. "Or a Reid's stout? As I recall that was always your poison of choice. I would like to have a word or three with you, if I may?"

Explaining that he was never missed unless there was an emergency, George pried his large frame out of his cubbyhole and let me lead him across the street to the Bag o' Nails tavern, a favorite of the Sadler's Wells' employees. He breathed laboriously and wheezed as though it were a great effort. I was always afraid that he might suddenly drop dead, but he had been that way as long as I'd known him. We had no difficulty finding a corner table at that hour, and he slumped down into the chair. Soon the two of us were sipping on large glasses of a good, dark stout. George finally looked up at me, a line of froth across his hairless top lip.

"So, what is it you're after, young 'Arry? You don't go buying me no liquid 'freshment without there being a reason."

I studied my drink for a moment before answering.

"Quite right, George. Not that I don't enjoy your company . . . occasionally. But I was wondering, what can you tell me about the Sadler's Wells' scuttlebutt? We opened Mr. Irving's new production of *Hamlet* last night. What was the reaction here? I can't believe Mr. Philius Pheebes-Watson doesn't have some comment." Mr. Pheebes-Watson was to Sadler's Wells what Henry Irving was to the Lyceum. He played the lead in all of their Shakespearean productions. To my mind Philius was a faint echo of the Guv'nor . . . and far too full of himself. He imagined himself the Guv'nor's equal, but his command of the stage was sadly lacking.

"Oh!" George allowed himself a broad grin, displaying a mouthful of rotting teeth. "Old Philly 'ad a comment or two, believe me! 'E's such an 'am, that man. Considers 'isself one of our nation's premier Shakespearean traggy . . . tragedy . . ."

"Tragedians?" I offered.

He nodded. "That's it. Mind you, 'e was beside 'isself at the thought of old Irving being poisoned."

I sat up straight. "He knew about that?"

George nodded and took another mouthful of Reid's. I waited.

"Ev'ryone knew about that," he said, finally. "The old lady—Mrs. Crowe—could talk about nothin' else. She fairly crowed." He chuckled at his weak joke.

I set down my glass and leaned forward. "Listen, George. And this is important. Just when was it that Mrs. Crowe first made mention of Mr. Irving's problem? Think carefully. Exactly when did she first say something about it?"

George's rheumy eyes fastened on mine and he was silent for a moment. He could see that I was being very serious. He even allowed the hand gripping his glass of stout to sink slowly down to rest on the table. He squinted his eyes behind his dusty spectacles.

"I can't be absolutely certain, of course, but I'd say I over'eard 'er tellin' Mr. Pheebes-Watson and Miss Stringer in the lunch break yesterday. She—Mrs. Crowe—always takes a spot of lunch at a card table in the OP corner when re'ears-als is going. Bit o' pork pie, as I recall. She was sayin' as 'ow they couldn't relax just 'cause Mr. Irving was going to be taken ill. They still needed to do a good job with our *Twelfth Night*."

"Mrs. Crowe regularly sits in the Opposite Prompt corner? And you're certain that was at lunchtime yesterday?"

"Oh yes . . . well, *fairly* certain." His glass was up at his mouth again, but finding it almost empty, he waggled it at me. "Throat's getting a mite dry with all this talkin', 'Arry. Oh, and a dozen oysters would slip down real easy."

I waved for the girl.

"The Guv'nor was not taken ill until the tea break. Am I not right, sir?" I asked.

Stoker acquiesced.

"How, then," I continued, "could Mrs. Crowe have known about it an hour or more before?"

"A very good question, Harry. One that we must pursue." He looked at me pensively. "Unless, of course, she is blessed with the sight." I didn't respond. It seemed to me that my boss frequently tried to lure me into discussion of his Irish superstitions and, especially, of his old granny's supposed second sight. When I didn't comment, he continued. "By the way, Dr. Cochran now is of the opinion that it was arse-nic that laid low our star."

"Rat poison!" I said. "Found in every house in London, I don't doubt, and most certainly in all the theatres."

The big man allowed himself a faint smile, something I seldom saw.

"What?" I asked.

"Nothing," he replied, and then smiled again. "I was just thinking back to that performance of *Macbeth* . . . when was it? 1879? About late autumn, was it not?"

I remembered and chuckled. "The rat?"

He nodded. "Act Two, Scene One. There was the Guv'nor, with John Saxon as I recall, as Banquo, when this huge rat comes scuttling onto the stage."

"Ah yes! What was it the Guv'nor said?" I asked.

"He pointed at the creature, swinging his arm across as it made for the prompt corner, and cried, 'Art thou for Duncan?'"

"I recall that half the audience believed we had trained a rat to play that part." I laughed.

"Well," he said, suddenly somber again, "there is certainly good reason to keep the rat poison on hand. The question is, Harry, how did it get into the Guv'nor's food and who was it who put it there?"

There was a tap at the door.

"Come!"

The door opened tentatively and Bill Thomas's worried face peered in. I knew something important must have happened to pry Bill loose from his cubicle.

"Well?" snapped the boss.

"Begging your pardon, Mr. Stoker. But we've just received word that the understudy, Mr. Richland, has been killed."

Chapter Two

I didn't know Peter Richland very well. He was the under-study to Mr. Irving for all of the Lyceum productions. Everyone knew that the Guv'nor would never fail to appear, so there was really no chance that Richland would ever have to stand in. If he had, I would hate to think of the reaction there would have been from both the audience and fellow thespians. It would have been a major disappointment not to see Mr. Irving as Hamlet, and to top that, Mr. Richland could never carry the part in anything like the manner of the Guv'nor. Exactly why Mr. Irving kept him on in that position I have no idea.

The man was—had been, I suppose I must now say—a pale-faced introvert whose only intercourse with his fellow actors and actresses was to complain that he was "ill used." He did, I must admit, somewhat resemble Mr. Irving in stature, which I'm sure is why he was first employed, but his voice had nowhere near the quality nor the carrying power. He would stand in the wings, dressed appropriately for the part being played by the Guv'nor, and mouth the words as Mr. Irving uttered them onstage. He even made gestures as he mimed the character. Then he would hurry off to his dressing room to change for the next scene and return to stand beside the prompt and continue his solitary work, just in case the Guv'nor should collapse in mid-performance.

Peter Richland was the only understudy employed as such. Other parts were understudied by other players— minor characters ready to take over for major players if necessary. Peter Richland had nothing else to occupy his time. I could see how that could wear on a man. Especially when Mr. Irving might meet with some slight injury—or even a major setback, as with this poisoning—and then, just as Peter Richland believed his chance at glory had come, the Guv'nor would shake off the pain and, in true theatre tradition, go on to give his usual outstanding performance, leaving Richland once again standing in the wings.

Mr. Stoker called the cast together onstage an hour or so before the next performance. Along with front of house staff and stagehands, I sat down in the front row of the stalls and listened to what he had to say. Above me, the gaslit chandeliers burned in wine-colored shades. The auditorium and front of house were still lit by gas; only the stage lighting had been changed over to the new electricity. I was surrounded by the myrtle green and cream and purple background of the gilt moldings, frescoes, and medallions. A truly beautiful auditorium giving an atmosphere of great luxury, it seemed to me. I was always impressed by it, as I'm sure were most of the patrons.

I was not a little surprised to see Mr. Henry Irving himself stride onto the stage. His face was pale, but then it was always pale without his makeup. He held himself up straight, as though to prove that he was not affected by the poison. I did, however, notice that he carried a tumbler of water, from which he sipped repeatedly.

"Ladies and gentlemen," he said, his face turning to look directly at his loyal cast. He always appeared to me to be acting a part, even when just being himself. He could be very dramatic on the most ordinary of occasions. But this was no ordinary occasion. "You have by now, I am sure, heard of the passing of our fellow thespian Mr. Peter Richland, a stalwart member of our company for some time. Some of you may not be aware of the fact that this good fellow served his time in theatres about this great country of ours, his formative years spent with the late, great Mr. Ronald Foxit's Shakespearean Company."

We all knew that Foxit's company was a ramshackle affair that operated on a threadbare budget and played only the smallest of provincial theatres. Mr. Irving made it sound as though it had been grand and noteworthy. I thought I saw some of the people onstage—John Saxon for one and Guy Purdy for another—smirking and winking at their neighbors. Mr. Irving seemed not to notice.

"How did he die, Henry?"

Miss Ellen Terry had joined the cast onstage, unnoticed by most, and now she stepped forward. Brought into the Lyceum to be Mr. Irving's principal actress when Mrs. Bateman left as manager, she had distinguished herself in the classical dramas. She was loved and adored by all: her fellow thespians, the Lyceum audiences, and even the critics. I had heard Mr. Stoker comment on her beautiful voice and claim that she was "endowed with one of those magnetically sympathetic natures, the rarest and most precious quality a performer can have." She now stood quietly, in a simple white dress with her long blond hair piled up on her head, and looked directly at the Guv'nor.

"He was run down by a carriage," said Irving, tossing off the line as though part of a theatrical scene. "I need not distress you with details of the trauma he apparently suffered, my dear. It would appear, from the Metropolitan Police report, that he may have left the theatre after last night's performance and then spent time—perhaps some considerable time—in our neighborly tavern, the Druid's Head."

There were murmurs and smiles, with heads nodding, since all at the Lyceum were familiar with that particular watering hole.

"From there," continued the Guv'nor, "he would seem to have blundered out into the late night traffic and . . . met his fate."

There were further murmurs and muttered comments.

"I understand that there will be a service of sorts on Saturday at St. Paul's Church, between the matinee and the evening performance."

John Saxon held up his hand, like a small boy in school trying to attract the attention of his master. Irving looked his way and inclined his head very slightly.

"Er, will there even be a matinee performance, I was wondering, Henry?"

Irving looked perplexed. "And why would there not be?"

"Oh! Er, I don't know. I suppose . . ." His voice trailed off.

Irving's steely gaze swept the theatre. "Any other questions?" No one said anything. "Then I would encourage you all to attend the church service . . . your duties allowing you to do so. That is all."

He turned on his heel and, with Miss Terry close beside him, strode from the stage, dismissing us with the wave of a hand.

I looked about for Stoker and saw him heading for the passageway that led from the stage to the office, a somewhat dark passage under the staircase leading to the two "star" dressing rooms above the stage on the OP side. I made off in the same direction.

I found the big man at his desk.

"The Guv'nor spoke of trauma suffered by Richland," I said. "What was that all about?"

"If you'd ever seen a man who's been trampled by a team of horses, you wouldn't have to ask, Harry," he said. "But now that you *have* asked, here's a chance to see it firsthand. The police at St. James's Division, Piccadilly, have the body. A Superintendent Dunlap is in charge. They want someone to officially identify it."

"Identify it?" I echoed, my voice sounding somewhat hollow, even to my own ears.

He nodded. "Hop on over there, Harry. Won't take you but a minute."

I had not previously had the opportunity, if that is the right word, to visit a morgue. The one at St. James's Division police station did not inspire me to repeat the effort at any time in the future. The morgue was in the basement, below street level, and was even colder than the February air outside. It reeked of a mixture of bodily excretions and stale tobacco smoke topped by liberal applications of carbolic soap. I held my scarf up over my nose and tried to breathe as shallowly as possible. The officer I had been handed over to was a Sergeant Samuel Charles Bellamy. He was in plain clothes, which he explained by stating that he was a detective policeman. He pointed to one of several sheet-covered figures lying on tables at the back of the white-tiled room.

"Strand fatality, approximately eleven thirty on the late evening of the 8th day of February 1881." The sergeant read from an oak and metal clipboard that looked as though it had seen many years of service. "Victim male, approximately thirty-five years of age; five feet and eleven inches in height; eleven stone four pounds in weight. Contents of pockets: none. Jewelry: none . . ."

"Yes. Thank you, Sergeant," I said. "I'm just here to identify the man. Can we get this over with?"

The policeman shrugged and advanced on a figure lying on one of the tables. A soiled grayish sheet covered the victim's head and body but allowed his feet to stick out incongruously from the bottom. The detective sergeant gripped the top of the covering and pulled it back. One of the dead man's arms flopped out and hung down over the edge of the table. I looked at it, trying not to focus on the victim's face. The hand seemed clean and fresh, almost as though belonging to someone alive.

I was not expecting what I saw when I turned my gaze to the head, though to be honest I didn't know what I expected. The man's face had been smashed and crushed almost beyond recognition. There had obviously been a great deal of blood, but this, mercifully, had been hosed off for the most part. The chest had caved in, and it looked as though one arm was at an unnatural angle. I glanced quickly at the destroyed features, nodded, and looked away again. I felt a great desire to vomit.

Upstairs in the office Sergeant Bellamy was kind enough to give me a cup of tea, which I clutched as I tried to absorb any and all heat from the liquid and from the steam it emitted. The sergeant wore his gray-flecked sideboards long and full in the old-fashioned muttonchops style, his thinning black hair brushed across the top of his head and plastered down with macassar oil. He had neither mustache nor beard. He was a tall man but had a slight stoop.

"You identify the body as this man Peter Richland?" he asked, a pen poised over the clipboard.

I nodded. I had been able to make out that the face—crushed as it was—had recently been shaved of beard and mustache. This was something Richland had reluctantly done to play—given the opportunity—the part of Hamlet.

It wasn't much but it was just about the only identifying factor available.

"How did you know he belonged to the Lyceum?" I asked.

"Not too difficult to a trained eye, sir," said the sergeant, in a superior tone. "We found that he had traces of that theatre makeup stuff on his face and he was only a short distance from the theatre."

"Of course." I nodded my head. "Of course."

The funeral took place on Saturday, with a mixture of rain and snow falling. It made the somber affair even more so. There were few mourners. There was normally a matinee performance on a Saturday, but despite what the Guv'nor had said to us, in his address onstage, it had been canceled after all, at Miss Terry's insistence, so as not to tax the Guv'nor after his poisoning. This then allowed Lyceum staff to attend the funeral, though it seemed that most of the people had found that they had duties of one sort or another that precluded them from being there. There were a few faces I recognized, however. Bill Thomas had abandoned his seat at the stage door. Miss Margery Connelly, the wardrobe mistress, accompanied by Miss Edwina Price, the prompt, were both there. A few of the actors, though none of the leads, stood about as though rehearsing a crowd scene.

St. Paul's Church—the Parish Church of Covent Garden—is known as the Actors' Church and has a long association with London's theatre community. The funeral was taking place in the churchyard. The rector was an ancient, thin rail of a man who looked to be in danger of sailing off into the stormy skies above, should the wind blow too strongly. He conducted the service in a high, reedy voice, on more than one occasion stopping to cough in such hollow, rasping fashion that many looked to see a second body join the one in the coffin. But he made it through the service and then, wrapping his cloak tightly about him, hurried off to the comparative warmth of the church, leaving the grave digger to finalize the event.

I noticed a small, plump woman whose hat and veil did not hide her red face and graying hair. She had been standing close beside the rector throughout the service. I made a small bet with myself that she was Richland's mother. I believe he had no wife to grieve for him. I approached and introduced myself.

"Good day to you, Mr. Rivers," she replied. "I appreciate your coming here today."

I couldn't help noticing that her eyes behind the veil had a twinkle to them, with no sign of tears. Yet as we spoke, her mouth changed rapidly from a slight smile to a thin, hard line.

"We shall all miss your son, Mrs. Richland," I said. "Such a tragedy."

"*Hamlet* is a tragedy," she said, her eyes boring into mine. "Peter wanted to play Hamlet. It seemed as though he might . . . at one time."

"Ah! With Mr. Irving's, er, mishap, you mean?" I said.

"Peter would have made a wonderful Hamlet. He was a very gifted child."

"Of course. Of course." I nodded my head and looked about me, hoping to see someone I could use as an excuse to break the conversation.

I had no need. Suddenly, without a further word, Mrs. Richland turned away and walked off in the direction of the Henrietta Street entrance to the churchyard. Her back was straight and she did not hurry.

Before returning to the theatre I caught up with Bill Thomas and he and I made a short detour to the Druid's Head. We were soon ensconced in a niche by the fireplace, each with a tankard of porter in hand.

"Speak not ill of the dead," said Bill, his face somber, "but I don't think Peter Richland will be missed nor mourned at the Lyceum."

"You are right there, Bill," I said.

"Was that his mother I saw you addressing?"

I nodded.

"I thought I recognized her."

"You've met her before?" I was surprised.

"She stopped by the theatre one time to drop off something for her son. Medicine he'd forgotten to take, or some such thing. I only saw her briefly."

"She seems to be taking it well. I expected to see a lot of tears and hand-wringing, but she had a determined set to her mouth and both eyes quite dry."

Bill took a deep drink from his tankard and then belched. He sat back on the settle. "You can never tell how a person will take a death, especially the death of your own son," he said quietly. "Just because there are no tears doesn't mean there is no sorrow." Quite the philosopher, I thought.

We sat quietly for a few moments. John Martin, the tavern keeper of the Druid's Head, loomed over us. If he could have acted, he would have made a magnificent Falstaff. His stomach preceded him as he steered around the tables and chairs of his establishment. His deep voice bounced off the low, blackened beams of the ceiling. His ruddy nose and cheeks reflected the red glow of the log fire in the hearth. He now stood before us clutching half a dozen empty tankards in his ham-sized fists.

"You at the funeral of that study man?"

"*Under*study," I said. "Yes, we were just there."

"Funny what 'appened to 'im."

"What do you mean, John?" I was suddenly curious.

He moved around and stood with his buttocks to the fire. I felt a sudden chill as the warmth was cut off.

"Why, 'e seemed sober enough when 'e left 'ere that

night. Walked out wif 'is friend, and the next fing I knew there was a commotion outside. When I looked out, someone by the road said as 'ow a gent 'ad been run down."

"You didn't actually see it happen, then?"

"No. Don't know as 'ow anyone did. Though there was a couple of toffs out there, wif too much wine in 'em. And then someone cried out about one man pushing the other, or somefing."

"One man pushing the other?" I was interested. "You mean, Richland didn't just get run down?"

John shrugged and, thankfully, moved out of the line of the fire's warmth. "Confusing stories," he said. "One of the gents said that your man, the study, blundered out into the road and was 'it by a growler goin' too fast . . . nufin' new there. The other gent was on about 'ow the study's friend 'ad *pushed* 'im in front of the four-wheeler and then—afterward—had dragged the body off to the other side of the road and then away down an alley." He sniffed. "All that matters, if you ask me, is that your man got 'isself killed." He somehow managed to add Bill's now empty tankard to those in his hands and sailed off toward the bar.

"But you say you didn't actually see this, John?" He had disappeared behind the bar and didn't hear me.

"Happens all the time," said Bill. "Those growlers are always going too fast. No consideration for others, especially when they've a few drinks in them. Bound to be accidents. Have another drink, Harry?"

I looked at Bill. "An accident?" I asked. "Or murder?"

"I think we have neither the time nor perhaps the interest to investigate Peter Richland's death," said Stoker when I reported my conversation with the owner of the Druid's Head. " 'Did he fall or was he pushed?' is the basis of many a theatrical drama, not to mention works of literature, Harry, as you well know. The police seem satisfied with the turn of events, I take it?"

"No mention of any fubbery at St. James's Division," I said. "All cut-and-dried, according to the detective sergeant at the morgue."

"You mentioned that there was nothing in Richland's pockets and no jewelry?"

"That's correct, sir. Strange, don't you think, though, the police didn't comment on it? You'd imagine that at the very least he would have had a pocket watch."

"But you spoke of an eyewitness saying that the man with him dragged his body over to the other side of the road and out of sight down an alley, did you not, Harry?"

"Yes, sir."

He shrugged. "Well, there you are, then. A simple case of robbing the corpse before making off. Opportunism, Harry. We see it everywhere." My boss paused, as though a thought had struck him, then nodded and pursed his lips. "Hmm."

"Is there something else, sir?" I asked.

"I hope there will not be."

I was puzzled. "Sir?"

He straightened up in his chair and looked me in the eye. "Mr. Richland was not, at least, killed within the confines of the theatre," he said.

"No." I was still puzzled. What was he driving at?

"It seems highly unlikely, then, that his *specter* will linger here; though there have been cases . . ." His voice trailed off.

"Are you talking about ghosts, sir?"

"Do not dismiss such things out of hand, Harry. I would draw your attention to the Man in Grey at the Drury Lane Theatre. Most certainly a well-known, if not famous, specter."

The ghost he referred to had been around as long as the Drury Lane Theatre had been standing. No one knew who he was . . . a onetime actor or perhaps an admirer of one of the early actresses. He would be seen sitting in a box seat or in the front row of the stalls. From all reports he appeared to be a man-about-town, but his three-cornered hat placed him over a hundred years behind the present times. In 1850 some workmen had knocked down a wall at the theatre, to enlarge the auditorium, and had exposed a hidden room. It contained a male skeleton with a dagger stuck between the ribs. Although the remains were given a proper burial, the ghost continued to appear at irregular intervals. I knew that there were many similar stories connected to other theatres in London and about various parts of England, Scotland, and Wales, not to mention Ireland.

"You are thinking that perhaps our Mr. Richland might become the Man in Grey of the Lyceum?" I asked.

Mr. Stoker shook himself. "As I say, he did not die within these walls, so don't be so superstitious, Harry! Let us keep our sights on the attempt to poison the Guv'nor. I am not willing to let that slide, and I still have great suspicions about those malcontents at Sadler's Wells."

"So I should just forget what I heard about Richland being pushed?" I didn't feel comfortable with that.

Neither, it seemed, did Stoker. After a moment's thought he said, "Well, as I said Harry, focus on the poisoning of the Guv'nor . . . but if you can also do a little digging into Richland's death, well, why not?"

"When you think about it," I said, "killing off our main understudy would add to any attempt to undermine our production. So it could be part of the same plan to do us harm."

"True. Yes, very true, Harry. And who, exactly, was this friend that Richland was with? Do we know that? Might bear some investigation, wouldn't you say?"

"I agree," I said. "So do you want me to make another trip over to Sadler's Wells?"

He again turned his gray green eyes on me and squinted

slightly as he tapped the side of his nose with his forefinger. My stomach lurched. I knew the sign. He had in mind some devious plan, and I was to be the instrument of it.

"You are well acquainted with our Mr. Archibald, I take it?"

I nodded. Mr. Archibald was in charge of makeup and personal props at the Lyceum. No one seemed to know if Archibald was his first or his last name. He was a short, thin man of indeterminate age, with a large head, who affected an almost feminine manner. Rumor had it that he wore one of his own much-curried wigs. He was inclined to wax poetic about the works, and actions, of Oscar Wilde. The twenty-seven-year-old Wilde had entered society just last year and, to complicate matters, had been a former suitor of Mr. Stoker's wife, Florence, though both gentlemen had long since settled their differences. Mr. Archibald lived in Chelsea, close to his hero.

"I would like you—if your stage-managing duties permit, of course—to visit with Mr. Archibald and see if you can affect some disguise that will permit you to enter the backstage area of the Sadler's Wells Theatre undetected and to mingle with the staff. See what the word is regarding Mr. Irving's affliction . . . and, now, Richland's 'accident.' I have the feeling that someone there is in on any malice that may have been directed this way. Do you think you can do that, Harry?"

"Of course, sir." The words were out of my mouth before I even considered it. I later thought to myself that perhaps I shouldn't be quite so eager to please.

As I made my way across the stage toward the dressing rooms, wardrobe, and makeup, on the far side, I wondered about my mop of carrot red hair. How on earth would Mr. Archibald hide that? It would take some monstrous wig, it seemed to me, to cover my head and still look natural.

There was a thud and I almost jumped out of my skin. Something had landed at my feet, right beside where I was walking. It had only narrowly missed me. Alarmed, I looked down on a heavy sandbag with a short piece of rope attached to its neck.

Up above the stage, on either side of it, are the fly galleries: working platforms where the flymen, or riggers, work scene changes by raising and lowering scenery flats. It had taken me a long time to learn the intricacies of this world above the stage. When I first came to work at the Lyceum, I had to learn and adjust quickly. It was a big theatre and there was much with which to familiarize myself. The fly galleries run back from the proscenium to the rear wall. They are connected, along the wall, by a bridge and narrow catwalks. All is accessible by ladders and rungs built into the walls. There is also the gridiron, or fly tower, high above the main stage, immediately under the roof of the building. It's called the gridiron because the floor consists of narrow wooden joists laid on beams with just enough room between the joists for ropes to pass through and connect to pieces of scenery. This vast network of ropes runs through multiple pulleys and up over two great drums rotating on shafts, just under the peak of the roof. The ropes go all the way down the walls to the stage floor. There they are wound around cleats when not fastened to the scenery. To counterbalance the weight of the scenery, the other ends of these ropes are tied around heavy sandbags that move up and down the walls as the scenery is manipulated.

It was one of these sandbags that now lay at my feet. I wondered how that had happened? Stooping, I saw that the short piece of rope had been cut through. This was tough, three-quarters of an inch, Manila hemp. Someone had deliberately cut it and dropped the sandbag, trying to hit me on the head! That would certainly have made a mess of my carrot red hair! As I peered up into the gloom above me, I heard someone scramble along the catwalk. It was far too dark to see who it was.

I am not one to move rapidly under normal circumstances, but someone had just tried to kill me. I leapt across to the closest wall and ran along to the ladder rungs set into it. I started climbing, gasping as I went, determined to catch the man. I reached the fly gallery and was halfway across the bridge when I heard a whooshing sound. Looking over my shoulder, I saw a shadowy figure clinging to a rope and descending rapidly to the stage floor below while one of the sandbags went flying upward to counterbalance him. As he reached the ground, he let go of the rope and ran off into the wings. The released rope immediately reversed its direction, and another sandbag hit the stage, this one bursting open and spewing sand in all directions. I started to slowly climb down again.

Chapter Three

Mr. Stoker was greatly agitated when he heard of my misadventure.

"So!" he hissed. "They have the nerve to bring their war into our camp. We can't let them do that, Harry."

"I could have been killed."

"Yes, Harry. Yes, of course." He paused, his brow furrowed. "I'll tell you what." I looked at him expectantly. "We'll forget about you going to Sadler's in disguise . . . for now, at least. We'll concentrate our attention here at home. Get up into the fly tower and check all the ropes. Make sure no other ones have been tampered with."

"All of them, sir? Couldn't the flymen . . . ?"

"Ah yes. Of course, of course. Tell Sam Green to get his men onto it right away. We don't need any mishaps at this evening's performance. Oh, and have a word with Bill Thomas. I want to know how a stranger got into the theatre."

"Probably happened while we were at the funeral, sir. Bill had to leave his post to go to that."

"Yes, well . . . someone should have been there to verify visitors."

The evening performance was fast approaching. I hurried off to catch up on my duties as stage manager. There seemed to be a lot that needed my attention. No time to dwell on what may well have been an attempt on my life. How often had I heard the old saw "The show must go on"? It must indeed and would, with or without me.

In *Hamlet* a majority of the scenes take place in rooms of the castle or in Polonius's house. The brief scene that is Act Four, Scene Four is "A Plain in Denmark," and so, rather than deal with major scene changing, a painted backdrop sheet of said plain is unrolled down in front of the main set and then pulled up again afterward. This sheet rolls down and up like a blind. I had watched while Sam Green unrolled and then re-rolled the sheet, to make sure that it ran smoothly. Little did I realize the part that this backdrop would play in the evening's performance.

The play was going well. The Guv'nor seemed to have regained most of his stamina and was charming the audience in his customary manner. They were eating out of his hand. Mr. Stoker was, as usual, ensconced in his office juggling paperwork: accounts, schedules, booking requests, front of house matters. While the performance was underway, the stage manager was in charge. I made sure the callboy was not slacking, quieted the chatter of the extras, ensured that props were where they needed to be. Many's the time I had to institute a frantic search for a dagger or sword that one of the actors had mislaid or I had to locate the wardrobe mistress because one of the ladies had stepped on the hem of her dress and torn it.

But tonight all seemed to be running smoothly. I stood behind the prompt and watched from the wings. Scene

Three finished and I saw Hamlet, Rosencrantz, and Guildenstern gathered opposite me, with Maurice Withers as Fortineras on my side of the stage waiting to go on. The lights were not dimmed for the brief scene change; it was a simple matter for the backdrop to come rolling down and the scene to start. At a cue from me, Sam Green and his men sent the backdrop rolling down. There was a sudden gasp from the audience, followed by a scream from Edwina Price, the prompt. The scream startled me, since Miss Price normally never uttered a word during a performance, unless called upon to prompt.

"Lights! Douse the lights!" Someone responding faster than me shouted the order, but the lights continued to burn steadily. I saw the reason for the commotion and leapt forward.

As the scene backdrop unfolded, something that had been rolled up inside it came bouncing out. It was a severed human head!

Detective Sergeant Bellamy examined the point of his pencil to make certain it was sharp. I'm sure he had a lot to write. The pencil was poised over his official notebook. He looked up again for the umpteenth time, his eyes only half open, and he seemed close to falling asleep. His mournful gaze rose to the vast darkness above the stage.

When Mr. Irving, onstage as Hamlet, had seen the head and realized what it was, he had run forward, kicked it into the orchestra pit, and then carried on as though nothing had happened. Miss Price's scream went unnoticed and the play had gone on to its conclusion with the usual number of curtain calls. It was not until the audience had cleared the theatre that Mr. Stoker notified the police.

"Rum do," observed the sergeant. "Rum do."

"Yes." I had to agree.

"So this wasn't a part of the play, we take it?"

"No," said Mr. Stoker. "The play is *Hamlet*. There are no severed heads in it."

My mind did go, fleetingly, to the churchyard scene and Hamlet musing over the skull of Yorick. It might, perhaps, have been more appropriate if the severed head had leapt out at that time, I thought.

"Whose head is it, sir?"

"Whose head is it?" Stoker echoed, incredulously.

"Yes. It must belong to someone."

"Well, of course it belongs to someone!" I exploded. "How would we know whose it is? I thought that was your job?"

He made a note in his book then looked at me through rheumy eyes. "No need to get testy, sir," he said.

"Testy?" It had been a long day and I was about to show him just how testy I could get when pushed . . . but I sighed and let it go. I was too tired to get into an argument. "You are going to take it with you, are you not?" I asked almost pleadingly.

"Oh yes. Yes. We'll remove the object, sir. Have no fear." Another note in his book. "Tell me, how did it end up in the orchestra pit . . . beside the bass drum, as we understand it?"

"The Guv . . . Mr. Irving kicked it there."

His eyebrows rose a half inch. "Kicked it there? Did he now? Now why would he do a thing like that?"

"So that the audience wouldn't get upset!" I said, exasperated.

"Look, Sergeant, can we not go over all these questions in the morning?" interjected Mr. Stoker. "It is getting late and we have all had a really long day . . ."

"Oh yes. Yes, sir, of course we can." More scribbling in his book, which he finally snapped closed. His eyes examined me for a moment, as though he thought I might be holding back some important information. Then he nodded in agreement with himself and turned to look down into the pit, where the head still lay. "Just come around to St. James's

Division before nine of the clock, if you would be so kind, sir, and we'll finish our report then. Do you have a bag, or something?"

The theatre was closed on Sunday. Not so the police station, so I made my appearance there and filed my report to Sergeant Bellamy's satisfaction. I was surprised to see him there on the Sabbath, but one of the constables suggested that the good sergeant had no other life.

"'E's married to the force," he said with a grin. "Ain't never 'ad no wife as I know, and not likely to get one, to my way o' thinkin'."

The good detective sergeant was about fifty years of age, and I surmised from his somewhat ruddy countenance that he was also married to the local tavern. I pondered whether or not that could be classed as bigamy.

It was a sunny day for February, though with no warmth from the sun. The bone-chilling wind that had blown through London for the past several days had died down to a whisper, and I felt almost exhilarated. I eschewed a cab or an omnibus, turned down Northumberland Avenue, and headed for the Embankment: Sir Joseph Bazalgette's vision of reclaimed river land. Up until twenty years ago this whole section had been twenty-two acres of mud and filth, with various sewer lines emptying into the river. Now it was a fine promenade fashioned from granite blocks brought by barge from as far away as Cornwall. It had rapidly become a popular venue for all Londoners.

A number of young couples strolled there beside the river, pausing now and again to stand close to each other and gaze out at the murky waters of the Thames. One or two nursemaids pushed their perambulators, clutching the hand of an older child dressed in his or her Sunday best. A young boy bowled a hoop along the Embankment while another boy enthusiastically whipped at a top to set it spinning. Most, I assumed, were fresh out of church. I was not a churchgoer myself, though I did duck into Christ Church in Marylebone once in a while, to keep on good terms with whoever might be in control "up there."

An old woman played a hurdy-gurdy at the corner of Northumberland, and not a dozen paces away a young boy fingered a pennywhistle at a furious speed, its notes clashing with those of the hurdy-gurdy. It was as I was turning away from admiring a slow-moving Thames sailing barge that I saw Ralph Bateman.

Ralph Bateman was the younger brother of Mrs. Crowe. Mr. Stoker believed that Mrs. Crowe (the Bateman daughter Kate) could be behind the poisoning of the Guv'nor. Her brother, Ralph, was a pasty-faced, overweight young man who had—so I had been led to believe—dropped out of Cambridge and, the last I had heard, journeyed off to the West Indies on the other side of the Atlantic. It seemed he had now returned, and it was indeed a surprise for me to see him here on so fine a morning. However, Ralph had always fancied himself something of a fashionmonger and before his travels used to hang about his mother's theatre passing his time by criticizing and complaining. His mother, and now his sister, fully indulged him. It was perhaps understandable that he would promenade along the Embankment, as did so many young bucks.

Right now Ralph Bateman was in deep conversation with a pair of unsavory-looking characters. One of them, a short man, kept his eyes firmly on Bateman's face, while the other, a tall and well-built dark-skinned man, constantly looked about as if to ensure that they were not being overheard. I didn't think that Ralph Bateman knew me, at least not by sight, so I casually strolled in their direction, idly wondering what they might be up to.

"You'll get your guinea when you've completed the job,"

Ralph was saying to the shorter of his two companions. "That's what the boss said; that was the agreement."

"That was afore I see'd the 'eight of that stuff! An 'undred feet above the stage, if'n you ask me."

"Nonsense. No higher than at Sadler's, and you know it. I hadn't realized that you were afraid of heights or I would have hired someone else."

"'Ere! I ain't afeared of nothin' and no one. I want me money."

"When you have completed the job." Ralph Bateman turned away as though the conversation was at an end. I stood there dumbfounded at what I was hearing and wondered who "the boss" he had mentioned might be. The short man took an impulsive step forward and Ralph swung back to stare at him, raising his cane and prodding him in the chest. "Don't even think it, Charlie Vickers. Don't even think it, especially if you want to get any part of your money."

The dark-skinned man stepped forward and nodded in my direction. Bateman glanced over his shoulder and then set off at a brisk pace away from the riverside and toward Whitehall Place. The two others hurried after him.

"Charlie Vickers, you say?"

Stoker peered at me over the gold rims of his reading spectacles. He was working on the accounts, and I felt guilty interrupting him so early on a Monday morning, but I wanted to report on my stroll along the Embankment the previous afternoon.

"That's what Ralph Bateman called him, I believe. I wasn't able to get too close before they took off, but I did hear that much. I don't know who the third man was, nor 'the boss' that Ralph referred to. The third man was a dark-skinned gentleman. Very well dressed. From across the ocean, I presume. I haven't seen him before."

Stoker's ponderous head nodded slowly up and down, as

it was wont to do while he digested my reports. "Could he have been a native of the Caribbean, joined up with Ralph when on his travels? And you think that they are concocting further mischief?" he asked.

It was my turn to nod. "Bateman said something about not paying Vickers until the job was completed. That's when he mentioned this 'boss.' "

Stoker laid down his pen and sat back in his office chair. "Charlie Vickers is a nasty piece of work, Harry," he said. "If the price is right, he'll do anything short of murdering his grandmother . . . and he probably has a price for that."

"You know of him, then?"

"Oh yes." Again he nodded his head. "A thrasonical scoundrel. One time, just before you came here, I believe it was, he sold counterfeit tickets to all of our best seats for the Guv'nor's production of *Richard III*. Caused no end of a problem. Then he was involved in the theft of the leading lady's jewelry at the Prince of Wales's Theatre on Charlotte Street. That leading lady, by the way, was our own Miss Ellen Terry, before she came to join Mr. Irving. Charlie Vickers is a small-time sneaksman with no inhibitions."

"Well, then there was that puzzling thing," I added. "Bateman said—and I think I heard him aright—that 'you'll get your guinea when you've completed the job. *That's what the boss said.*' In other words, it sounds as though someone else is actually in charge, giving the orders, and yet Ralph doesn't usually pay attention to anyone other than his mother. And she's no longer with us. He pays no heed to his sister."

There was a long silence while Stoker digested that.

"I must admit, I thought this a little ambitious for Mrs. Crowe's brother, Ralph. Yes, Harry, it would make sense that there be a smarter mind behind these attacks on the Lyceum. The question is, who could it be?"

"I've alerted Bill Thomas to be especially vigilant," I said, "and I've also paid a crossing sweeper and an itinerant musician to keep an eye open outside and report anything that strikes them as being out of the ordinary."

"Good. Good." He looked back down at the accounts book as though anxious to get back to it. "What news from your Sergeant Bellamy and the head?"

"Oh! Here's a surprise. I looked in on St. James's Division on my way here this morning. That head . . . according to their morgue records, it belongs to our deceased understudy, Peter Richland. The very man we buried a couple of days ago!"

Stoker did not seem surprised. When Sergeant Bellamy had told me, I had been astounded, but not so my boss. "I rather suspected as much," he said.

I gaped at him and then, when nothing else was forthcoming, closed my mouth. Perhaps this wasn't the time to pursue the matter. I could see that our theatre manager wanted to get back to his work. "What would you like me to do, sir? I've got plenty of Lyceum work to get on with but . . ."

"What plans do you have for after tonight's performance, Harry?"

The question took me by surprise.

"Why, none, really. Back to my rooms and a hot supper, if Mrs. Bell can fulfill her obligations. Why do you ask?"

He removed his spectacles and rubbed his eyes, then replaced the glasses and again studied me over the rims.

"Fancy a bit of grave robbing, Harry?"

Chapter Four

The moon was full that night. I would rather it had been a new moon or something less than its complete self, so that our actions might not be obvious to anyone who would be passing the cemetery. This was also Saint Valentine's Day—not that the celebration of lovers had anything to do with me, a confirmed bachelor. I did, however, wonder what excuse—if any were needed—Bram Stoker had given his wife to explain his absence on such a night.

Stoker led the way between the tombstones as though he was familiar with the path, his great figure casting a huge shadow on the ground behind him. I had myself forgotten exactly which grave we had stood about, two days earlier, but he seemed not to hesitate as we rounded the rear of the church and he struck off at an angle along the tall brick wall separating the church property from the street. This was all the more surprising since he had not been at the funeral.

Stoker stopped close to an ancient yew tree, whose branches

brushed the wall. "I think it's here, Harry," he said, pointing to the far side of the tree.

He was right. The grave had not yet been sodded down, and loose earth confirmed the recent excavation. There was as yet no memorial stone, but only a wooden marker. In the bright light of the moon I could make out the painted notation: *B34R8 PETER RICHLAND 12Feb1881.*

"What is the plan?" I asked.

"I arranged to have a pair of shovels left here," said the big man. "Ah! There they are—behind the tree. Now then . . . As you observe, Harry, there is a moon too bright for our enterprise. However . . ." He looked up and scanned the sky. I followed his gaze. "There are plenty of large clouds. We wait until the moon goes behind one of those and then we dig until it comes out again . . . Dig when it is dark and conceal ourselves behind the tree when it is brightest. It is almost midnight, so I doubt there will be many passersby, but it will be best if we are not observed."

I agreed with that. I had no desire to meet with Sergeant Bellamy with my wrists in a set of darbies and accompanied by a constable. "And why is it, again, sir, that we are grave digging?"

"The head, Harry. The head." He slipped off his surtout and his jacket, placing them in a neat pile at the foot of the tree, and rolled up his sleeves. He took hold of one of the shovels and, as the light suddenly faded, moved forward and started digging. "The head that truly belongs to our Peter Richland should be inside the coffin, attached to the body. I want to see if it has really been spirited away."

We alternately dug and secreted ourselves behind the tree. It was harder work than I had expected, the grave deeper than I felt certain was necessary. At one point, as we paused to get our breath, Stoker leaned on his shovel and looked up at the cloud-enshrouded moon.

"What do you know of the Roma, Harry?" he asked.

"Excuse me?" I said, puzzled.

"The Roma. Known generally as the Gypsies. They were not truly from Little Egypt, you know, but the name stuck."

I had no idea what he was talking about, but who was I to question the ramblings of my boss?

"You know about Gypsies?" I asked.

"Oh yes."

I was not really surprised. Stoker was a writer and storyteller at heart. He spent a great deal of what little spare time he had researching the most obscure subjects. He told me that one day they would all be worked into novels that he planned to write . . . when he had the time. In 1872, before coming to England, he had had a short story, "The Crystal Cup," appear in print, and then, shortly afterward, "The Chain of Destiny" was published in four parts. I didn't doubt for one moment that he would one day be the author of a major literary work.

Just then the moon escaped the grasp of the clouds and we retired once more behind the yew.

"A superstitious lot," he said. It took me a moment to realize that he was referring to the Gypsies. "It was the full moon made me think of them. They attribute divine properties to it, you know? Worship it. The Gypsies of Transylvania, so I am given to understand, claim that thousands of years ago the Sun King married a beautiful golden-haired woman. His brother the Moon King also married a silver-haired beauty. Then there was some sort of dispute that ended in the Sun King chasing the Moon King across the sky for all eternity." He paused, looked up, and signaled me to follow him back to the digging. As he sank his shovel once more into the dirt he continued his story.

"Superstitious people, yes. Take vampires, for example."

"Vampires?" I stopped digging.

"Don't stop, Harry. I have a feeling we are very close."

I resumed the work. "There's really no such thing as a vampire, is there, sir?" I asked, peering about me and wishing I could see into the shadows.

He grunted. "The Roma believe in them. And for good cause, it would seem. The Romanes word for the living dead is *mullo*." He suddenly chuckled.

"What?"

"Nothing, Harry. I was just recalling that the Roma obviously have little respect for our medical profession. Their word for doctor is a *mullomengro* . . . literally translated as a 'dead-man maker.' Hah!" He chuckled again but then grew serious. "Gypsies believe that the dead will rise from their graves to seek revenge, in the form of vampires, if they have been killed by an enemy. Such a vampire may just go after the one who caused his death or may go on an indiscriminate killing spree. There's just no telling." He glanced around, peering into the darkness, as did I. I shivered and wished to be finished with our morbid work.

"Ah!" Stoker stopped as his shovel hit something. "I think I may have struck what we seek." He moved close beside me as I took over the digging. "Carefully does it, Harry. There's no need to abuse the wooden lid. Though heaven knows it is only going to be buried again."

We gently brushed the dirt from the top of the wooden casket. The faint moonlight glinted on the brass nameplate that adorned the lid. I peered at it.

"Well, at least we've got the right one," I said, making out the engraved *Peter Wilberforce Richland*.

In another ten minutes we had the top cleared with enough room to kneel beside the casket. Stoker uttered a mild curse.

"What is it?"

"I didn't bring a levering tool. We need something to pry up the lid."

I reached for my shovel again. "I think we can use the

head of this," I said. "It may not leave a clean edge to the coffin, but I don't think anyone will complain." I heard him chuckle.

It seemed that the lid was not fastened down as tightly as it might have been, and I had no difficulty getting the head of the shovel into the edge and began lifting the exposed top. My boss moved around to the far side and did the same there. Suddenly, with a loud crack that must have been audible as far away as Fleet Street, the lid came free. We both stopped moving as the echo of the sound bounced off the church walls.

After what seemed a very long time to me, Stoker laid down his shovel and, taking hold of the edge of the lid, lifted the top up and away. We both leaned forward to look inside. Just at that moment the moon came out from behind its cloud and we saw nothing in the bottom of the casket but a large log.

"We have Mr. Richland's head—or the police have it—but where is the body?"

Stoker sat in his office chair and looked at me, his brow furrowed. We had departed the cemetery that morning, leaving the grave and coffin open, revealing its arboreal contents to anyone curious enough to investigate. I now sat opposite my boss, trying to stifle a yawn, and pondered the same thing.

"Perhaps it was dumped in the Thames," I suggested. "So many bodies are."

"It is possible, Harry. But something tells me that it was not. The question is, why go to the trouble of having a funeral and burying a tree trunk in place of the man, when you can simply steal the body and hide it for your nefarious desires without the need for the ceremony? Presumably—to answer my own question—the tree trunk was so that the coffin would seem sufficiently heavy and no one would realize that the body was missing."

"But who would do that and why?" I asked.

"Precisely." He was silent for a moment. "Why deposit the head in our scenery, Harry?"

"To disrupt our production, I suppose. And I imagine he was not expecting us to recognize whose head it was."

The big man nodded agreement. There followed another silence, this time longer than the previous one. Eventually, I felt impelled to break it.

"Where would one start looking for a headless corpse?"

"Of course there may be another totally different explanation."

Bram Stoker gazed, unseeing, at the blank wall opposite his desk and ignored my question. I recognized the look that enveloped his face when he was plotting one of his short stories or mulling over some obscure facts or folklore.

"What do you know of zombies, Harry?"

I said nothing . . . What was there to say?

He continued. "The empty coffin got me thinking. In certain Caribbean countries—one immediately thinks of the Republic of Haiti—an empty coffin signals the creation of a zombie. The 'undead,' as they have been called."

"I thought that was vampires?" I said, trying to sound intelligent.

"They also have been so termed."

"So what's the difference, sir?"

"Ha!" He shook his head as though in despair. "Vampires spend their 'waking' hours sucking blood from human victims, to sustain themselves. They then return to their graves, which they use as a base for their nightly sojourns."

"And zombies?"

"Zombies do not return to their graves. Neither do they drink blood. Once resurrected, they will work, sustained not by blood but by normal food—albeit any type of rotten garbage containing sufficient nutrients to support their strength. They are, in effect, slaves to their masters, requiring no pay, clothing, or entertainment, and minimum sustenance. Extraordinarily cheap labor, Harry."

"So what exactly *is* a zombie?"

"It's an abomination, Harry. No two ways about it."

"Yes, but more specifically . . . ?"

His focus came around to me and he ran his fingers through his beard, a gesture I envied.

"In that black republic there are men we would call magicians. They are known as *bokos*."

I was beginning to feel uncomfortable and wondered what the time was. I'd been hoping to take a nap before the day progressed much further, but I had to admit that Stoker's tales of the undead held me captive. His stories always did.

"The word 'zombie' comes from the Congolese *nvumbi*, meaning a body deprived of its soul." He suddenly yawned. He, too, it would seem, was feeling the effects of our late-night outing to the cemetery. He stretched and yawned again. "It is the boko who creates the zombie, Harry. When a person in the islands is considered dead, because of the climate they are not embalmed but are placed in the grave as speedily as possible. At nightfall, after a funeral, the people of the villages lie in their huts and wait with bated breath to see what may happen."

"L-like what, sir?" I was on the edge of my chair.

"Drums, Harry. Drums."

I swallowed.

"When the drums start sounding, and resonate down from the hills, the villagers know to stay safely inside their huts and not to venture forth."

"What is happening?"

"At the cemetery, at the fresh grave, the boko takes a handful of meal or flour and allows it to trickle through his fingers onto the earth in the design, or the representative, of Guédé, the god of the dead. He lights four candles and sets them about the grave site. Then he pours libations of rum. The boko's drummer starts pounding out the traditional rhythm of the Petro dance, and the boko stands and watches as his minions dig through the freshly turned soil and unearth the coffin. They bring it to the surface and remove the lid. It is said that then, when the boko calls the name of the deceased, a hand will appear on the edge of the coffin and gradually the corpse will stand up, climb out, and follow the boko wherever he may lead. From then on he is a slave to his new master." Stoker yawned again. "But enough of this, Harry. Let us leave it for the moment."

I was speechless, in my mind seeing the enactment under the light of a Haitian moon. I didn't want him to stop. My tiredness seeming to have abated. I finally blurted out, "But is this true, sir? I mean, are there really such things as zombies?"

He looked at me long and hard. "An alternate explanation, Harry, is that the boko has surreptitiously introduced an alkaloid drug to his intended victim. The drug would bring about a cataleptic state easily mistaken for death. As I've mentioned, with the heat and humidity no time is lost in getting a corpse—real or imaginary—into the ground. By the night following the burial the drug would have worn off sufficiently for the boko to rouse the victim and lead him away."

"What sort of drug could do that?" I asked, my interest piqued.

He thought for a moment. "A zombie is said to move in a slow, jerky manner, Harry. In just such a manner as does one who suffers from catalepsy. Such a person may be unable to recognize loved ones and unable to speak or register emotions. He—or she, for there are female zombies—must eat to obtain the strength to work, however. Local herbs that can bring about such a state are *Terminalia catappa, Spondias dulcis,* and one or two others—all deadly poisons if used incautiously. But cigars and pipes are commonly smoked in Haiti, by both men and women. What simpler method to introduce the soporific to the victim than by using the dried leaves rolled in the form of a cigar or crushed like tobacco? But . . . enough of this, Harry!" He sat back, seeming to have reached some sort of conclusion. "Talking of poison, I think it best we concentrate on our original question, who tried to poison the Guv'nor? I still strongly suspect Mrs. Crowe, or her brother, Ralph."

I was a little disappointed that the storytelling was over, but he was right—we needed to get on with more practical things.

"I may yet send you off to Sadler's Wells in disguise," he continued, "but for this morning we have other work to do. The Guv'nor is not happy with Act Three, Scene Four. He thinks that Mr. Sampson's Polonius is not all it should be when he gets stabbed through the arras. He wants to walk through that whole scene again."

"The whole thing?" I said, "Miss Grey is not going to take kindly to that."

"Oh, Meg won't have to do it, Harry. Miss Edwina Price can read in the Queen's part for her. Now, while I think of it, Harry, I need you to run an errand."

I couldn't suppress a sigh. There was always a lot to do in the theatre when preparing for an evening performance. And I should certainly be there if the Guv'nor was going to be making any changes to Act Three. It seemed like I'd been running errands not directly connected with the Lyceum's production for a long time now.

"Yes, sir," I said, dutifully. "What is it?"

"It's for the Guv'nor, so you needn't look so put-upon."

I sat up straight.

"He wants you to take a cab around to his house and

fetch back his Brodie edition of *Hamlet*. He's worked from that for years, apparently, and it's full of his penciled notes. Mrs. Cooke, the housekeeper, will let you in. Make sure you leave everything tight and secure when you depart, you hear me?"

I nodded and stood up. I had never visited Henry Irving's home before so this would be interesting.

I had somehow missed my breakfast that morning, so I stopped briefly at the Druid's Head for a quick bite to eat before heading for Mr. Irving's residence. As I watched John Martin carve a thick slice of ham and slip it between two slices of home-baked bread, I thought back to his comment about Peter Richland being with a friend the night he got killed. I asked him about it.

"Lor' bless you, Mr. Rivers," he said. "I gets far too many folks in 'ere to recollect 'em all. But yes, now that you asks, I did take note as 'ow your man seemed over generous—if I may put it that way—when it come to buying drinks for this other feller."

He spoke with his face screwed up as he tried hard to recollect that night. Not paying attention, he piled a particularly ample portion of mustard on the ham before slapping the top slice of bread back on it and pushing the plate across the counter in my direction. He continued talking as I lifted that top slice and carefully scraped off much of the dressing.

"Don't rightly know as 'ow this feller *was* a friend of your Mr. Richland, o' course. Could 'ave been long-lost cousins for all I was to know. Or they could've just met that night as they was drinkin', which is 'ow I sees it."

"So you think Richland simply got to drinking with another man who was in here?"

"As I said, that's the way I sees it. But 'oo's to say? You like a nice glass of porter to wash that down, then, 'Arry?"

I nodded. "But you did say that they left together?"

"Oh aye. Staggered out of 'ere the best of friends. Then your man got 'isself run down."

I ate my sandwich and drank my stout and had John go over things one more time. It seemed he'd never seen the other man before, nor had the man shown up since, which I thought strange.

The hansom let me off outside 15a Grafton Street, Mayfair, on the corner of Bond Street. Asprey's Jewellers occupied the ground floor, with display windows showing their expensive silver plate and jewelry. A small black door, around the corner on the Grafton Street side, was the entrance to the rooms above, where the Guv'nor lived. He shared the household with his friend Mr. Henry G. Barker, a leather merchant, and a staff of six. The cook was—perhaps appropriately—Mr. Henry Cooke, and his wife, Eliza, was the housekeeper. There were three young female servants plus a fourteen-year-old boy servant. It was the boy who answered the door to my knock. When I told him of my errand, he turned away from me and shouted up the stairs behind him.

"Mrs. Cooke! Mrs. Cooke!"

A young servant girl shortly appeared at the head of the stairs and looked down on us.

"What is it, Timmy? Mrs. Cooke is occupied."

I spoke up the stairs to her and again explained my errand.

"Oh, I'm so sorry, sir. Timmy! You know better than to leave the gentleman standing! Come on up, sir. I'm sure Mrs. Cooke will be with you in just a moment." Then she turned and scurried away, presumably to alert the housekeeper. The boy stepped back and allowed me to precede him up the narrow staircase.

As I reached the top, a short, stocky woman in a tight black dress, her hair pulled back in a severe bun-chignon, came bustling along to the landing. For the third time I explained why I was there.

"Of course, sir. Come this way, if you please. Timmy, get on and fill the coal scuttles, they're all 'alf empty. Jenny, you take this gentleman to Mr. Irving's study and see as 'ow 'e's comfortable." She turned back to me. "Jenny'll see to you, sir. You must excuse me but we're all be'ind today, some'ow." She picked up her skirts and hurried away as the young housemaid smiled at me and led the way down the corridor and into a room on the right.

"This is Mr. Irving's study, sir," she said. "Let me take your hat and coat. Timmy should have done that. Oh dear."

She seemed momentarily distressed at the oversight. I felt I had arrived at a most inopportune moment and tried to make amends.

"Please don't fuss, Jenny. It is Jenny, is it not?"

"Yes, sir." She blushed and bobbed a curtsey.

It had been a long time since anyone had curtsied to me and I held up my hand. "Please! Don't stand on ceremony. I work for the Guv'nor just as you do. I'm Harry Rivers, by the way. You can call me Harry. I'm the stage manager at the Lyceum."

She was a pretty young thing and I envied the Guv'nor having such a servant. Not much more than five feet and two inches in height and small bosomed, she was slim-waisted and had dark brown ringlets that escaped her cap. Her eyes were deep brown wells that drew me in. Her mouth, devoid of any artificial color, was full and red. I wondered what the other maids were like.

"I've never been to the theatre," she said wistfully.

"You haven't?" I was astonished. Here was a young woman who worked for England's finest actor and yet she had never been to the theatre. I made a mental note to talk to Mr. Stoker about that. Perhaps an evening out for the Irving residence staff might be arranged? Glancing again at Jenny, I must admit I hoped it could come about and that I might, in some way, facilitate it. She bobbed again and turned for the door.

"Wait!" I blurted out. Then, as she turned back, "Er—didn't Mrs. Cooke ask you to—um—to see that I was comfortable?" It was a lame attempt to keep her there, and I think she recognized it as such. She came back into the room, her cheeks very much colored.

"Can I fetch you a cup of tea, sir?" she asked.

"Harry," I said.

"Can I fetch you a cup of tea . . . Harry?" she repeated, her eyes cast downward.

"Thank you, Jenny. I'd like that very much."

While she was gone I started my search for the book I had been sent to retrieve. But my mind was not on it. It had been a long time since I had looked twice at any young lady. One of the penalties of working all hours as stage manager for a busy London theatre. Yet Jenny had really captured my attention. I knew it was a useless fancy . . . she being the maid for my main employer. I knew nothing about her. Perhaps she had a young man? Someone as pretty as she must surely . . .

My thoughts were interrupted as she came back into the room, bearing a small silver tray on which rested a cup of tea and a plate of biscuits. She still avoided my eyes as she set it down on an occasional table.

"Will there be anything else, sir—er—Harry?"

"Yes." I tried to sound businesslike. "Yes, Jenny. Mr. Irving sent me here to collect a book of his. Perhaps you can help me find it? It's a small red-bound book of Shakespeare's play *Hamlet*. You may have seen it about."

"Oh, I seldom have occasion to come into the study." She looked all around her. "It could be anywhere."

"Let's start with the desk," I said. We both reached out to lift the lid and our hands touched. Jenny snatched hers away as though she had been burned. She hurried across to one of the bookshelves.

"I'll start here," she said. "It's a book so it should be on the bookshelf, right?" She giggled, a sound that made my heart skip a beat.

"Good idea," I said. "But if he's been studying it recently, it may be in the desk. You look there and I'll look here."

We settled to the search. As Jenny ran her fingers slowly along the leather backs of the volumes on the shelves, reading the titles, I realized that in fact she could read. So many maids and other belowstairs staff could not. For some reason I was pleased.

I moved papers and memos in the walnut and burl Davenport. There were a couple of the small Brodie editions of Shakespeare's plays in there—which gave me hope—but neither was *Hamlet*. There were bills marked *PAID* and receipts, lists of things that the Guv'nor apparently planned to purchase, short notes on different productions, written both by Mr. Irving and Miss Terry. I also recognized Mr. Stoker's handwriting on some items.

I turned my attention to the drawers in the sides of the desk. In the top one on the left there was a bundle of letters from Mrs. Florence Irving, the Guv'nor's estranged wife. They bore postal marks over the past several months. None of them had been opened; they had just been stuffed into the drawer. I recalled what my boss had told me about Mrs. Irving.

Born Florence O'Callaghan, she was the daughter of Surgeon General Daniel O'Callaghan of Her Majesty's Indian Army. The O'Callaghans' Irish roots went back to the tenth-century king of Munster. It was no surprise, then, that the surgeon general hoped for a good marriage for his daughter. Instead, a chance encounter in 1869 caused the rebellious young lady to become romantically infatuated and involved with Irving, then a young actor and the drama critic for the *Sunday Times*. Irving's prospects were far from promising, but Florence was too much of a rebel to care. Despite her parents' objections, she married Henry Irving in July of 1869.

But it seems that she had never really cared for her husband's profession. Despite the birth of a son, husband and wife grew apart. After the opening night of Irving's first big success—as Mathias in *The Bells*, just ten years ago—he and his wife were driving home when she said to him, "Are you going to go on making a fool of yourself like this all your life?" Mr. Irving stopped the carriage—it was at Hyde Park Corner, according to Stoker—and he descended to the pavement. At the time his wife was pregnant with their second child, but the Guv'nor walked off into the night and never saw her again. *The Bells* went on to run for 150 nights, and Mr. Irving's name became one to be reckoned with in the English theatre.

"No luck here," said Jenny, breaking into my thoughts. "I'll try the other bookcase." She crossed the room.

I turned to the drawers on the other side of the desk. I found the book I was looking for in the top drawer: a well-worn, slim, red-leather-bound volume. I don't know why but, for some reason, I continued peering into the other drawers below it. (Curiosity about the great man, perhaps?) In the bottom drawer I found another bundles of letters addressed to him, though these had all been opened. The top letter was stuffed very roughly back into its envelope, and I could read the signature on the bottom of the letter. It was Peter Richland's name. I have no excuse . . . I took out the letter and read it.

Chapter Five

"Tell me again, Harry."

"I was tempted to bring at least one of the letters to show you, sir, but on reflection I realized I should not."

"Quite right, too."

"They were letters from Peter Richland to the Guv'nor referring to some episode that occurred before Mr. Irving's marriage. It would seem that he had strayed from the bachelor path, as it were, or possibly been led astray by a young woman named Daisy."

"Don't beat about the bush, Harry."

"He'd had an affair."

"Ah!" Stoker nodded understandingly.

"It was in 1866 when he was playing Doricourt in *The Belle's Stratagem* at the St. James's Theatre."

"He would have been twenty-eight."

"Yes," I agreed. "It seems that Peter Richland recently met this Daisy person and she spun him a yarn about the Guv'nor dallying with her and then abandoning her."

"Abandoning her? Doesn't sound much like the Guv'nor to me!" said Stoker.

"Nor to me. But apparently Richland made a very real threat to spread the story. It seems that this is why the Guv'nor took him into the Lyceum company as understudy, to keep an eye on him."

"Sounds suspiciously like blackmail!" Stoker's eyes narrowed and his mustache fairly quivered.

"My thinking exactly," I said. "I'd often wondered why Richland was taken on. It certainly wasn't for his acting ability."

"I think there must be more to the story, Harry. If it had been me I would have beaten the scoundrel and sent him on his way with a flea in his ear," said Stoker darkly. "But the Guv'nor is too softhearted." He scratched the top of his head and looked at me with one eye closed. "If our Mr. Richland was up to those sorts of tricks with other people also, he may very well have been pushed under that growler."

The same thought seemed suddenly to strike both of us. For just a moment we looked at each other. The Guv'nor . . . Would he? . . . Could he? . . . No! We both mentally shook our heads.

"About this Daisy person?" I said.

"Hrmph! The Guv'nor had a hard training. For almost a decade he played in a wide variety of stock companies around the country, mainly in the north. It was his first break when he played the St. James's Theatre, here in London, in '66. As a young bachelor, he might have been tempted to an occasional brief flirtation with one or more of the young ladies treading the boards in those days. It would be only natural. But I doubt very much that he would have taken advantage of this Daisy in any way. Much more likely that the young woman in question has seen his rise to fame and was looking—perhaps through our Mr. Richland—to gain monetarily."

"Yes," I agreed. "That does sound reasonable."

"Besides, it is my understanding that Henry was devoted to the stage and to fine-tuning his acting abilities even to the extent of living an almost monastic existence. No, I think we can dismiss those letters, Harry," continued Stoker, turning his attention back to his crowded desk. "At least for now."

"Oh! There was one thing, though." I suddenly remembered something. "There was reference in one of the letters— I didn't read the whole thing, you understand? Just glanced through it—there was mention of Ralph Bateman."

"Bateman? Are you sure?"

"Yes, sir."

"What did it say about him?"

"As I said, sir, I didn't actually read the letter. Just glanced at it. After all, sir, this was personal correspondence of the Guv'nor's."

"Right." Stoker's brow furrowed. I knew he didn't trust Ralph Bateman. And now it seemed there was a connection between Bateman and the late Peter Richland. "Perhaps we are being a trifle hasty in simply dismissing those letters," he said, thoughtfully. "I'm thinking it may not be a bad idea to verify whether or not there's anything there that might affect the well-being of the Lyceum."

"Would not the Guv'nor have brought such a thing to your attention?" I asked.

"Maybe; maybe not. He always has a lot on his mind, of course. He may have dismissed out of hand much of what Richland wrote. And probably didn't even read all of it. No, on reflection I rather wish you had borrowed one or two of these epistles." He sighed. "But I suppose we have enough to worry about with the poisoning and the attempt on your life with that dropped sandbag."

I thought for a moment before asking, "If it is Sadler's Wells at the bottom of this, sir, what would be their motive?"

"Motive?" He gave a short, sharp laugh. "We beat them to the opening night, Harry! Our *Hamlet* started a good couple of days before their *Twelfth Night*, so we got the lion's share of theatre-goers for the all-important start of the season. The pit customers gave us resounding approval. You know how these things go. Now, if Sadler's Wells can manage somehow to disrupt our advantage—to perhaps cause us to close *Hamlet*, if only temporarily—then it would allow them to catch up and probably take over as the number one London production. Big houses mean big profits, Harry. You know that."

"Yes, sir. I do."

"There's a lot of money at stake here."

"So there may very well be some sort of a vendetta being waged against the Lyceum and its production?"

"That there may, Harry. That there may. And I'm wondering just where Ralph Bateman stands on that score."

I was able to get some of my regular work done for an hour or so after that. I must admit that I did have occasional thoughts of young Jenny but tried to put them out of my head and concentrate on Lyceum work. I remembered the fact that my mother had been a scullery maid before she met and married my father. I did make a point of suggesting to Mr. Stoker that the servants at 15a Grafton Street might benefit from a visit to the theatre. "Benefit" was the word I used, though I wasn't able to elaborate on exactly how such a visit would advance them. Happily, Mr. Stoker didn't press me on the matter. He merely grunted, as usual, and said he'd look into it when he had the time.

I was standing in the wings contemplating some changes that had been made to prop placement for Act Three, Scene Four, when suddenly Bellamy appeared beside me.

"Goodness, Sergeant! You startled me."

"We're sorry about that, sir, but we have a question or two that bears answering."

"Of course."

Out came the inevitable notebook and pencil.

"It would appear that someone—and we do stress the word 'someone,' sir—has entered the churchyard of the Parish Church of Covent Garden—namely, St. Paul's Church—and has seen fit to interfere with one of the interments at that location. In a word, sir, they have dug up a grave and removed the corpse from the coffin." He fixed his bright, beady eyes on me. "Would you happen to know anything about that, we were wondering?"

"Removed the corpse?" I said, not willing to admit to anything. I found that my mouth had suddenly gone dry and I was aware of my face growing hot. I swallowed and tried to look surprised.

"There was no body in evidence, sir. A short, stout tree trunk of elm wood was lying in the place normally reserved for the deceased."

"Dear me," I murmured. "And this was Mr. Richland's grave?"

"Did we say that, sir?" The pencil hovered and then scribbled in the notebook.

"Er, no." I cursed myself, conscious that I was now sweating profusely. "No. But I presumed, since you have come here to the Lyceum, that it must be he." I felt better. That made sense, at least to me.

"Mmm." The sergeant was noncommittal.

I pressed my slight advantage. "And was this log of elm wood placed in the coffin before or after the interment?" I asked, innocently.

More scribbling. "That, sir, has not yet been ascertained."

"Then you had best be about your business and ascertain

it," I said triumphantly, and turned my back on the policeman. After a brief pause he walked away.

It was another day before Mr. Stoker got around to sending me off to Sadler's Wells again, looking for clues as to who might have poisoned the Guv'nor.

"If they did it once, they could do it again," he said. "Perhaps poison the whole cast! That would certainly slow us down."

I don't know that I was quite so suspicious myself, though that heavy sandbag that had only just missed me did give some emphasis to the possibility of a war that might well be developing. Such thoughts passed back and forth through my head as I sat in the red "Favorite" omnibus that would let me off outside the Sadler's Wells Theatre.

I was mentally somewhat numb from the transformation that Mr. Archibald had performed on me. He had completely agreed that any wig that would hide my bright carrot hair would have to be so large that it would draw more attention than the hair itself. His solution? To instead *color* my hair! I had been prevailed upon to dip my head repeatedly into a bucket filled with some odious brown liquid that smelled of garlic, coal tar, wood ash, and vinegar. The result was a drab, brownish red mop that, under certain light, I swear had a purplish tinge to it. Mr. Archibald had claimed that he could have done a far better job by adding walnuts to the mixture but that it would then have taken two to three months of washing to get it out again. I balked at that. I was just glad that Jenny couldn't see me like this.

To complete the transformation, Mr. Archibald dabbed on spirit gum and affixed a stringy mustache and an equally stringy beard. He clipped a pair of pince-nez spectacles on my nose, patted me on the shoulder, and sent me off.

The two big shire horses brought the omnibus to a halt and I jumped off the vehicle and sauntered along to the stage door of Sadler's Wells. Outside the theatre a trio of musicians played a desultory selection of popular tunes. I suspected that they were members of the Sadler's Wells' theatre orchestra and they were there seeking to expand their earnings. I slipped around the violinist, cracked open the stage door, and peered inside. As I expected, George Dale was wedged into his booth and was sitting with a slice of pork pie in one hand and a copy of *Sporting Life* in the other. His eyes were half closed, the lids drooping. Even as I watched, his head nodded down and then he jerked it up again. He was obviously fighting sleep. The hand holding the half-eaten pork pie slowly descended to the countertop in front of him. I took a chance and slipped into the narrow passage in front of him as quietly as I could. I ducked down below the level of his window and crept along, hoping no one else would appear. As luck would have it, I made it all the way to the end of the passage and turned the corner without being seen.

I headed for the scenery bays. I knew that the stagehands were anonymous in most houses. They did their job and the actors rarely thought about them. Consequently, during rehearsals and before performances the stagehands would many times pick up gossip overheard from actors exchanging what they believed to be confidential tidbits.

I knew a couple of the Sadler's Wells' scene changers, though not well. One was Jack Parsons, and I was pleased now to see him in the scenery bay, measuring a flat that needed restoring. I knew him to be an honest man who always thought the best of his fellows.

"How's it going, Jack?" I asked.

He glanced up, squinting a little as he tried to place me. I was thrilled that my disguise held up. "'Oo's asking?"

"Just came aboard," I said, playing the part of a new employee. "Someone said that Jack Parsons could be found back here. I take it that's you?"

He nodded and returned to his measuring. "Didn't know as 'ow they was 'iring?"

"Not much," I said. "I was just lucky to apply at the right time. What you doing? Building or rebuilding?"

"Some clumsy actor managed to put 'is foot through this flat," he said, sniffing. "Don't ask me 'ow 'e did it! Just got to patch it."

"Can I help?"

For the next hour or so I helped repair and repaint a number of pieces of the *Twelfth Night* sets and got to chatting with Jack Parsons till we were like old friends. I got him talking about the principal actors and—more importantly, from my point of view—about the management.

"So who's really in charge, then?" I asked "This Mrs. Crowe or the lead actor, Mr. Pheebes-Watson?"

"Old Philly *thinks* 'e's in charge." Parsons chuckled. "Leastwise, you'd believe 'im if you 'eard 'im. But it's Mrs. C as pulls the strings. Trust me, she's the one you need to pay attention to."

"What's this I heard about someone poisoning the Lyceum man?" I tried to make it a casual question. "That Henry Irving."

Parsons laughed out loud. "Ha! It's amazing 'ow stories gets around."

"It's not true, then?"

He shook his head. "They was talkin' about 'ow they needed to get *Twelfth Night* going afore the Lyceum's 'Amlet, and speaking of Mr. Irving, old Philly said somethin' like, 'Someone should poison the blighter!' Not serious, o' course."

"But someone *was* serious," I said. "I mean, Irving did get poisoned. So who do you think did it?"

Parsons paused with his paintbrush in his hand and gazed off into the wings, thinking. "Don't know as 'ow it was anyone from 'ere, though I'm supposing it could 'ave been. But it could just as well 'ave been someone from the Lyceum for all I know."

"You haven't heard any tittle-tattle?"

"There's always tittle-tattle," he said, resuming painting. "I try not to listen to it, though sometimes you can't 'elp it. Take that young Mr. Bateman, for example . . ."

"Ralph?"

"Right! 'Im! 'E was 'anging about with a couple of the lighting blokes and was braggin' as to 'ow 'e could bring the Lyceum folks to their knees if 'e 'ad a mind. Just boastful talk, mind you."

"You think so?"

"Oh yes. Though come to think on it, 'e was pretty tight with one of the Lyceum 'ands wot got 'isself the mittens; got booted out! Too fond of the bottle, I 'eard. What was 'is name now?"

"Willis?" I offered.

"That's 'im! 'Erbert Willis. Nasty piece o' work. 'Im and Ralph Bateman made a fine pair of scalawags."

"Is that right?"

"Well, I'm thinkin' our young Mr. Bateman 'as 'is fingers in a lot of dirty pies, if you follow me?"

I nodded. I followed him only too well.

"What about that other Lyceum man?" I said. "The understudy who got run down and killed."

"Ah!"

There was a wealth of meaning in that word. Obviously Jack Parsons knew more than he had so far divulged.

"Can I buy you a drink, Jack, when we get through here?"

He was no fool. He realized I wanted to know more on the subject. I arranged to meet him later at the Bag o' Nails.

Meanwhile, I had a quick word with one or two others of the Sadler's Wells backstage staff.

Jack and I were soon settled at a table away from the bar; he with his favorite India pale ale and me with my inevitable porter. It didn't take long to draw him out on the running of Sadler's Wells and the comings and goings of Ralph Bateman and his cronies. Jack gave the impression of being a quiet type who just did his job, but I had long ago learned that he was well able to keep up with the gossip and chitchat that takes place in any large theatre. He told me, as I already knew, that Ralph had been abroad for a while but had recently returned, bringing with him a new friend from Haiti named Henry Ogoon, who seemed to have made himself at home. Not just made himself at home, but seemed to have some sort of "power," as Jack put it, over the young man. It wasn't like Ralph to take orders from anyone, yet according to Jack he did anything and everything that Ogoon suggested.

Jack said that the rivalry between Sadler's and the Lyceum was something everyone was aware of but that no one other than the Batemans really took seriously.

"Oh, old Pheebes-Watson likes to dream about showing up 'Enry Irving, but I think even 'e realizes that it'll be a cold day in 'ell afore 'e is actually recognized as the better actor."

I agreed. "But tell me, what do you hear about that understudy's death?" I asked. "You seemed to hint that there was more to it than meets the eye."

"I did?" Jack was suddenly playing innocent. "Oh, I don't know as I'd say that. Mind you, Ralph was crowin' somethin' awful after it 'appened. As though 'e knew more than anyone else. But I didn't take 'im serious, and I wouldn't think you would, neither."

I let it go for now. I was sure all would come out eventually.

"What are Ralph's cronies like?" I asked as innocently as I could, after a long draw on my porter. "You hear of him running around with them, but I'm wondering just who they are. Anyone I'd know, do you think?"

Jack stared down into his now-empty tankard for a moment. I signaled for a refill for both of us.

"A lot of 'em come and go. They're all sorts, I suppose you'd say. O' course there's one or two as is real thick with Ralph. That understudy as you just talked about f'r instance. The two of them was pretty thick, it seems to me. As well as that Willis fella."

"Was Ralph thick with Richland?" I was surprised.

"Was that 'is name? Richland? Yes. Ralph and 'im spent a lot of time together, right 'ere in this same watering 'ole."

I made a mental note.

I left Jack in the public house, having his lunch, and started back to the Lyceum. As I came onto the street, a figure approached and stood blocking my way. Smartly dressed in a fashionable topcoat, with top hat and carrying a cane, it was the West Indian man I had seen with Ralph Bateman on the Embankment.

"Mr. Harry Rivers," he said.

I was startled that he not only knew who I was but that he could see through my disguise when even my old friend Jack Parsons had not done so. However, Jack had told me the man's name. I thought to throw it back at him.

"Mr. Henry Ogoon," I said.

It didn't faze him.

"There is a saying in your country, Mr. Rivers. It is 'a word to the wise.' You are familiar with the expression?"

"Of course." I nodded.

"A word to the wise, then, Mr. Rivers, assuming that you have some wisdom. Do not go prying where you are not welcome. Do I make myself clear?"

I took a deep breath. I didn't know this man nor was I aware of what he might be capable. But I was not going to be browbeaten. After all, I represented the Lyceum, Mr. Irving, and Mr. Stoker.

"That cuts both ways, Mr. Ogoon," I said. "You are familiar with the expression 'to cut both ways,' I take it?"

His deep brown eyes—almost black—bored into me. He said nothing for a long moment, and then he raised his hat, turned, and walked away. I saw that his head was completely shaved; not a hair on it nor on his face. I don't know why, but I shivered.

"So nothing definite, I'm afraid, sir," I reported back to Mr. Stoker as soon as I returned to the Lyceum. "Just wild talk and boasting by Ralph Bateman." I felt myself loath to report on my meeting with Henry Ogoon. I tried to put it out of my mind. If necessary I would mention it to my boss later, I told myself.

"Nothing new about that," grunted Stoker.

I had caught him in his exercise period. Perhaps with memories of his invalid childhood, when he had been confined to a bed and unable to walk, Bram Stoker observed a strict regimen of exercise. This involved pounding a large, stuffed canvas bag, which he had suspended in a corner of his office, and—as he now was—the swinging of heavy Indian clubs. I was always afraid that one would escape his powerful hands and fly off in my direction, so I tended to keep close to the door when I found him so engaged.

"Oh, and it seems Bateman is close with our ex-stage-hand Herbert Willis who, I'm sure you recall, sir, cursed the Lyceum when he was fired from it for excessive drinking," I said from around the doorpost. "And Bateman was definitely involved with Peter Richland."

"Involved? How so, Harry?"

I took a chance and eased myself into the room.

"Bateman and Richland were thick as thieves both before Ralph took off for the Caribbean Islands and, it seems, more so since his return. Right up to the time of Richland's death."

"Indeed?"

"And it seems that this Caribbean man who has turned up exercises some sort of power—if that's the right word—over Ralph." I felt suddenly uneasy as I said that. I could see the man's eyes boring into me.

"Explain yourself." Mr. Stoker put down the Indian clubs.

"Influence, I suppose it is." I searched for words. "Jack Parsons says that ever since Ralph got back from foreign parts, he has been more subdued and seems eager to please this man, whose name, by the way, is Henry Ogoon, or some such."

"Ogoon?" Stoker seemed surprised.

I nodded. "So Jack said. You know the name?"

"Just a coincidence, I'm sure." He placed the clubs carefully in the corner of the office. "It's just that Ogoun is the name of the storm god of Voudon. One of the deities, or *loa*, as they are termed." He thought for a moment. "You spoke to more than this man Parsons?"

"Oh yes," I said, and indeed I had. "I got into conversation with lighting men, props, even the wardrobe mistress. I figured she would hear anything worth hearing."

The big man sighed. "All right, Harry. Thank you."

"Can I get back to my own hair color now then, sir?" My head was starting to itch and I was sure it was Mr. Archibald's concoction that was responsible.

"Of course. Hopefully we won't be asking you to do that again."

I hurried off to the dressing rooms and got one of the

wardrobe assistants to boil up some water for me. I couldn't wait to wash my hair.

I thought about the situation. It was doubtful that Ralph could have sneaked into our theatre without being discovered, though that didn't go for Willis. We were very much more aware of strangers in our midst than Sadler's Wells apparently was. But even if Ralph had managed it, he was too portly and out of shape to have climbed to the fly tower and dropped sandbags. Again, not so with Willis. Other than his beer belly, he was a skinny scurf. As to the poisoning, we still were not certain as to just how that had been accomplished. Miss Terry's theory—and it seemed the most logical—was that the arsenic had been introduced to the hot lemonade that the Guv'nor always drank with his lunch. Yet that lunch was prepared by Mr. Turnbull, the caterer, an ancient gentleman who had been providing victuals for the Lyceum actors for longer than anyone could remember.

The more I thought about it, the more I became convinced that Ralph Bateman was not the culprit for the poisoning. Much as I hated to admit it, Jack Parsons could be right; it may well have been someone right here among the Lyceum's own staff, and although now dismissed, Herbert Willis did fit the bill.

There are over three hundred people employed by the Lyceum, including front of house and backstage staff. Yet few of them, so far as I could see, would have access to actors' provisions. And anyway, it was only the principals who were catered for; the extras and lesser roles invariably retired to the Druid's Head for their refreshments. So that would seem to rule out Willis. I found myself thinking around in circles and getting nowhere.

I was interrupted in my ruminating by remembering that my boss had suggested that we should—by which he meant that *I* should—do the decent thing and apprise Mrs.

Richland of her son's empty coffin. Not a task I looked forward to completing.

The evening performance went off without a hitch . . . if you didn't count John Whitby, as the sexton in the churchyard scene, dropping Yorick's skull and having to scamper across the stage to retrieve it. (Shades of that loathsome severed head!) It did provoke some laughter from the audience, but the Guv'nor quickly brought them back to the scene. Yet there were no falling sandbags, nor any other untoward incidents . . . until later.

The American actor Edwin Booth had arrived in London in January, destined for the Princess's Theatre. Regrettably, the manager of that establishment was more at home with crude forms of melodrama rather than higher standards of true drama, hoping for quick financial return. Mr. Booth, therefore, so it was reported, suffered from this bad presentation. Mr. Stoker and the Guv'nor decided to step in and offered to have Booth perform at the Lyceum in one of the Guv'nor's productions. It was decided that *Othello* would be the ideal vehicle, with Booth playing the title role and Irving playing Iago. The production was planned for late April, after *Hamlet* had run its course. I felt in two minds about this. I knew, of course, that we would be starting a new production when *Hamlet* came to an end, but the added pressure of hosting an American alongside Mr. Irving presaged all kinds of complications. I was not happy about it.

Since the start of the century, American actors had been coming to England to make an appearance. I think a lot of them came just to say that they had appeared in the homeland of Shakespeare, though some few wanted to be compared to the best that England could provide. In turn, many British actors had crossed the Atlantic Ocean to show off our talents in what used to be "the Colonies." The Guv'nor had himself talked to Mr. Stoker about the possibility of one day taking a Lyceum production across to America. Not just himself but the whole theatre: actors, stagehands, scenery, lights . . . a very ambitious project never before attempted. All the more reason, Mr. Irving said, for us to do it. Well, I wasn't holding my breath. Neither, I suspected, was Mr. Stoker.

As luck would have it, this very evening Colonel Wilberforce Cornell, Mr. Booth's business manager, attended our performance of *Hamlet*, to acquaint himself with our standards of excellence. He sat with my boss in the royal box, both his bald head and his monocle gleaming, and apparently thoroughly enjoyed the performance . . . despite John Whitby's blunder. The colonel, who was almost as tall as my boss, had a longish dark beard and a mustache that drooped on either side of his petulant mouth. I wondered if all Americans wore the wide-brimmed hats that the colonel carried. Such headgear would seem to promise far more sunshine than we enjoyed in these British Isles.

After the final curtain had fallen and the audience had dispersed, Colonel Cornell was brought onstage and my boss introduced me. I quickly ran over my duties but could sense that the gentleman was well acquainted with what had to be accomplished backstage during a performance. He was far more concerned about the specifics of Mr. Booth's role in the new production. Mr. Stoker pointed out details of the projected set that had been designed, and explained exactly where it would be erected after the *Hamlet* set was struck. My boss pointed out the details of the present scenery. Mr. Irving had brought a new sense of realism to the London stage with the sets presented at the Lyceum, and word of this had apparently crossed the Atlantic Ocean. Stoker and the Guv'nor stood admiring the present set and discussing ideas for *Othello*. I was close by, in the wings, and saw what happened next.

Suddenly, above the three of them, there was a clang and Mr. Stoker, with a quick upward look, pushed the colonel to one side. A short wooden batten, with three heavy lights tied to it, came crashing down. It smashed into the colonel's left shoulder but would surely have split his head had it not been for Mr. Stoker's quick reaction.

I shouted to the stagehands, still moving scenery, to watch for anyone descending and once again rushed to the ladder up the back wall. I started to climb as quickly as I could.

"Get him, Harry!" shouted Stoker.

I was too out of breath to reply but hurried on upward. Above me I heard someone curse as they hit against an obstacle, then there was a loud, rasping noise and a clang. I looked up as I climbed. I saw what looked like a bright light shining down from the fly tower, though with little in the way of actual illumination. I only glimpsed it through the slats of the gridiron, so I couldn't really make it out. Then something seemed to cover the light before moving off it again. I gritted my teeth and climbed till my heart was thumping in my chest.

I reached the fly gallery and dashed across the bridge to continue on upward on the central rear ladder. Across the top of the wall stretched the old gas table. This is where the gas used to be regulated, with a complicated system of valves, for the stage lighting. The stage area had been converted to the new electricity, but the gas table had not yet been removed. It was my guess that the intruder had bumped into it as he moved around.

I eventually reached the gridiron and stepped onto the slatted floor. My eyes were drawn back to the circle of light from above. I realized that a roof vent had been pried open—the sound I had heard—and that what I was seeing was the moon, just three days past full. Our intruder had blocked the light momentarily as he climbed up onto the shaft of the drum and exited through the vent, out onto the roof. I followed.

Chapter Six

B y the time I had got up to the fly floor inside the theatre, my eyes had adjusted to the low light. It, therefore, took only a moment, when I broke out on the rooftop, to be able to focus on the figure I was chasing. The moon, sliding in and out from behind the clouds, helped. The intruder was dressed all in black—which didn't help me—and had a good start, but I spotted him disappearing over the ridge of the roof on the north side toward Exeter Street. The front of the theatre was on Wellington Street, and I didn't think he would attempt to get down that façade with its big Gothic columns. But on the north side there was a variety of possibilities, with gutters and rainspouts, sloping gables, mansards, and dormers. Crestings, decorative eaves, and embellishments could afford handholds for a desperate man. I rushed after him, slipping and sliding on the ice-covered roof. I part fell and part threw myself down at the corner where I had last seen him, and peered over the edge. There was no sign of the man. He had either fallen to the street below or he had somehow managed to hang on and claw his way to freedom.

I struggled upright, which turned out to be a very bad move. My feet suddenly slid out from under me and I pitched over the side. Instinctively I reached out and managed to grab hold of the decorative cresting along the edge of the roof, quickly bringing up my other hand and hanging there, swinging like a pendulum. My feet scrambled to make purchase on the slope of the curved mansard roof below me, but there was nothing to give support. I have no idea what the temperature was, but it was icy cold and I was not wearing gloves. My fingers protested as I hung there, frantically trying to pull myself up.

I don't know how long it took, but my fingers finally gave out. I dropped from the top ledge and slid down the outward sloping mansard roof to suddenly come up short against the same decorative cresting on the lower edge. I was facedown, flat against the cold curve of the roof, my shoes hard against the wrought ironwork. I prayed that the decorative edge was not so old that it would give way.

I slowly turned my head first one way and then the other. To my left I saw a dormer projecting from the mansard. I vaguely recalled that there were some attic storage rooms, where spare ropes, pulleys, and the like were kept. If I could manage to edge along to that, I might be able to break the window and get inside. Slowly and very carefully I eased myself along toward the dormer, carefully placing my feet against the decorative spikes and whirls and sliding my body and face along the roof.

After what seemed an eternity I reached the protruding window. How, now, to break the glass? What did I have with which to hit it? The obvious thing was one of my shoes. Very, very slowly and carefully I took my weight on one leg and slid my other leg up until I could get to my shoe. After a struggle I got it off. The next issue was that it was in my left hand, with the window to my left, and I am right-handed. That should not be a problem, I told myself. Glass is fragile; windows are easily broken.

My first attempt somehow turned out to be not much more than a tap. I was cold. My hand was cold. My shoeless foot was now becoming extremely cold. I tried again, hitting as forcefully as I was able. The shoe bounced back off the glass, out of my hand, and disappeared over the edge of the roof.

I lay for several minutes flat against the roof, my head twisted to the side, my left foot not only cold but suffering from the pressure against the pointed iron of the cresting. I am not a religious man, but it did occur to me to pray. However, I could not see the hand of God reaching down and plucking me off the side of the building, so I tried to be practical. I very carefully eased myself around, turning over so that my back was now against the roof and my good right hand was closest to the defiant window. I struggled and contorted myself to remove my other shoe, realizing that this would be my last chance. I got it off and held it as securely as I possibly could. I reached out and smashed it into the glass.

The window exploded and jagged pieces flew in all directions. Happily, since I was flat against the roof and out of the line of fire, none of them struck me. I used the shoe to hit the glass several times more and removed the dangerous shards still attached to the window frame. Then I worked on getting myself inside the dormer, through the hole.

Colonel Cornell sat in a seat in the front row of the stalls, a doctor tending his smashed shoulder. His winged collar had broken free of its stud and stood out from his bruised face while his silk cravat was dragged to one side. The silk lapels of his jacket were severely creased. He had screwed his monocle back into his eye and now fixed me with a fierce stare as though it was all my fault that he had been so dishonored.

"No luck, Harry?" My boss stood to one side of the visitor and, happily, seemed more concerned about me than he was about the American. I told him what had happened, as one of the stagehands wrapped a blanket around my shivering form.

"Luck was a large part of it, sir, I'm sure," I said ruefully. "But it was all on the side of our visitor—our would-be assassin. There was no sign of him on the street, when I finally got down there. And no one standing around in the snow to be witness to anything. Not that I think they would have seen our man. He seemed to know what he was doing."

"Any sign of your shoe?"

I thought I caught the hint of a smile on my boss's face. "I'm sure it is now a welcome cover on the foot of some street arab," I said.

"D'you know this—this assassin?" spluttered the colonel.

I noticed that the Guv'nor had departed and left our visitor for Mr. Stoker to handle.

"There's the rub, as the Bard would say. We have been plagued by this miscreant before but have yet to detain him," said Stoker.

"Mr. Booth would not be willing . . ."

"Mr. Booth must make his own decisions." Stoker towered over the seated, disheveled figure. He could be very forceful when necessary. "I can only add my own apologies to those already expressed by Mr. Irving for this unfortunate occurrence. As he explained, we are working with the police to detain the person responsible. I am sure the matter will be resolved long before Mr. Booth might set foot on our stage, so he may have no qualms on that score."

"I would rather we had kept this in-house, Harry," said Stoker the next morning, frowning at the open newspaper laid out on the desk in front of him. "But these damned Americans are always looking for publicity—good or bad."

The *Morning Herald* had published a report of last evening's events with the bold caption *Mysterious Intruder Attempts to Kill American Actor's Manager*. Happily—as I pointed out to my boss—it appeared on page three rather than the front page, being displaced by a lengthy report from Dungannon, Ireland, about a continuation of riots in the Catholic village of Listamlaght brought about by a party of Orangemen. The description of the breaking of windows and doors in Listamlaght, along with the frightening and beating of villagers and the setting on fire of one of the cottages, took pride of place over a falling light in a London theatre.

"How did the newspaper get hold of the story, sir?" I asked.

"Our Colonel Cornell himself, I'd wager, Harry. None of our people would have spoken to any newspaperman."

I nodded. "It will be interesting to see if the colonel's philosophy is valid," I said. "If we get a full house tonight, it could conceivably be because of the story."

"Hrmph! I think—and I'm sure the Guv'nor would agree—that we would far rather depend upon more positive publicity." He crumpled up the newspaper and tossed it into the wastebasket. "What are your plans for the day, Harry?"

I got up from my seat, ready to go back to work. "First is to get Sam Green's crew checking ropes and pulleys again. The closing of the vent onto the roof I personally supervised before going home last night. I'm doubling theatre security for tonight's performance and we'll especially keep our eyes open for Saturday."

"If you can fit it in, Harry, it might not be a bad idea to get together with that police sergeant. I'd feel a bit more comfortable if he has a couple of his constables keeping an eye on the place as well."

"Yes, sir. Good idea. I'll make a point of seeing him this morning."

"Oh! And the Guv'nor wondered if you'd mind running around to his rooms again? His friend Mr. Barker, who shares the rooms with him, apparently came up with an old recipe his mother used to use that has helped the Guv'nor settle his stomach since the poisoning. It seems he forgot to bring the bottle with him this morning. He doesn't think he'll have time to go back home again before this evening's performance."

"He wants me to pick it up for him?" Suddenly the day brightened.

"If you have time, Harry. I told him I could send any one of the lads around, since you are so busy . . ."

"Oh no, sir! No, I'll be happy to do it. I could do it on my way to see Sergeant Bellamy, in fact."

Stoker smiled and gave me a knowing look. I swore that he knew my thoughts before I knew them myself! I left the room before he might change his mind.

I stood outside 15a Grafton Street, brushed the light sprinkling of snow off my shoulders, and straightened my tie. I felt a little like a giddy schoolboy infatuated by a girl in his class. I mentally shook my head and stood up straighter. Not the time to get carried away! I was there simply to pick up the Guv'nor's medicine. I lifted the polished brass knocker and let it fall.

Mrs. Cooke answered the door. She wore what appeared to be the same black dress she had been wearing on my previous visit, though perhaps she just had a number of such garments, much like a uniform. I explained my errand and hoped that she would not simply ask me to wait and then bring me the bottle. I was in luck.

"Do please come up, sir. I'm sure I don't know what bottle you are talking about but mayhap one of the girls will know."

"The young lady who assisted me in finding Mr. Irving's

book last time I was here," I said as I climbed the stairs. "She seemed a bright young person."

"Young Betsy, are you meaning, sir?"

"No!" I said quickly. Then added, more calmly, "I think her name was Jenny."

I was left standing on the landing but it was only a moment before Jenny appeared. She looked pleased to see me, with a slight blush to her cheek. I grinned broadly, like a fool, and then tried to look serious.

"I'm on another errand for Mr. Irving," I said.

"Yes, sir."

"Harry. Remember?"

I swear her blush deepened. "Yes . . . Harry." Her voice was little above a whisper.

I told her what I needed. "I hope I'm not being a bother," I said.

"Oh no, Harry. Not at all." She gave me a quick smile. "I think I know the bottle you mean. Mr. Irving keeps it on the table beside his bed. I'll go and get it."

While she was gone I racked my brains to think of an excuse to linger. I'm sure I could have suggested I be offered a cup of tea, but there would be no reason for Jenny to join me or even linger while I drank it. Suddenly she was back, holding a small stone bottle in her hands.

"That was quick," I said.

We stood a long moment just looking at each other. Suddenly she seemed to realize that she was still holding the bottle. She reached out her hand as I did the same, and we touched. She almost dropped the bottle but I quickly caught it. We both smiled.

"I—I suppose I must be on my way," I said. "I, er, I hope Mr. Irving thinks of other things for me to come for. Oh! By the way, I did speak to Mr. Stoker about you and your fellow employees visiting the theatre one of these days. He said he thought it a good idea."

"Oh, that would be lovely!" She looked deep into my eyes, and it was my turn to almost drop the bottle. "Thank you so much, Harry."

I had a sudden thought that perhaps I could somehow get another look at the mysterious letters from Richland to the Guv'nor. They were right there in the room next to where I was standing. But on what pretext could I again invade Mr. Irving's desk? No. It was not to be on this visit.

I caught Jenny studying me from under lowered eyelashes. I blurted out: "If I may be so bold, do you receive a day off during the week?"

"Yes, I do." She nodded her head vigorously. "Sunday, after ten of the clock."

"Sunday at ten?" I said. "I'd like . . . I mean . . . if I may . . . ?"

"Yes, Harry."

I have no recollection of leaving the house nor of hailing a cab. I suppose I must have done so, for I found myself bowling along the Strand, smiling into the blowing snow and clutching the medicine bottle as though my life depended upon it. I raised my stick and tapped on the trapdoor. It was opened and the driver looked down.

"What was the address I gave you?" I asked.

"Lyceum Theatre, sir. We're nearly there."

"Drop me at the Little Vine Street police station instead, would you?" I remembered that I had to catch up with Sergeant Bellamy.

It was actually lunchtime before I did get to see him. At the station I learned that he usually took a liquid lunch at the Stag's Head on Sackville Street, and I made my way there for my own repast. I found the sergeant sitting at a corner table consulting the *Sporting Times* as he downed a pint of the black Whitbread porter that was the speciality of the public house and nibbled on a wedge of Cheshire cheese.

"I'll have the same," I called to the barman as I dropped into the chair opposite Bellamy.

"The bread's stale," observed the policeman, indicating the thickly sliced hunk of homemade brown bread he'd left on the side of his platter.

"Doesn't look it," I observed, peering down at it.

"Trust me. They don't put out the good stuff till about two of the clock. They need to get rid of yesterday's leftovers."

I accepted the glass of stout brought by the serving girl and tasted the bread. I made a face and, like Bellamy, stuck with the cheese by itself.

"What brings you here, sir?" he asked, his eyes still running down the columns of the *Sporting Times*. "Wouldn't be that affair with the falling light at your theatre, would it?"

"Indirectly," I admitted. "Mr. Stoker wondered if you might be able to put a couple of your constables out there, to keep an extra eye on things tonight and perhaps for a day or two?"

He nodded. "We think we can manage that, sir." He put down his newspaper, folding it neatly down its length to leave visible a listing of horses running the next day. "You a betting man, Mr. Rivers?" he asked, nodding at the paper.

"Only when it's a sure thing." I smiled. He did not return it.

"We hear tell that this falling light 'accident' is not the first thing to upset the Lyceum applecart."

"Where did you hear that?" I was curious and somewhat annoyed. Mr. Stoker had spoken of keeping things "in-house."

"Oh, word gets around, sir. Word gets around. We always keep our ear to the ground, as it were."

I thought it wise to keep on good terms with the police sergeant. I signaled for the girl to refill his almost-empty glass. He watched her do so with one eye closed, as though measuring the amount she poured. He said nothing for a while as she walked away. He sat staring at the brimming porter.

"Just being neighborly," I said, suddenly realizing that a police officer might see such a simple gesture as an approach to bribery. Though why I would need to bribe him, I have no idea. Why was I getting nervous?

"Indeed." He lifted the glass, drank a considerable amount, and then set it down again.

"Any news on the head?" I asked, hoping to change the subject.

"Ah! The head," he said, enigmatically.

"Have you found out how and why it got into our theatre?"

"One thing at a time, sir. As to how it got there, no, we have not yet ascertained that piece of information."

"What about how and why it fell out of our scenery?" I persisted.

"There again, sir, we are afraid the answer is in the negative." He sank his teeth into more of the cheese.

"In other words, you've got nothing?"

Sergeant Bellamy took a moment to wash down the cheese with a good mouthful of stout.

"When you put it like that, sir, you are correct. We are still working on it, of course."

I had some cheese and porter myself. I couldn't really fault the sergeant. I suppose there are few clues on a severed head to indicate who placed it where. Then I had an idea. "If there is a bodiless head floating around," I said, "then there must also be a headless body out there somewhere."

"Logical."

"You have no reports of such a thing?"

"Not at C Division, no."

"What about the other divisions?"

He actually paused with the last of his cheese halfway up to his mouth. "We will make a point of checking on that, sir."

"Good." I returned to my own cheese and porter. I realized that tomorrow would be a good day to visit Mrs. Richland, to advise her about the empty state of her son's coffin.

Mrs. Richland lived out at Twickenham, west of the City, in a house close to the villa once lived in by Alexander Pope, the eighteenth-century poet famous for his use of the heroic couplet. Pope's beautiful home had been purchased with the money he had made from translating Homer's *Iliad*. Mrs. Richland's abode was nowhere near as impressive as Pope's, yet it did back onto an exceedingly beautiful stretch of the River Thames, upstream from the popular Eel Pie Island. I had learned that Mrs. Richland's late husband, Henry, had been some years her senior and had passed away two years ago, from a heart attack. I was sacrificing almost a day of precious time in order to visit Mrs. Richland, but Stoker did feel—and I had to agree—that it was only right and proper that we let her know what we had discovered regarding her son's body, so Saturday morning found me in Twinckenham.

The driveway curved around to give the visitor a glimpse of the long, narrow garden behind the house, stretching down to the riverbank. I could not help but notice that the once manicured lawn had been sadly neglected and the small boathouse in the distance was leaning sideways at a slight angle. I thought I saw someone disappear into the boathouse as I glanced at it. I hoped it was not Mrs. Richland, since I wanted to make this visit as brief as decently possible.

An aged maid answered my second knock on the front door. The large brass knocker, I observed, was due a polish and the doorstep a whitening.

"Yes, sir?"

"Is Mrs. Richland at home?" I enquired. "I would like a few moments of her time, if possible."

I handed the maid my card, its corner appropriately turned down, which she took and disappeared, leaving me standing on the doorstep with the door ajar. It was some time before she reappeared and ushered me inside. She took my hat and coat and then led the way up to the first-floor drawing room, where I found Mrs. Richland seated at a small table close to a very low fire. She was well wrapped in a tea gown with no less than two woolen shawls held tightly about her shoulders. I found this understandable when I discovered little heat coming from the fireplace.

"An unexpected visit, Mr. Rivers," she said, holding my card in her hand as though it were somehow tainted. She studied it at length through a tortoiseshell-framed lorgnette. She did not ask me to sit, despite the number of chairs scattered about the room. "To what do I owe this encounter?"

"I have some news regarding your son's . . . er, regarding your son," I said.

"My son is dead and buried, Mr. Rivers, as well you know. You were at his funeral, were you not?"

"Yes. Well, that is the point, ma'am."

"Then kindly get to it. I have matters that need to be attended and time is irrevocable."

She smelled strongly of camphor; her shawls were probably kept in a camphor chest for much of the year. I could not imagine what business she might have that was in the least bit urgent, but who was I to question her?

"Mrs. Richland, your son's grave was recently opened and the coffin . . ."

"What?" She looked up sharply and her eyes were ice. "What do you mean, my son's grave was opened? Pray explain yourself, sir!"

I was afraid I'd make a mess of trying to explain things. *Thank you, Mr. Stoker*, I thought, *for leaving this task to me!*

"The police . . ." I began. Best to bring in mention of the authorities, I thought. "It was apparently necessary to determine . . . that is to say, to confirm that the body . . . that your son . . ." I took a deep breath and plunged in. "It would appear that your son's body is missing, Mrs. Richland. I'm sorry to have to let you know in this way but Mr. Stoker felt—we all felt—that you needed to be informed. There was nothing in the coffin but a tree trunk. The body is gone!"

I don't know what sort of reaction I expected. I was certainly prepared to call the maid should the administering of smelling salts be necessary, but they were not. Mrs. Richland rose to her feet—happily, still a couple of inches shorter than myself—and stared me in the face.

"I do not know what you are saying, nor implying, Mr. Rivers, but I think I should advise you that I do retain the services of a competent solicitor. My son's remains were placed in consecrated soil by a respected church minister. They should remain there, undisturbed, for all eternity. If you have somehow interfered with that repose, then I must remind you that a higher authority than that of the Metropolitan constabulary may bring you to task. Bodies of the deceased do not transmute into tree trunks. If what you say is true, then it sounds to me like the shenanigans of a theatrical production. I will look into this affair, and believe me when I say that you will be hearing further from me. Good day to you, Mr. Rivers!"

I got back to the theatre just in time for the matinee performance. During the first interval I was backstage talking with old Margery Connelly, the wardrobe mistress, who was sewing on a button for Meg Grey. As we chatted, Miss Connelly mentioned seeing Peter Richland in the wings before curtain up.

"This afternoon?" I asked, perplexed.

"Yes. He wasn't in costume," she said. "Everyone was scurrying about, as they do before curtain-up, you know?"

"Yes." I was still trying to take in what she said. "Are you certain it was Mr. Richland?"

"Oh yes. Well, fairly certain, Mr. Rivers. My eyes are still good for close-up work—which is what you need, you know, working in wardrobe—but they are not all they once were for distance, I'm afraid. Why one time I . . ."

"Yes. Yes, sorry for interrupting, Miss Connelly, but you do know that Peter Richland died? You were at the funeral, I believe. He couldn't possibly have been here."

She stopped her sewing and her face went white. "Oh dear me! Yes, of course! How silly of me. Oh dear! Perhaps . . . perhaps . . . No, it must have been my eyes. But it did look like Mr. Richland. Of course, he was on the prompt side and I was opposite prompt. But still . . . Oh dear!"

"It's very dark in the wings," I said. I could see her worrying that she was starting to lose her faculties, and I tried to set her mind at rest. "Don't worry about it, Miss Connelly. I'm sure it was a natural mistake." Then I had a thought, and laughed. "Of course, it could have been Peter Richland's ghost. Perhaps the Lyceum has now got its own Man in Grey to match the one at the Drury Lane Theatre."

Margery Connelly did not laugh with me.

Chapter Seven

"I've been thinking about our missing body, Harry," said Stoker later that afternoon, when the matinee crowd had cleared out.

"Yes, sir?"

"If whoever emptied Richland's coffin of his body was responsible for separating top and torso, and then planted the head here in our scenery, would it not make sense that he'd also secrete the body right here in our theatre?"

I thought for a moment. "That does seem to make a certain sense," I admitted. "Why deposit them in two different places when one will do, albeit with head distinct from body? So, what's the plan, sir?"

"Why, we must search the theatre, of course!" He got up and slipped off his jacket. Mr. Stoker always dressed well, and his clothes were expensively tailored. I could understand that he wouldn't want to go digging around backstage and elsewhere in his best coat. He carefully hung it from the mahogany clothes tree by the door. "I suggest we start at the bottom and work our way up. Lead on to the understage, Harry!"

I led the way out to the stairs heading down to the dressing rooms, wardrobe, and green room. I led on through the opening that put us underneath the stage itself. It was a large, low-ceilinged space filled with boxes, pieces of furniture, hampers of clothing, and assorted properties. In the few short years I had been at the Lyceum, I had never fully explored this vast, dark area. For some reason I felt uncomfortable down there, a remnant of childhood fears. I had vague memories of once being inadvertently locked inside a large trunk I had climbed into, in the attic of the Hounslow Masonic Institution for Boys. The attic was, of course, out-of-bounds, but that hadn't deterred an adventurous spirit such as myself. The experience of being locked in complete darkness for three hours did, however, leave its mark.

Many of the old oil lamps and floats, and a pair of broken limelights were piled in one corner. I had honestly been meaning to get down there and clear up one of these days . . . but I never seemed to find the time. Happily, I didn't have to give any excuses to my boss; he knew the score.

"Check the trapdoors, Harry."

"You think the body might be in one of them?" I asked.

"No. Not likely. But it struck me that if our villain can cut ropes coming down from above, he can certainly cut ropes working on trapdoors coming up from the bottom."

I should have thought of that and mentally kicked myself. The traps were important, and most stages had a number of them. For this production of *Hamlet* we had three: two placed one on either side of the stage and the third at the rear. Climbing up, I saw that the rear one, used for the Ghost of Hamlet's Father, was fine. The one stage right was the grave trap, the section of stage that was lowered just sufficiently for the actors to appear to step down into the open grave in Act Five, Scene One, where the skull of Yorick is unearthed. I climbed up the stepladder beside the mechanism. Ropes attached to the platform ran over pulleys so that the stagehands could pull on them and lower or raise the platform.

"This one seems to be all right," called Stoker, from stage left.

My blood suddenly ran cold. "Not so this one," I said. "The ropes have been cut partway through. Whoever stepped onto this tonight, their weight would cause it to let go. It would drop like a stone to the bottom!"

"Probably not enough to kill anyone, but certainly sufficient to cause serious injury," said Stoker, coming over to join me. "Get someone on this, Harry. Right away! We don't need any more accidents."

I rounded up Sam Green and got him and one of his men to replacing the ropes. I rejoined Stoker, who was standing holding up an oil lamp and studying a small flat lying on its side at the back wall of the area. There was little lighting in this whole section.

"What is this doing here, Harry? Why isn't it in the scenery bay?"

I looked at the flat. "I'm quite sure it's not part of any scene we have for *Hamlet*. Leftover from a past production, I'd say. I don't know why it was put here."

It was painted to look like a section of stone wall. Although it didn't exactly match the stonework of the basement wall under the stage, the flat did tend to blend in and thus—I presumed—that was how it had got overlooked and left there. I called to Sam, who was just about to leave the trapdoor platform.

"Sam! See that this flat gets back up to the scenery bay, would you? It doesn't belong here."

"Sure thing, 'Arry!"

I turned back to Stoker, who was now digging through a trunk full of assorted pieces of Roman armor from *Julius Caesar*—breastplates, greaves, vambraces, and assorted togas, tunics, and cloaks.

"Think the body might be in there?" I asked.

"You just never know. Look everywhere, Harry."

"Yes, sir."

"'Ere, 'Arry! What's this, then?" Sam Green's voice caught my attention and had Stoker standing upright from the trunk of Roman props. "This is a dodgy do an' no mistake," muttered Sam. "I ain't never see'd that afore."

He had moved the flat away from the wall and revealed a hole in the stonework behind it that was about two feet square.

"Looks as though it might be for drainage," said Stoker uncertainly. "You know how damp it can get down here."

"Big 'ole just for drainin', beggin' yer pardon, Mr. Stoker," said Sam, removing his cap and scratching his head.

"You are right," agreed my boss.

There was a mesh grill covering the hole, but when I touched it, it came free. It did not seem to be fastened at all.

"Get a better light, Sam," Stoker said. "Let's take a look."

When Sam returned with a bright naphtha lamp, we moved inside. Behind the grill a larger space opened up that extended back to a corroded iron pipe that had once carried away any water that might have seeped into the theatre's foundations. Between the grill opening and the pipe was what amounted to a small room, albeit with little height to stand upright. A soiled, torn mattress lay in one corner of the space, two threadbare blankets across it. There were one or two upturned wooden boxes, one bearing the stub of a candle, and on the floor a tin plate on which sat a large rat. I kicked at it and the varmint scuttled away, disappearing into an unseen hole in a dark corner.

"What have we here?" said Stoker. "It would seem to be a hideaway; an abscondment for some Lyceum rapscallion."

"This opens up all kinds of possibilities," I said. "I would doubt it was used by any employee of the theatre . . . Why would they need it? No. There is the strong possibility of someone from outside making use of this."

"Someone who would not then have to pass the scrutiny of our vigilant Bill Thomas."

"Exactly."

Sam pointed out an old tin of rat poison. "Some rat catcher, d'you think, sir?" he asked.

"None that I know of," I said. "Leastwise, not an official one for the theatre."

The three of us examined the whole area, which didn't take long. We found no clues to the occupant, though Stoker did find five or six empty liquor bottles in one corner.

"Could be this is an *old* 'idey-'ole, sir," volunteered Sam. "May'ap no one's been 'ere in years."

"I think not, Sam." Stoker prodded the blankets with his foot. "These blankets may be old, but they are not covered with dust. And the burnt wick of the candle is still flexible. If it were ancient, it would be brittle and snap off. No, this place has been used, and fairly recently at that."

We sent off Sam, with the oil lamp, to return to his work, and Stoker and I continued a survey of the below-stage area with the brighter illumination. There was a section far from the descending steps and not far from the newly discovered hole where it looked as though a circular area of the floor had been cleared.

"What's this, then?" I said.

Burnt-down candles stood around on the ground, apparently to mark the area. There was a liberal amount of sawdust in the center, with some dark substance mixed in. It looked as though it had once been liquid and had now congealed. I noticed an unpleasant pungent odor but with a second, slightly sweet, smell lingering. I sniffed, as did Stoker. I looked at him quizzically.

He prodded at the sawdust with the toe of his elegant boot. "If I am not mistaken, Harry, this may be the residue of blood, with the sawdust put down to absorb it."

"Blood?" I was aware of a tremble in my voice.

He nodded. "And that slightly sweet smell, judging from those bottles that we found in the hiding area, is rum."

"Rum?" I felt like a fool standing there repeating the words as Stoker said them.

The big man stroked his beard and paced around the area.

"Is this another case for Sergeant Bellamy?" I asked. Then I had an idea. "Would the blood be from the severed head?"

"No. No, in fact it probably is not even human blood, Harry. A chicken, perhaps. A rooster."

"What?"

As we moved about the cleared area, my foot kicked against something. I picked it up. It was a small metal cup. I saw that it was probably silver and was handleless. It looked vaguely familiar, possibly from the prop box. I put it down again.

Stoker stopped his pacing and beckoned me, leading the way back to the hiding hole. He took the naphtha lamp from my hand and we entered. Stoker stood for a moment in the center of the space, crouched down because of the low ceiling, and slowly swung around in a circle, studying the walls.

"Aha!"

He moved forward and pushed aside a box. I was able to make out a crude design painted on the wall in red paint . . . or what I assumed to be paint.

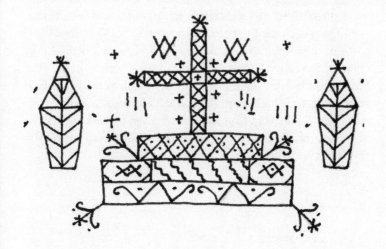

"As I suspected," muttered Stoker. "Come, Harry. Let us return to my office. There is nothing more we can do here for now. We have much food for thought."

When we did get back, Bill Thomas brought us each a cup of his strong tea. I was grateful for it but wished he was more liberal with his milk and sugar, to assuage the bitterness of the bergamot in the Earl Grey.

"Thank you, Bill," said Stoker as the old man went back to his station. "Now then, Harry. Let's get our noggins to work. Have we stumbled upon the home of a Lyceum ghost, d'you think? Perhaps the one that Miss Connelly thought she saw? If so, it's a very earthbound one that requires some form of habitation. No! My instinct tells me this hiding place we just discovered was used by whoever dropped sandbags on you, and even the one who poisoned the Guv'nor. And my old granny always told me to listen to my instinct. 'It's the true voice of your spirit,' she used to say." He shrugged back into his swallowtail coat, ran a hand quickly through his thick, dark hair, and sat down.

I nodded, inured to Stoker's Irish beliefs and traditions. "Do you think he'll return to it, then, sir?"

The big man shook his head. "I very much doubt it, Harry, though you never know. He must surely know that we'll search every inch of this old place. It probably served him well for a long-enough period." He paused before continuing. "However, if he *does* return, then I think he may be a much more dangerous personage than I had originally believed."

Chapter Eight

"Herbert Willis," I said suddenly.

"I beg your pardon?" Stoker looked surprised.

"Herbert Willis. That stagehand that we had to let go. Bill Thomas may be right," I said, warming to the idea. "Willis cursed the Lyceum when he left. He was always sneaking off somewhere to tilt the bottle while he was here, and you found bottles down there. He could well have discovered that drainage space and made use of it, for God knows how long, for his imbibing. Then, after he was dismissed, he could have slipped back into the theatre—perhaps while we were away at Richland's funeral—and ensconced himself there while he waged his war against us. What do you think, sir?"

"Mmm!" The dark red head nodded up and down. "It is possible," was all he said. He drank deeply of the dark, strong tea, seeming not to notice its slightly bitter taste. He eventually put down his cup and looked at me. "What you say of Mr. Willis may or may not be the answer, Harry. But

I think there is far more going on here. Your Mr. Willis may have been a drinker, but most of those bottles we found were empty *rum* bottles, which could be very significant."

I didn't follow, and my face must have registered it. Stoker continued.

"You remember what I told you of zombies, Harry?"

How could I forget? I'd had some very disturbing dreams for the last couple of nights.

"Are you saying that the Lyceum has become a home for zombies?" I asked.

He gave one of his mirthless chuckles. "Not exactly, Harry. No. But . . . not far from it!"

A sudden chill swept over me and I shivered. Bram Stoker's wild stories were one thing, and I could listen to them all day, but to suddenly find myself in the middle of one? No! That was not what I had signed on for.

"What was that design on the wall down there, sir?" I asked.

I moved my chair a little closer to his desk as he settled in and cleared a space on the tabletop. "That and the bottles are what suggest an alternate scenario to me," he said. "The latter, as I said, are rum bottles."

"That is significant, you say?"

"Highly." He laid down a sheet of paper on the desk and started drawing on it. I quickly recognized—even upside down from where I sat—the design we had found on the wall below stage.

"You certainly memorized that fast enough," I commented.

"That's because I know it well," he said, cryptically. "I've mentioned it to you before, Harry, and now you can see it. It is what is known as a *vévé*, the symbol of one of the deities of Voudon. These gods, or loa, each have such a particular pictorial representation. This is the symbol for the god of the dead: Guédé."

I made no comment. I sat with my eyes focused on his drawing.

"Notice that it looks something like a gravestone, with a stylized cross atop the base. On either side are representations of coffins. All the little swirls and marks have meaning, Harry. And in the rituals of Voudon—a polytheistic religion, I might add—the use of rum is important when drawing down the chthonic deities. The rum is distributed to the four 'corners' of the ritual space."

"The cleared circle we found?" I suggested.

He nodded. "Marked by the candles. That was the consecrated space. The *houfor* for the ritual."

"What ritual would that be?" I asked, already suspicious as to the answer.

"It involved sacrifice to the loa. In this case, the killing of a white rooster."

"You—you're talking primitive ritual," I protested. "This is London, England, in Her Imperial Majesty's year of 1881. Modern times!"

"You think all primitive religion has ground to a halt just because Victoria is on the throne?" His eyes bored into me.

"No. No, of course not! It's just . . ."

"No, Harry. All I am saying is that it appears this is no mere slapping at the Lyceum by a discontented stagehand. This is something I would hazard to say is far beyond the comprehension of our Mr. Willis. Something far more serious indeed."

"You are surely not suggesting that our Peter Richland has been turned into a zombie?" I said, thinking of Marjorie Connelly's vision of what may have seemed like Richland's ghost. Could it have been a zombie of Richland? I shuddered at the thought.

"No, nothing like that. Simply that a perhaps similar Voudon ritual, aimed at the downfall of the Lyceum, may well have been performed in our very under-stage area."

I said nothing.

Stoker sat deep in thought for a long moment before finally saying, "It is not unlikely that further rites may yet be held there."

There was another silence that stretched on. I did not want to break it, to interrupt his thought processes. Finally, he looked up at me from under his bushy eyebrows, his eyes questioning.

"If—and I do say 'if,' Harry—it is necessary to undertake more midnight activity, may I count on your help? This would be a very different enterprise from our last adventure. It is perhaps unfair of me to ask you, since this is far outside the borders of your appointed employment, but . . ." He let the words hang there. Then he sighed. "We will talk further on this should the occasion arise."

I felt uncomfortable but at the same time drawn in to whatever nefarious scheme my boss had swirling around inside his head. I felt as a mongoose must feel when locked onto the eyes of a cobra. I was repelled but I was fascinated; I could not look away.

"Where do zombies fit in?" I finally asked, in a quiet voice.

"Where indeed, Harry? If, in fact, they do. But they are a product, if you like, of Voudon. A tool of the evil side of that practice. And I would hasten to add that Voudon is not a purely malevolent religion. It has its benevolent side also, bringing healing and well-being to its many followers. But, as I have told you, zombies are created by a Boko—the representative of the evil side—working in just such a ritual circle as we have found under the stage of the Lyceum." He studied his drawing for a long moment before, with a sigh, he looked up at me and smiled, breaking the spell. "But this hasn't helped us find the body, has it?"

"No, sir. It has not." I was unsure as to whether or not I wanted to stop this discussion of the working of evil in our midst, but I think I did need a change of direction for a while.

Stoker reached around for one of his leather-bound ledgers and dropped it, with a thump, on his desk, covering the drawing. "I can't spend any more time on this right now, Harry. I need to think things through a little more. I'll have to leave you to continue the search of the theatre. Get a couple of front of house people to check that side of the footlights and take any hands you need to comb backstage. I'd like to have a clean sweep before curtain-up tonight."

"Yes, sir."

"Oh, and Harry . . . ?"

"Yes, sir?"

"Be careful."

Dismissed, I got three of the stagehands started on searching for the body along with any additional attempts at undermining the production and passed the word to Herbert Gardner, who ran the commissariat, to start going over the front of house. Gardner grumbled, since there is not a lot of time between the matinee and the evening performance. I told him to get others involved and do the best he could.

I went back to my own little office. Not that it could truly be so called. It was a large alcove—much like a small room with one wall missing—that held my own greatly battered desk and chair together with an open bookcase stuffed with scripts and reference works. There was no carpet on the floor. A single gas jet jutted out from the wall . . . The electrification for backstage had not yet included me. Untidy piles of assorted props spilled over from my desk onto the floor. It was a mess, I admit, but I felt comfortable and safe there. With no wall or door, people passed freely to and fro in front of my space, often stopping to ask a question or lodge a complaint. I spent the next hour catching up on complaints, suggestions, directions, and assorted notes from everyone from the Guv'nor on down. The whole time, at the back of my mind, the worry about what sort of a midnight adventure Mr. Stoker was dreaming up plagued me.

I slipped out for a quick bite to eat, getting back an hour before curtain call. Reports from backstage and front of house confirmed that there was no headless body or further signs of trickery anywhere in the theatre. I breathed a sigh of relief and sent word to my boss.

Half an hour before curtain-up the Guv'nor always had either a hot lemonade or a cup of tea and three arrowroot biscuits. It was a tradition of his. At that time he would be in costume and makeup but was then able to relax and run over any lines or other business before curtain. Sometimes Miss Terry joined him, though she was more often refining her makeup until receiving the first page.

As I sat at my desk I saw the aged figure of Mr. Turnbull passing my office bearing a tray holding the Guv'nor's snack. Mr. Turnbull has been with the company for more years than anyone could remember. He retired from the front office a decade ago but couldn't abide being away from the theatre. He became unofficial personal caterer to the theatre's star actor when Mr. Irving first appeared at the Lyceum in 1871 in *The Bells.* This was under the management of Ralph Bateman's now deceased father, Hezekiah Bateman, and long before my time or Mr. Stoker's.

I saw Mr. Turnbull stumble slightly and got up from my desk to go to him. But he recovered and moved on to start the climb up the stairs to the two stars' dressing rooms. I followed, not a little concerned about the old man. When we got to the Guv'nor's door, I reached around Mr. Turnbull and tapped on the door, then opened it and let him go in. He tottered forward to put the tray down on the table beside Mr. Irving's makeup bench.

When Turnbull came back out he thanked me.

"Not at all," I said. And then I had a thought. "Tell me, Mr. Turnbull, last week when the Guv'nor got poisoned, was anyone else here when you brought up Mr. Irving's hot lemonade?"

His white head rose from his stooped shoulders as he pursed his lips and wrinkled his already well-creased face, thinking back the past few days.

"I usually manage quite well, Mr. Rivers, by putting down the tray on the floor so that I can open the door, but I do recall that on that day someone did reach around me and open the door for me—just as yourself a moment ago."

"They opened the door for you?"

"No, wait! I tell a lie!" He smacked his forehead with the flat of his hand. "I had placed the tray down on the floor and opened the door myself. Then, as I turned back to get the tray, someone handed it to me."

"Who was it?" I asked. I realized that whoever it was could well have dropped poison into the Guv'nor's cup while Mr. Turnbull was opening the door.

"Ah! Now there you have me, I'm afraid. My old eyes are not what they used to be, and besides, I don't know half the people who now move around here. Not like the old days. Not by a long chalk. Why, I remember when . . ."

"Yes. Thank you, Mr. Turnbull. So you didn't recognize the man but did he seem familiar, however vaguely?"

"Oh yes. Yes, I had seen him around. He was of the Lyceum and no mistake."

"Can you describe him?"

"Tall. Leastwise, taller than me, though that probably doesn't tell you a great deal, Mr. Rivers, does it? Clean shaven, I do remember that. So many young men these days like to . . ."

"Age?" I interrupted.

"Age? Oh, now there you have me again. I am never very good at guessing a person's age. Young ladies especially. But then, there you have to be circumspect, do you not? Young people generally . . ."

"Thank you, Mr. Turnbull. Yes. If you should recall who it was who handed you the tray, please let me know at once, would you?"

"Of course, Mr. Rivers. Of course."

He stood a moment as though getting his bearings and then shuffled off to the landing. Clutching the handrail, he descended once again to the stage floor. I watched him go. Well, at least his story seemed to confirm that someone had had access to the Guv'nor's lemonade enough to poison it. But the question remained . . . *who* had done it?

The evening performance went smoothly. John Whitby kept a firm hold on Yorick's skull, Anthony Sampson's Polonius was well stabbed through the arras, and nobody dropped sandbags or lights on anyone. We had a full house and the Guv'nor took seven curtain calls. I felt cheered as I headed back to Chancery Lane and my rooms at Mrs. Bell's. The wind had picked up and I knew I'd hear it screaming past my poorly fitting window all night, but I felt tired enough I didn't think it would keep me awake. Besides, I comforted myself, I was to see Jenny in the morning.

After the wild and windy night, Sunday was fair and mild. A very light snow fell, but the sun struggled to break through the low overcast, occasionally peeking through the clouds like a muted spotlight seeking to highlight an actor.

As I alighted from the omnibus, I found Jenny waiting for me at the corner of Bond Street. She was wearing a midnight blue cape trimmed with gray squirrel fur. Although obviously far from new, the cape complemented Jenny's bright face, dark hair, and sparkling eyes. On her head was a fur-felt walking hat, draped with velvet on the brim to match the blue of the cape; folds of taffeta around the crown finished with a knot and a light blue fancy quill. Her three-button kid gloves echoed the gray of the fur. I almost gasped at the picture she made, standing with a slight if nervous smile on her face. I quickly opened my umbrella against the light snow and moved close beside her.

"You look beautiful, Jenny, if I may say so," I said.

She blushed prettily and looked down. "Thank you, Harry."

"Where would you like to go? How long before you have to be back?"

"I'm free until two of the clock," she said. "Mrs. Cooke doesn't like for us to be late getting back."

"Have no fear, Jenny. I'll see you are on time. Why don't we go somewhere where we can talk? I'd love to find out more about you, if you don't mind me asking?"

She nodded, still looking down, but she tucked her hand into the crook of my elbow and we crossed the road where a crossing sweeper was at work. I gave the boy a penny. We turned into Conduit Street and proceeded through to Regent Street. It felt wonderful to have Jenny's hand tucked into my arm, and to any passing pedestrian I must have looked incredibly foolish with the huge grin that was spread across my face. But a brief glance sideways showed me that my expression was matched by Jenny's.

It didn't take us long to find an Aerated Bread Company and to settle into a table by the window, where we could see the slight amount of traffic on Regent Street. I slipped off my overcoat and Jenny her cape and we relaxed in the warmth of the café. I ordered a pot of tea, some sandwiches, and an assortment of cakes for us, and soon Jenny was pouring tea for us both as though we had been together for years. My smile did not diminish.

"I don't even know your last name," I said.

"Cartwright," she replied.

We talked as we ate and drank our tea, not noticing the time passing. I told Jenny of my own upbringing. With the death of my mother and younger brother in childbirth, I had remained an only child. Then when my father died, when I was fourteen, I became an orphan. I liked to believe that my father's death was from a broken heart at the death of my mother, but I later learned it was from scarlet fever. We had lived in Isleworth, Middlesex, and I had gone to school at the Hounslow Masonic Institution for Boys. There was much I could tell Jenny of my schooldays and immediately thereafter, but there was plenty of time; I was anxious to hear her story.

"Nothing so exciting," she said, nibbling on a petit four. "I never truly learned what happened to my parents, but I believe they both died of the diphtheria that was all about London at the time. So we are both orphans, Harry! I was raised by a spinster aunt in Bermondsey. She was strict but kind, having little money. She worked for some years as a parlor maid at a house in Putney. There she had known Mrs. Cooke and so got me placed when Mr. Irving first took up residence in Grafton Street and Mrs. Cooke became housekeeper. I started as a scullery maid, at thirteen pounds a year, which seemed like a fortune."

I smiled. "I'm sure. But that was hard work, was it not?"

"Oh yes," she said ruefully. "Very hard. But in a funny way I enjoyed it."

"I know what you mean," I said. "I enjoy working, especially at the theatre. Mr. Stoker keeps me busy doing a wide variety of things. And, of course, Mr. Irving occasionally has errands for me to attend to."

"But you are much more than just an errand boy, Harry, are you not?" A slight frown rippled across her normally smooth forehead.

"Very much so." I laughed and was pleased to see the frown disappear. "The job of stage manager is a rigorous one, keeping me busy from early morning until long after the final curtain of the evening." I found myself explaining to Jenny the strengths and the many little foibles of the theatre. Somehow I ended up relating recent occurrences and how I had discovered Peter Richland's letters to Henry Irving and the suspicions that Bram Stoker and I harbored regarding them.

"But that is terrible, Harry." Jenny stopped in the middle of pouring a second cup of tea for me. "Do you really think this Peter Richland was blackmailing Mr. Irving?"

"Yes, I do." She finished pouring and I accepted the cup from her. "I just wish I had 'borrowed'—if that's the right way to put it—a few of those letters for Mr. Stoker to study. He would know what to do."

Jenny was silent for a long while, and then she looked up at me with that same quizzical expression on her face. "Harry . . . do you think *I* could 'borrow,' as you put it, what you need? I have access to Mr. Irving's desk, as you know. I would do that for you. I couldn't do anything that might make me lose my employment, but . . ."

"Oh, have no worries about that, Jenny!" I cried. "Yes! Oh yes, that would be wonderful if you would. I know that Mr. Stoker would ensure that no harm came to you if ever it was found out, but yes, Jenny! It would be a big help if we could just examine those letters, if only for a short time."

"I could then replace them." She smiled, looking very mischievous. "No one would ever know, would they?"

Chapter Nine

"Let's just call it a presentiment, Harry," said Stoker. "A guess, if you like, albeit an educated one."

He looked off into the distance—so far as his office walls would allow him—and squinted in his thoughtful way. I could almost hear the wheels turning in that large and educated head.

"But you think there's a good chance, sir?"

"I think there is a very good chance, Harry, for I do not give up my night's sleep in so cavalier a fashion."

He said nothing about me having to give up my night's sleep, I noticed.

"So we are to meet back here at midnight, sir, after the last house?"

"Outside the stage door, I think. We can then effect our entrance together, with due caution. I don't want you stumbling about in here in the dark while you're waiting for me."

Two thoughts sprang to my mind. One concerned the charge that I would be "stumbling about" and the other the implication that I would get here early and have to wait for my boss. But I held my tongue. I knew he didn't exactly mean what he said.

"Would you care to make me privy to the whole plan, sir? Just so that I might be prepared for any eventualities?"

"Of course, Harry. Of course!" His mind came back to join me in the office. His bright gray green eyes shone with anticipated excitement. "It is my belief that the Voudon practitioners who have made so free with our premises in the past may well be returning tonight to carry out a further ritual."

"That seems awfully risky for them, doesn't it?" I asked.

"They thrive on risk," he said. "But you are correct. To anyone else this would seem foolish. But think, Harry! Who would ever guess that they would do such a thing?"

"Well, you for one, sir."

"Thank you for that. But no, I mean the ordinary person."

I let that slip.

"We are right now in the dark half of the moon. The full moon was, as you were aware, on St. Valentine's night. We are now, then, about halfway through the waning cycle. This is the time for negative magic, Harry. If they are working their wiles to bring down any particular aspect of the Lyceum Theatre or its minions, then this is the time that they will act."

"And we are going to stop them . . . how, sir? Should we be armed with garlic bulbs, or something? I think you once told me . . ."

Stoker laughed, though not unkindly. "No, Harry. We don't need cloves of garlic or sharpened stakes, or anything like that. Believe me, we will, in point of fact, be no match for them if they are as I believe. No. We will simply be observing."

"You mean, we'll be in hiding?"

"Very definitely."

I breathed a little easier. Then I had a sudden thought. "How will they be getting into the theatre? I can't imagine that they will also use the stage door."

"This is one of the things I will be most interested to find out, Harry. The theatre is not locked up until close to midnight, so I'm sure they won't be planning anything before the early hours of the morning. The night watchman will have made his rounds. I want us to be inside—down in that under-stage area—with plenty of time to secrete ourselves and then to note their means of ingress."

"And we'll be staying for their full production?" I said.

"We will indeed."

After the midnight visit to the cemetery with my boss, to dig up a coffin, it somehow didn't seem too strange to be talking about breaking into our own theatre to watch a Voudon ceremony, even one aimed at us. If I was going to participate in any such endeavor, I could be with no better person than Abraham Stoker, I knew. I tried to relax.

I got away from the theatre as soon as possible after the final curtain that evening and hurried around to Chancery Lane and my humble rooms at Mrs. Bell's. I downed the foul-tasting gruel that she had prepared for my supper, being grateful that at least it was hot, and then prepared myself from Mr. Stoker's instructions by dressing both warmly and in dark clothing. I sat on the edge of my hard bed and studied the clock as it slowly ticked off the minutes. I aimed to be at the stage door at midnight exactly. I was on time.

"Harry!"

A whispered voice that seemed to come out of nowhere made me jump and brought on a case of the hiccoughs. The large bulk of Mr. Bram Stoker, dressed all in black, materialized at my side. I had neither heard nor seen him coming, although I had been looking about for him.

"Sir—*hic!*" I said.

"Shh!" He looked carefully about us and then took a key from his pocket and unlocked the stage door. "Quickly! Inside."

We both slipped in and he closed the door behind us. I felt a chill as I heard the lock click closed again, though the sound was enough to still my hiccoughs.

"With me!" he hissed and set off along the passageway.

It was pitch-black, but I could sense the cubicle where old Bill Thomas spent his life. It seemed strange to pass it knowing it was empty. Happily, both my boss and I had traveled this route enough times that we could proceed in the dark with just a light touch of the fingertips on the wall as we advanced.

It was a different story when we got to the stairs down to the dressing rooms. Stoker stopped and stood perfectly still for a long time, listening. Apparently satisfied, he fumbled at his coat. I heard the scrape of flint and then saw a spark. After a moment we were both blinking at the light from a policeman's bullseye lantern.

"A dark lantern, courtesy of our friend Sergeant Bellamy. I thought it would come in useful."

"Very comforting, sir," I said, nodding approval.

Within ten minutes we were down beneath the stage with my boss swinging the light about the area, focusing in on the entrance to the hiding hole.

"Where had we best place ourselves, sir?" I asked.

"I've been giving that some thought, Harry. I want to be able to see the ritual area, but I also would like to learn exactly how they get in and out."

"How many of them will there be, sir?"

I sensed him shrug. "Your guess is as good as mine, Harry. It could be as many as a dozen or more, or it could be just one or two."

"A big crowd wouldn't give us many places to hide."

"I know it. I think it more likely that there will be but a few of them, but we can't know until they get here."

He swung the beam of the lantern around the area. He let it settle on the rearmost trapdoor, the one used for the ghost of Hamlet's father.

"The trap?"

"Why not?" he said. "There would be no reason for them to use it, and it's upstage enough that it's not too obvious. You and I could both settle down in the base of that, Harry, and still command a good view of the whole area."

I thought—I hoped—that was brilliant. We moved over to the trap and carefully positioned ourselves.

"Make yourself as comfortable as you are able, Harry, without setting yourself up to fall asleep. We will need our wits about us, make no mistake."

I was certain of that. I found some old stage curtain to put down in the bottom of the trap so that we would both have a relatively soft bed to lie on. Mr. Stoker chose the stage left end, which was closer to the ritual area.

"Sir? Suppose they decide to create a whole new ritual area, over the other side from where they last performed?"

"Good thinking, Harry. Well done. Yes, it's always a possibility, and if that's their preference, then we'll just have to adapt. But I'm reasonably certain that they will work in the previous area if only because of the energies that they have already built up there. They will consecrate it again, I'm sure, but it will be to reinforce the older blessing."

I pulled out my old half hunter and caught the light from the dark lantern. It was already half an hour past midnight. I wondered how long we would have to wait. My boss saw my action.

"It will be at least an hour yet, Harry, so you can put away your watch. I am going to extinguish the light, if only to conserve fuel. We won't be using it while they are here, of course, but it will be invaluable after they leave."

As the light faded I seemed to be suddenly aware of the

chill in the air. I rubbed my arms to increase the blood circulation. There had been no heat coming from the lantern, but as the light went out I felt as though the temperature had dropped a number of degrees. I huddled down in the curtain material to begin the long wait.

Chapter Ten

 My eyes had not closed, I was sure. Well, I was fairly certain. Yet apparently some amount of time had managed to slip by me. I was awakened—and I use the word advisedly—by Mr. Stoker's elbow digging into my ribs. His large hand over my mouth ensured that I did not cry out.

I listened, my eyes unable to penetrate the Stygian blackness that engulfed the whole under-stage area. I thought I heard something. I sensed Mr. Stoker, close beside me, nodding his head, conscious of my sudden awareness.

The sound we'd heard made me think—I know not why—of the lid of a stone sarcophagus being maneuvered into place. It seemed to come from the direction of the hiding hole. I turned my head that way. Suddenly I saw a glimmer of light. I heard Mr. Stoker's intake of breath.

It took me a moment to comprehend what I was seeing. Apparently a large slab of stone in the back wall of the hiding place had been slid to one side, revealing an opening through which shone a soft, low light. That light was momentarily blocked as a figure emerged through the opening. It was followed by a second figure. I had no idea from whence the opening came, but apparently it connected to some area outside the Lyceum Theatre. I tried to recall what buildings abutted our walls, if any. I immediately thought of the Lyceum Tavern, a favorite with some of our front of house staff. It would appear that a secret passage existed between the two establishments, known only to these followers of the Haitian religion while unknown to native Londoners. I made a mental note to go through the records with Mr. Stoker and track down any architectural drawings that may be in existence.

As I watched, one of the figures moved forward and started lighting the candles we had noted lying about the ritual area. He was revealed to be a short, hunchbacked, dark-skinned man. The stone slab was slid back into place, and any light from that source was extinguished. More candles were lit and soon we were able to get a better idea of what was to ensue. The taller of the two figures strutted about the area; he was obviously the one in charge. The hunchback scurried to and fro, arranging candles and other items. A sweet, slightly sickly smell of incense began to permeate the area. A covered wicker basket was placed in the center of the ritual circle, and fresh bottles of rum were stood about the cleared space.

Suddenly the shorter man squatted down and I saw that he had a drum, which he started to beat. It was a soft, gentle rhythm that, if continued for any length of time, I am sure would have sent me to sleep. I made out the silhouette as my boss gave his head a good shake, probably to keep himself awake.

We were both saved when suddenly the drummer changed tempo and started a rapid, staccato beat that immediately lost any soporific value. I noted that the tall figure now started moving about the area as though performing some sort of dance. I was surprised to note that at some time in the proceedings he had divested himself of his clothing and now danced nearly naked. I strongly suspected that it was, in fact, Mr. Ogoon.

Masked by the steady rhythm of the drum, Mr. Stoker leaned across and whispered in my ear, "Keep your eyes on that dancer, Harry. Commit to memory everything he does. We will need to write down all of this later on."

I knew, of course, that the only "we" who would be writing it down was myself, so I tried to pay attention.

Ogoon—if Ogoon it was—took up one of the bottles of rum and tipped it up, filling his mouth. He then strutted around the area spitting out the fiery liquid onto the ground, following the pattern of the circle. I realized that he was marking the sacred space. He then took up a large saber sword, such as I knew to be in one of the prop and costume hampers near the area. He waved the blade through the air and then moved it to form a particular pattern at each of the four main cardinal points. As he did so, he called out some rhyming verse in a language unknown to me. In this manner he worked his way around the great circle. Then he laid down the saber. All the time his companion kept up the staccato beat.

Ogoon next lifted an earthenware bowl filled with some white powder. Dipping in his fingers, he scooped out the substance and allowed it to run down through his fingers onto the ground. As he rapidly moved his hand about, even from where we were hidden, I could see that he was using the cornmeal, as I later learned it to be from Mr. Stoker, to describe the self-same vévé we had found painted on the wall of the hiding place; the vévé Stoker had said was representative of Guédé, god of the dead.

Then the drum suddenly became silent. We lay there and waited. Ogoon and his partner sat like statues. The minutes ticked by.

The drum suddenly started up again, very softly but gradually building in both volume and tempo. It was not long before the stentorian tones of Ogoon rang out to complement the drum, echoing off the low ceiling of the understage area. The sound assaulted the ears and brought me a throbbing headache that I did not lose until much later that night. Ogoon suddenly sprang to his feet and started an intricate dance about the center area, treading in the white design till it became absorbed in the dirt of the floor. He then grasped the lid of a basket that had sat in the center of the circle for so long. Flinging the lid from him, he reached into the wickerwork and pulled out something jet-black and noisy. As it flapped its wings and crowed, I saw it to be a black rooster. Ogoon snatched up a dagger from the ground at his feet and, flourishing it in ritual gestures, swept it around and down to sever the head of the bird. Even in the low light of the candles, from where we sat a short distance away, we could see the blood.

I felt nauseated by what I saw but knew I had to keep watching. Ogoon smeared the blood of the fowl on his body before flinging the carcass from him. I remembered my boss saying that he thought there had originally been a white rooster sacrificed. If so, then the present offering of a black one would seem to indicate some sort of advancement in the purpose of the rituals. I wondered what that omen might be. Nothing good for the Lyceum, I was certain.

The sacrifice would seem to have been the climax of the rite. From then on the drumming slowed and Ogoon's perambulations equally cooled. Eventually, with a long and comparatively tenuous chant, he sank to the floor and lay there unmoving. The drum settled into a dull, monotonous beat and all was still. After what must have been about ten minutes, both men got up and started clearing away the evidence. Candles were extinguished and the mysterious sliding panel was reopened to allow the participants to exit.

The stone slid back into place, leaving all in darkness, and Stoker and I breathed a little more easily.

"Do you . . . ?" I started to say.

"Shh!" Stoker hushed me. "We must give them plenty of time to leave. It would never do for them to come back for some forgotten item and discover us. Rest easy awhile longer, Harry."

"Rest *easy*?" I whispered.

When my boss and I finally dragged ourselves up from the depths of the theatre, it was by mutual consent that we made for our respective homes, to wait until the following morning, in the warmth and safety of Mr. Stoker's office, to discuss what we had witnessed.

I actually welcomed Bill Thomas's extra-strong tea the next morning. I had eschewed Mrs. Bell's watery version, together with her greasy bacon and eggs, and had not yet broken my fast as I hurried around to the theatre. I think Bill guessed as much since he also brought in a chipped plate bearing two large slices of toast, albeit burned black around the crusts. Without comment, Stoker and I sank our teeth into them. We then set to, going over the events of the previous night, with myself writing down the account as Stoker explained the actions of the Voudoist.

"The long, plaintive song, or chant, was the Petro song," he said. "A paean to the gods. And spitting rum to the four corners was the blessing, or consecration, of the area."

"And the sacrificing of the black cockerel?" I asked, scribbling as fast as I might.

"If you want something from the loa, then you need to offer them something in return."

I laid down the pen. "What do you think they were asking for, sir?"

He looked at me steadily, his face as serious as I have ever seen it. "I very much fear they may have been asking for someone's death, Harry."

"The Guv'nor's?"

"Let us hope not, though any death would be tragic. Of course, they may not have been specific, simply asking for death to strike in our midst, without naming names."

"Is there anything we can do?" I asked.

"I am already on it, Harry," he said, a note of weariness in his voice. "As soon as I got here this morning I roamed about the whole theatre strategically placing certain herbs and roots. You laughed at the notion of garlic . . ."

"I didn't laugh, sir," I protested.

He waved a hand. "No matter. The point is, Harry, that there are associations with certain plants, herbs, and minerals that are centuries old. In this modern age we may tend to laugh at them, but they have served in good stead for generations."

I could believe him. Mr. Stoker's many superstitions must be rubbing off on me, I thought, because I could not only believe but actually had some kind of faith in all of his mumbo jumbo. It gave me a sort of comfort in an area where otherwise there was none.

"We need to go through the architectural drawings for this building to trace that very clever connecting passage they were using. You might also send Sam Green below stage once again to have a close look at the sliding doorway. In fact, alert me when you are going to do that, Harry. I would like to have a closer look myself."

"Yes, sir."

We were both tired but we worked through till lunchtime, going over the details and verifying that we had each witnessed the same things. I was almost certain that the main figure we had watched was Ogoon, though it was difficult to visualize the elegant, smartly dressed Haitian as the prancing figure with blood smeared across his chest.

On revisiting the scene of the nighttime ritual, we found

that the dead rooster had disappeared and, as had seemed apparent from the previous rite, sawdust had been sprinkled over the worst of the bloodletting.

"It is indeed as well that we did not linger last night, Harry. Someone did return to make their exploits less obvious."

"Either that or there is a person in the Lyceum staff who is aligned with them and has taken care of this side of things," I said.

"Excellent thinking, Harry." I glowed at my boss's praise. "With so large a number of employees it is not possible to swear to the loyalty of all, I am sure. However, we will need to examine their names and see if anyone appears doubtful."

"Yes, sir," I said.

With Sam Green's help we discovered the sliding stone panel. It was cleverly arranged and, even knowing of its existence, was far from obvious. In fact it took Sam's prying with a crowbar to eventually reveal it.

"'Ow on earth did you come to know about this, then, Mr. Rivers?" Sam asked, wiping the sweat from his brow. "Weren't no easy thing to see."

"We had been furnished with certain information," said Stoker. "It is some ancient passageway long since fallen into disuse and disrepair, Sam. Time, I think, to close it up permanently."

"Oh yes, sir!" he cried. "I'll get some of the boys onto it. Though seems to me a bit of a shame to put an end to a quick way into the old tavern!" He chuckled to himself.

"That's as may be, Sam," I said. "But by the same token we don't need half-drunk tipplers finding a quick way into the theatre, do we?"

"Ah, you're right there, sir."

Chapter Eleven

It was quite by chance that I bumped into Jack Parsons, the Sadler's Wells scene changer, as I was taking a quick bite of lunch at the King's Arms on Carey Street.

"'Arry Rivers, I do believe!"

Jack seemed genuinely pleased to see me. I remembered that he lived with his invalid mother somewhere close to Fleet Street. He obviously hadn't recognized me in my disguise when I had visited Sadler's Wells so recently.

"How have you been, Jack?" I asked. "How's your mother?"

He shrugged and shook his head. "Not much change there, I'm afraid."

We spent our lunch time catching up on each other's recent activities.

"I 'eard about your man's death," Jack said. "Run down by a growler! I swear, the traffic these days is somethin' terrible. Omnibuses, cabs, carriages, carts . . . it's never ending!"

"How goes it at Sadler's?" I asked, always hoping to hear something that might contribute to our investigation.

He shrugged. "*Twelfth Night* is going all right, I s'pose. Old Pheebes-Watson still thinks 'e's the cat's meow. And 'er ladyship Miss Stringer is right up there with 'im." He sniffed. "Never a word of thanks for us backstage folks. And that young Mr. Bateman is another thing, believe me!"

"Oh?" I pricked up my ears.

"Like a bear with a sore 'ead, 'e is! Lost a lot of money thanks to your Lyceum, so they say."

"What do you mean?" This was starting to sound interesting, I thought.

"Speaking of your man what got run down, 'e was the one as put Mr. Bateman on to betting on things."

I laid down my knife and fork and held up my hand. "Whoa, Jack. You've lost me. What's going on? Who is betting on what?"

Jack gave a loud belch, which was ignored by the serving girl passing by.

"You know 'ow our two theatres are, with Mrs. Crowe's mother, Mrs. Bateman, 'aving been running your Lyceum until your Mr. Irving took over?"

I nodded. "Yes. The two have been at each other's throats ever since," I agreed. "And it seems Mrs. Crowe has taken up her mother's torch in trying to out-do the Lyceum. Our getting *Hamlet* going before your *Twelfth Night* could not have gone over well."

"That's it. That's the 'ole thing," said Jack. "It seems your man—what was 'is name? Richmond, or something . . . ?"

"Richland," I said. "Peter Richland."

"That's 'im. Well, your Richmond tells our Ralph Bateman that there's no way the Lyceum can get going afore Sadler's. So what does young Mr. Bateman do? 'E puts a big fat bet on it! Thinks to make a lot of money 'cos your Richmond man works at the Lyceum and should know what 'e's talking about."

I began to see the whole picture. Richland had tried to delay the opening of *Hamlet*, thinking that the Sadler's Wells' production would then be first. Ralph Bateman, on Richland's word, had placed a large bet on that assumption, probably hoping to make money both for himself and for Richland. But when Henry Irving refused to lie down, *Hamlet* opened and Bateman lost his bet. A thrill ran through me. Did this then mean that Peter Richland was the one who had poisoned the Guv'nor? Did Richland, perhaps, kill himself when his plan didn't work? I couldn't wait to get back to the theatre and run this by Mr. Stoker.

"It's an interesting theory, Harry. But there's more here than just the poisoning of the Guv'nor. Someone has been in the theatre, dropping sandbags on you and lights on our American guest, climbing our rigging, and running over our roof. They have even sneaked in to perform black magic rituals, as we well know. All this *after* Peter Richland's death. How does that fit your story?"

"It could be Ralph Bateman trying to make us pay for him losing his bet," I suggested. "Bateman and his cronies. You said yourself that if they could close us down then they'd be ready to leap into first place."

He nodded his head. "Quite right, Harry. So I did. But I don't think any of this can definitely lead us to the conclusion that Richland was the poisoner, not without some help at least. Perhaps Herbert Willis had some hand in it, as you suggested. But I think you're right that the would-be murderer is the one behind the sandbag and the lights falling."

I had to agree. Richland was dead, but someone was still hard at work, and it didn't look as though there would be any immediate end to it. As if to make my thoughts prophetic, there came a commotion in the passageway outside Mr. Stoker's office.

"See what the fuss is, Harry, would you?" he said.

I went out to investigate.

John Witherspoon, one of the stagehands, was there talking excitedly to Margery Connelly. He looked up as I came to them.

"I was just on my way to Mr. Stoker," he said. "It's old Mr. Turnbull. I think he was taking a cup of tea to the Guv'nor when he suddenly dropped his tray and fell down. Sam Green said to come and get Mr. Stoker. Looks as though the old gent has played his last house."

I rushed past him and up the stairs toward Mr. Irving's dressing room. Broken crockery lay on the steps, with the tea tray at the bottom. Mr. Turnbull's body was in a crumpled heap at the top of the stairs, close to the main dressing room. The door was open and the Guv'nor himself stood there looking down at the old gentleman.

"Alas!" he said, as I arrived on the scene.

Offstage Mr. Irving never seemed to display a lot of emotion, but I saw that he now wore what I thought of as his "tragedy face." His hand rested on his chest to complete the effect.

With scarcely a glance at him, I knelt down by the body and tried to listen for a heartbeat. There was none. Poor old Mr. Turnbull breathed no more. Unexpectedly, a wave of sorrow swept over me. I did not know Mr. Turnbull well. I don't think anyone did. He kept very much to himself, trying to be as unobtrusive as possible yet still be a part of the theatre and its operation. I would miss seeing his stooped figure and snow-white hair pass by my office area. I would miss his wrinkled face and watery blue eyes.

As I got to my feet again I heard the Guv'nor quietly close his door. Life—the life of the theatre—must go on. I made my way back down the stairs and then sent John Witherspoon around the corner for Dr. Cochran. When the doctor came, he confirmed that Mr. Turnbull was dead.

"What was it, doc?" I asked. "Heart attack?"

He stood for a long moment, thinking. "It would seem so, Harry. Certainly at his age . . . But he was into my office just last week, for a minor sore throat. I took the opportunity to give him a complete physical at that time, since it had been a while. He was fit as a fiddle, considering his age. A little unsteady on his feet perhaps, but he was better than many of the young men you have working here. His heart was strong." He pulled on his lower lip and wrinkled his brow. "I will have to let you know after I get the body out of here and have a good look at it. And I'll have to let Dr. Entwhistle, the coroner, take a look. Such a shame. A really nice old gentleman."

After the shock and the commotion, I eventually got back to my boss's office to bring him up to date.

"Dr. Cochran said it could be a heart attack," I said, "but he sounded a little uncertain." I explained what the doctor had said about Mr. Turnbull's earlier examination. "I know Mr. Turnbull was old and frail, but it seems strange that he should suddenly drop dead, especially after he had been declared 'fit as a fiddle,' as Dr. Cochran put it."

Stoker sat back in his chair and did his trick of pursing his lips and squinting his eyes as he gazed into space, obviously thinking hard.

"What is it, sir?" I could see doubts forming all about the big man.

"What did I tell you about Voudon magic, Harry?" he asked. Before I could reply, he continued, "I told you of the Boko, I recall, and the creation of a zombie."

I nodded.

"Did I tell you of the working of magic and, especially, of curses?"

I shook my head. "No, sir. You didn't." I wondered what, if anything, this could have to do with the death of Mr. Turnbull. I waited. Stoker obviously had some other thoughts on the matter that he wished to share.

"In Voudon there are often unexplained deaths," he continued. "A boko will obtain something belonging to his intended victim and use it in some way to focus his evil magic on that person. Shortly afterward, the person dies mysteriously and for no apparent reason."

"Good Lord," I murmured. Then something struck me. The old silver cup we had originally found in the basement, in the circle that contained the chicken blood . . . That cup was old Andrew Turnbull's! I remember it now; he used to drink three cups of water a day from it, he once told me. Belonged to his grandfather. How had it got down into the under-stage area, and into that infamous circle?

There followed a very long silence. Finally, Stoker continued.

"If a person in the Caribbean has an enemy, or wants to get rid of someone for whatever reason, he can employ a boko to do so magically. The boko, being a good businessman, will then go to the intended victim and explain that a curse has been placed on him and offer, for a fee, to remove that curse. Then the boko will return to the original man and say that he will reinstate the curse for a higher fee! So he will play one against another, ending with the demise of the underbidder."

"Enterprising," I said.

"At other times the boko may simply place the curse, especially if the victim is not easily accessible."

"And does the curse actually have any effect?" I asked.

"Oh yes, Harry. Yes, it does. The victim may suddenly drop down dead and with no apparent explanation. Doctors have examined such cursed people and not been able to find any hint of poison or trauma of any kind."

"This is beginning to sound very much like the death of Mr. Turnbull," I said.

"Exactly, Harry. And did we not witness a Voudon ceremony for the dead just last night?"

"But you're surely not suggesting that someone paid to get rid of Mr. Turnbull?" I was aghast. "Whoever would do that?"

"I am not suggesting anything, Harry. Merely observing. I am certainly not, for one moment, suggesting that there was such bargaining involved in Mr. Turnbull's death . . . I am merely acquainting you with the ways of Voudon."

He thought for a long moment. "I think we need to track down Herbert Willis," Stoker finally said, "and see exactly what he is about, now that he is no longer in the Lyceum's employ. Perhaps we can eliminate him as a suspect."

Once again I heard Mr. Stoker say that "we" needed to do this . . . and knew that he meant me. I sighed. Well, that was what I was here for: to assist Mr. Stoker and do a variety of jobs for him. Track down Herbert Willis? It could be a challenge, I thought, but a rewarding one, and I loved a good puzzle. I repaired to my office and decided upon a plan of action.

I first went to talk with Bill Thomas, tucked away as usual in his cubbyhole by the stage door entrance.

"Bill, you're a betting man," I began.

"Here! Who's been talking?"

I glanced down at the *Sporting Times* that was spread out in front of our doorman, as it always was. I tapped my finger on it. "It doesn't need anyone to talk," I said. "Your choice of literature speaks for itself."

He grinned and rubbed the stubble on his unshaved chin. "Just joking, Harry. What do you need to know? The two thirty at Sandown? Three fifteen at Kempton Park? I can give you a good tip for Hurst Park if'n you've a mind?"

"No, nothing like that, Bill. Though I do appreciate your

offer. No, I need to know with whom Ralph Bateman might have placed a bet, and whether I might be able to get information from that gentleman, if I can locate him."

Bill scratched the top of his head with one hand and pushed his spectacles up on his nose with the other. "Not really your territory, I wouldn't think, Harry. And not very salubrious surroundings for the likes of you, if you catch my meaning."

"I do indeed," I said. "And I thank you for your concern, but I would like to speak to such a person if possible."

Bill was quiet for a few moments, obviously shuffling thoughts through his head. He finally drew his mouth into a tight line and looked me hard in the eyes. "The sort of person who would handle bets from someone such as Ralph Bateman is not your regular bookie, Harry. As you well know, such things as bear baiting, bull and badger baiting, cockfighting, ratting, cudgels, and even good old bare-knuckle fighting have been banned these many years."

I nodded.

"That's not to say that such things are no longer indulged in by those cognizant of such sports."

His eyes wavered away from my face. I got the distinct feeling that Bill was himself one of those "cognizant of such sports." I encouraged him to continue. "Go on, Bill," I murmured.

"Well . . ." He seemed to regain his self-assurance. "For them as is into such things, there are certain individuals as will take bets on, shall we say, unusual wagering opportunities."

"Like, which theatre will open first?"

"Even that." He nodded. "Though that's somewhat 'tame,' you might say, compared to some I might mention. Still, it isn't your usual wager."

"So who handles these bets?"

"A flash cove that goes by the name of Ernesto Arroyo y López. Spanish!" He spat out the word.

"Spanish?"

"So he claims. I've heard rumors that he's been no farther from Piccadilly than Brighton, but live and let live I say."

I nodded. "Quite right, Bill. Now, where am I likely to find this character?"

"Oh, that's not easy. He's not one as can be pinned down. But, as it happens, I have heard of a—er—not quite proper confrontation between two gentlemen that is due to take place this very afternoon. I think you might find your Mr. Arroyo y López in attendance for that."

I understood. "Thanks, Bill. I really appreciate it."

"Not that I think you should go there, Mr. Rivers. It could get out of hand—some of them fights do, you know. And also, it could be raided by the police, and then you'd find yourself wearing a nice pair of darbies and riding a Black Maria to Brixton prison. We couldn't have that now, could we, Mr. Rivers?"

"Don't worry, Bill. I'll be careful. Now, where exactly is this confrontation to take place?"

Chapter Twelve

The underground railway let me off at the Angel in Islington. The bare-knuckle fight—and I had gathered from Bill that that is what it was—was due to start at three thirty of the clock. I should just make it in time, I thought, and hopefully get back to the theatre before curtain-up. I exited the station and made for the road through the old turnpike gates.

I knew of Islington principally from the Collins Music Hall, a conversion of the Lansdowne Arms public house. It backed onto an old burial ground called New Bunhill Fields. I made my way there, following Bill's directions. It seems that on the far edge of New Bunhill Fields there stood an old stone barn, much run-down and seemingly abandoned. But as I came in sight of it, I saw a number of sportingly dressed fellows, along with many obvious locals, making their way into the barn through the old cattle doors on the end. When I got to the doors I was looked over closely by a big bruiser of a man, obviously keeping an eye open and touting for the police.

I followed the others into the foul-smelling structure and up a set of rickety wooden stairs to the upper floor. I could hear the crowd already there talking and arguing about the respective merits of the two combatants. These I discovered already in the makeshift ring: a thick rope stretched around rotting hay bales that marked the corners. One man, billed as the Camden Town Mauler, was dressed in the traditional silk drawers, in this instance bright crimson. His hands, hardened with lemon and vinegar, were coarse and red, the knuckles enlarged. His trainer was down on his knees working on the Mauler's legs, massaging his thighs and calf muscles.

Across the ring was his opponent, the Bermondsey Basher, said to have killed a man in one of these illegal brawls. His drawers were a dirty green. While his trainer worked his thighs, the Basher glared around at the crowd and sneered at his opponent. I wouldn't have wanted to get in the way of either of these combatants. To step into a ring with them would have been suicide. But I wasn't there for the fight.

I climbed up on a rusting piece of farm machinery, alongside several other men, and looked all around the barn. The air was thick with cigarette and cigar smoke. It made my eyes water, though it seemed not to bother the two pugilists. I spotted three men, each with a satchel over his shoulder, working amongst the crowd. They were obviously taking the wagers. One was a black man with a cheery grin and a battered brown bowler at a rakish angle on his head. The second was a thin-faced, bald, hatless person who kept his eyes down on the money being passed back and forth. The third I took to be my mark, Mr. Ernesto Arroyo y López. He wore a top hat and black frock coat, a fancy waistcoat, and had a diamond pin flashing from his cravat. Despite the crush, people seemed to pull back as he passed. He kept to the side of the crowd that seemed to be the better class of punter. I got down from my perch and started making my way around to where Mr. Arroyo y López operated.

A bucket was struck repeatedly with an iron spike and the crowd fell silent. A short, bowlegged man who looked as though he should be working with racehorses climbed up on a box someone had placed in the center of the ring.

"The Camden Town Mauler weighs in at fourteen stone ten pounds. The Bermondsey Basher at fifteen stone two pounds."

There was a buzz of conversation. The Basher had an advantage of six pounds. How significant that was, I had no idea.

"The Basher 'as the choice of corners," continued the announcer.

The big man in the dirty green drawers took his time walking around the ring. He found a spot where the sunlight—weak as it was—streamed in through a chink in the wall. He moved to the corner where his back would be to the light and held up one huge fist. The Camden Town Mauler, with a muttered curse, shuffled across to the opposite corner.

The announcer resumed. "No butting or gouging, no biting or kicking," he said. "Down on one knee and wif an 'and on the ground counts as down. Seconds can then 'elp their man back to 'is corner. They stays out of the ring till then. Thirty seconds between rounds. This 'ere's all as the 1866 London Prize Ring Rules. Any questions?" He didn't wait to see if there were any but scrambled down off his box, which was retrieved by a young boy who ducked under the rope. From the sidelines the announcer finished, "When I 'ollers, 'Time,' both men to the scratch and 'ave at it."

I had managed to get near to Mr. Arroyo y López and kept close as he took the last bet pushed at him and then retired to the back of the barn. There he climbed up onto one of a number of hay bales placed strategically for the three bookies. As I moved in and waved to Arroyo y López, the announcer called, "Time!"

"Too late, my good man," Arroyo y López said to me. "Now get out of my way. Let me see the action."

I had no choice but to wait and hoped it would not be a long contest. I had heard of these things going on for two or three hours but trusted that would not be the case here.

The two men went at each other with incredible energy. The strategy favored by both seemed to be to plant themselves firmly in one spot and punch the opponent with blows and jabs that would fell an ox, receiving and absorbing similar punishment to that meted out. They moved their feet but little and simply rocked backward and forward.

The first down went to the Bermondsey Basher. A punch that seemed to come up from the floor smashed into the other man's jaw and the Mauler was lifted off his feet and crashed to the ground. The Basher got in a surreptitious kick to the ribs before pulling back and allowing the Mauler's seconds to drag their man over to his corner. There a bucket of water was dumped over his head and the seconds went into action, slapping his face and rubbing his body. As the time ticked away, the giant of a man, incredulously to my mind, gave his head a shake and clawed his way to his feet. Just in time, he staggered out to the line scratched across the center of the ring. The Bermondsey Basher was there waiting for him.

They again went at it as though nothing had interrupted them. I shook my head and wondered how long this could possibly continue.

The Basher suddenly gave a forceful one-two-three series of jabs into the Mauler's ribs and forced him to take a step backward. The Basher followed up and swung his great fist around in a wide arc. If it had connected I am sure it could have removed the other man's head from his shoulders, but the Mauler was ready. I wondered if he had in fact faked his first takedown. As the Basher's fist came around, the Mauler ducked his head underneath it and came back up with his own fists moving. They beat a tattoo on the other man's chin, snapping his head back with a crack that was heard throughout the barn. There was a sudden total silence from everyone, and we all watched in disbelief as the Bermondsey Basher's arms dropped to his side; he stood wavering for a moment and then crashed to the floor, never to stand up again. I learned afterward that he had indeed had his neck snapped.

It was a sobering sight and one I would not care to repeat. How anyone could watch this sort of thing on a regular basis I had no idea. How the crowd could also make bets on the outcome of such a contest I also had difficulty comprehending. It all seemed far removed from the civilized world of the theatre. Fleetingly, I gave thanks that Jenny would never have to witness such a barbaric spectacle.

Near chaos ensued. It seemed that the Bermondsey Basher had been the favorite and no one had expected the Mauler to last more than a few rounds. There were shouts and boos, and hay bales and farm tools were angrily thrown into the ring. I saw the bowlegged announcer making himself scarce, running and jumping down the wooden steps to get out of the building. In all the commotion the three bookmakers made their own way out, clutching their bulging satchels to them. I followed, keeping up with Mr. Arroyo y López.

"I just need a few words," I said, as we emerged from the barn. "I'm not looking to bet or to cash in. I just want to ask you a couple of questions."

He looked at me suspiciously. "Was you bettin' on this fight?" he asked, belying his claim to Spanish ancestry.

I shook my head. "No. I only came here to find you. I understand you know a man named Ralph Bateman."

"Bateman? Never 'eard of 'im."

"Yes, you have," I persisted. "Think for a minute. He

placed a bet about the Lyceum Theatre and the Sadler's Wells Theatre, a fortnight ago."

He stopped and his forehead wrinkled as he thought about it. "Theatre bets? Oh yes. I do recall 'im now. Friend of a reg'lar of mine name of Willis."

"Aha!" I cried. "Now that is actually the person I'm trying to find. Herbert Willis. You do know him, then?"

Arroyo y López's face grew dark. "What's this leading to? You connected with the peelers? What's this all about?"

I waved a dismissive hand. "Nothing to do with the police. This is strictly personal. I'm trying to find Mr. Willis. I thought that if he was a regular punter with you, then you might know how to contact him?"

"'E contacts *me*, if'n he wants to lay a wager."

"But surely you also have a way of getting in touch with him? What about when he wins?"

"Hah!" His face broke out in a grin and he shook his head. "That ain't never goin' to 'appen!"

Chapter Thirteen

"According to Mr. Ernesto Arroyo y López, Willis did place the occasional bet and had been instrumental in introducing Ralph Bateman to the bookie." I passed on the information to Mr. Stoker as I hurried backstage for the evening performance. "He gave me an idea as to where we might find our Mr. Willis."

"Excellent."

"I'll get onto it first thing in the morning," I continued. Then I remembered something. "Actually, second thing . . . I have to call on Jenny to see if she acquired those letters you want to study."

Stoker nodded and tugged on his mustache. "I really am of two minds about this, Harry. It doesn't seem right to pry into the Guv'nor's personal correspondence, but at the same time if there is some reference there to young Bateman, and if this blackmailing of Richland's affects the Lyceum, then I do feel it my duty to verify what is contained in the letters."

"I agree, sir. Wholeheartedly."

"Thank you, Harry."

I hurried off to attend to my stage-managing duties.

As I opened the front door of Mrs. Bell's establishment on Wednesday morning, eager to be out and on my way to see Jenny, I was surprised to find Sergeant Bellamy on the pavement outside, just stepping down from a hansom.

"Good morning, Sergeant. Not come for breakfast I take it?" I smiled. He did not.

As the cab pulled away behind him, he glanced up and down the street before giving me his full attention. I almost expected him to pull out his inevitable notebook, but all he did was fix me with his stare. I found myself wondering if policemen are especially trained to make one feel guilty no matter what one may have done or not done.

"We have not been idle, Mr. Rivers," he said, and laid a finger alongside his nose.

"N-no," I replied. "No, I never for a moment thought that you had been."

"No, sir. We have not been idle." He dipped a hand into his pocket and—almost to my relief—pulled out his note-book. He flicked through a couple of pages to find what he needed then looked at me again and cleared his throat. "One headless corpse," he said, reading from the book. "Male, indeterminate age, clad only in underclothing."

I was both surprised and delighted. "You've found it! That's wonderful. Well done, Sergeant. Might I ask where it was?"

"Well you might, sir. Well you might."

"All right, then . . . ?" I waited, but Sergeant Bellamy was not to be hurried. He obviously savored his success.

"It appears that at approximately ten thirty A.M. this past Saturday, 19 February 1881, one Arthur York, rag-and-bone merchant of 27 Webber Street, Blackfriars Road, was making his usual rounds, accompanied by his assistant William. Somewhere along the way—and he claims he cannot recall exactly where—he acquired a large bag of rags. William, who is age ten, assured us that it had been left at the side of the road somewhere in Southwark. He particularly remembers it for two reasons. One: it was 'just layin' there like it 'ad fallen off some other ragger's cart,' as he stated. And two: as he also stated, 'it was bleedin' 'eavy.'"

"Go on," I urged.

Bellamy cleared his throat. "They got the bag back to York's place of business but didn't get around to emptying it until late yesterday, which is when Mr. York came to us."

"The body was in the bag?" I couldn't wait, but the sergeant still insisted on taking his own time.

"It would appear that they empty such bags of rags that they have collected 'out and about' as they put it, but don't do this until they have dealt with the people who bring rags directly into the shop. These they weigh and pay tuppence a pound for."

"Go on."

"When they emptied out the big bag they had discovered in Southwark, what should tumble out but a headless corpse. Young William was all for keeping it, while Mr. York admitted that he contemplated dumping it in the Thames. However, he knew that young William would not be able to remain mum on the subject, so he finally informed his local constabulary. And rightly so."

"Of course," I agreed. "So this is Peter Richland's body, then?"

"Preliminary examination would seem to confirm that, Mr. Rivers. Yes."

"So, now that you have both head and body, I presume you can refill your empty coffin and put it back in the ground?" I asked.

"Not so fast, sir. Not so fast."

I sighed. I was anxious to see Jenny and I also had to go searching for Willis. Delighted as I was to learn that the body had been discovered, I really wanted to get on. "What is it?" I asked.

"We can't have people digging up graves, separating heads from bodies, and then leaving bits and pieces in theatres and on curbs for casual pickup by rag-and-bone men."

"No," I said. "No, I suppose you can't."

"We need to find the person or persons responsible and to bring them to account."

"Of course."

"It was your theatre that called us in when the head rolled out of your scenery, was it not?"

"It was," I agreed.

"So we need to conclude that case, Mr. Rivers. Need to find out who did it and why. That's all part of our job."

"Yes, Sergeant. Yes. Thank you. I think that an excellent idea and no less than I would expect of the Metropolitan Police. You will, then, keep us informed as you proceed?"

"Oh, that we will, Mr. Rivers. That we will."

It would certainly be good to know who was behind it all, I thought. Might this, too, come back to Willis? And what about Ralph Bateman? Yes, it was good that the police were keeping on with their investigating. I watched the detective sergeant walk off down Chancery Lane. As I hailed a cab, I briefly thought of offering to give him a lift wherever he was now proceeding . . . but decided against it.

I had arranged with Jenny that I would stand on the corner of Grafton Street, opposite the house, at nine of the clock and that if she had acquired the letters, she would signal me from the corner window. She would then send them down to me by the boy, Timmy. If I saw no signal I would return the following day, and so on till the end of the week. I would see her again the following Sunday, but I hoped to be returning the Guv'nor's property by then.

It was just past nine when I got to the corner of Bond Street and Grafton Street. I prayed that I had not missed Jenny's signal but felt sure she would keep an eye open for me. Sure enough, I had not been there but a few moments when I saw the corner window open a fraction and a feather duster thrust out and vigorously shaken. I raised my hat in acknowledgment and casually crossed to stand by Asprey's Jewellers. I had scarcely taken up my position when the black door accessing the upstairs rooms opened and Timmy stuck out his head. He saw me and grinned.

"Sum'at for you from Jenny . . . sir," he said. He waved a brown-paper-wrapped parcel.

I hurried over and took it, slipping him a silver thru-penny bit. "Thanks, Timmy."

I dropped off the parcel at the theatre before continuing on my way to track down Herbert Willis. Mr. Stoker was not in his office—Bill said that he was with the Guv'nor—so I left the package and a note in the middle of his desk, where I was certain he couldn't miss it.

On Thursday morning I took the light green omnibus to Paddington. I paid my tuppence fare and found myself crammed between a corpulent hurdy-gurdy man balancing his instrument on his knees and an emaciated curate. The clergyman appeared alarmed to find himself in the midst of such sweaty, odiferous creatures as filled the vehicle. He tried to keep his eyes downcast but was constantly jerking his head up to gape at some male or female and expressing indignation at somebody's manners or lack thereof.

There was a brief episode when the curate discovered that the hand of a young lady pickpocket had been slipped surreptitiously into his pocket. He recoiled at touching the young lady's hand just as she recoiled at being discovered. Both let out a shout before the young lady managed to vault off the slowly moving vehicle to disappear among passing pedestrians. The clergyman was left without his wallet and his fellow travelers had a good laugh.

Mr. Ernesto Arroyo y López had said that he'd heard Willis was currently with a penny gaff in Paddington. Quite a step down from the Lyceum, or from any legitimate theatre if true, I thought. The penny theatres were the bottom of the theatrical scale, catering to the sensation seekers and the illiterate. Although a few of the establishments could hold several hundred persons as their audience, the majority were no more than shop fronts that had been converted into miniature theatres to entertain juveniles and the virtually impecunious. Offerings were melodramas, pantomimes, and comic songs, frequently all on the same bill. What Willis might do at any one of them was beyond my imagining. They used little in the way of scenery, but perhaps he could handle the primitive lighting required. The management was usually so dedicated to providing as many seats as possible that the stage was often a narrow, cramped segment that barely held the actors.

I extricated myself from my fellow passengers at Paddington and quickly walked north to Bishop's Road, where I knew there were a few gaffs. It didn't take me long to check them; all were open and I managed to have a word or two with the managers. No one had heard of Herbert Willis. It passed through my mind that he may have taken an assumed name, but then I thought, why would he do that? It's not as though he were a fugitive, just a constant tippler who was frequently obfuscated. Even if he was the one responsible for poisoning the Guv'nor, he probably wasn't trying to hide but only seeking work.

I turned down Gloucester Street. There were few places of public entertainment there, though it seemed dotted with street singers, each trying to outdo the others. Some sang the latest songs in the hope of getting a penny or two, while some rendered a single song ad nauseam in the hopes of being paid to go away. At the bottom of Gloucester I came to Praed Street and, stepping around two of the singers, remembered that there was a prominent penny gaff on Praed just past London Street. I found it almost immediately and got onto the end of the queue that was forming for the next performance.

I felt a nudge and a push at my back. As I turned, a young boy of about ten ducked his head and ran off, his bare feet slapping the pavement. I instinctively felt for my purse and found it gone. I cursed myself for a fool. *Welcome to Paddington*, I thought. Now I would have to walk home.

There was now no point in standing in line for the performance—and I didn't really have the time to sit through one anyway—so I made my way around the corner to where I could see the equivalent of the stage door. This gaff boasted a small stage with the rudiments of scenery. As I looked about me it became obvious who were the actors and who were the stagehands, though the latter were no more than three men. One of them was Herbert Willis. I had struck gold.

"Mr. Bleedin' Rivers!" His red-rimmed, watery blue eyes locked onto me and he glared. "What you want? Not content wif takin' m'job, you're followin' after me, now?"

I had rather expected this. It was Mr. Stoker who had done the actual firing, but Willis knew me as the Lyceum's stage manager and, ergo, one of his "enemies."

"Glad to see you've found another place of employment, Herbert," I said.

"Wotcha want?" He jutted out his chin in defiance.

"Just a word or two," I said.

Mr. Herbert Willis was of average height, which is to say

slightly taller than me. He had dirty blond hair with a straggly mustache but no beard. This had always surprised me, since he had a nasty scar on his chin. If I had borne such a disfigurement I would have grown a beard to hide it. But Herbert Willis was little concerned with personal appearance. He was painfully thin, but I noticed he was developing a large stomach, almost certainly from the amount of drinking he indulged in.

"That bastard Stoker send you?"

"No, Mr. Stoker did not send me."

"Well, whatever 'tis, you'd best get on wif it. I've got a show to do." He tilted his nose up in the air, as though he had a full London theatre to run rather than a ramshackle affair out in the wilds of Paddington.

"What do you know about the attempted poisoning of Mr. Irving?" I asked, deciding to get straight to the meat of my questions.

He looked surprised. "Wot? I thought that was old 'at. You still chasin' that scratch?"

"Answer the question," I said. "What do you know about it?"

He had a nervous tick that caused his right eye to twitch when he got exited. It now began to work overtime. He gave a scornful laugh. "No more'n you, I'm sure. An' even if'n I did, you don't fink I'd be tellin' you, do you?"

No, I didn't think he would. But I had to ask. "You are an associate of Ralph Bateman," I said.

"Wot you mean, a 'sociate?"

"What exactly is your relationship?" I pressed. "I can't really see the two of you as close friends."

"That's none o' your nevermind! We 'ad a workin' setup, is all." He peered around the corner to see if he was needed inside, then turned back to me.

"Did he supply you with money for drink? Is that what it was?" Then I had a thought. If this man's loyalty revolved around the bottle, then I could work with that. I dug around in my pockets and managed to locate a solitary shilling. I pondered a moment, since I had lost my purse, as to whether I should hold on to it to pay my fare home, but I decided that information from Willis was more important. I held the coin in my hand. "Are you still working for Bateman?"

"Nar! 'E says as 'ow 'e don't need me no more." He spat into the gutter.

"But he used to employ you to run errands?" I let him catch a glimpse of the money.

"Yes, if'n you must know. I'd take messages for 'im and 'e'd pay me for doin' it. An' where I spends me money is my business. Wot's wrong wi' that?"

"Nothing," I said. "If that's all you were doing."

I held up the silver coin where he could see it. "A last question for you, Mr. Willis . . . for now. You were taking messages from Mr. Bateman to whom?"

"'Oo was the other geezer, you mean? Why, that was Mr. Richland, the actor feller."

"The understudy?" He nodded. "Thank you, Mr. Willis. That's all for now. You may get about your job here." I reluctantly let him have the coin.

"'Ere! You ain't got no peelers out after me, 'ave you? I ain't done nofink, y'know."

"No," I said. "You're safe . . . if you're telling the truth. But I will be checking further on you, I can tell you that much."

Content that I now knew where to find him, I walked off, heading back toward the omnibus stop, until I again remembered that my pocket had been picked. I changed direction to start the long hike back to the Lyceum. As I swung around to cut along London Street, I caught sight of Willis dashing away from his place of employment and hailing a passing growler. He was leaving, and with my money! Without stopping to think, I ran after the cab and had the good fortune to find a hansom only a street away. I jumped into it even before it had come to a stop.

"See that growler?" I cried to the startled cabbie. "Follow him, will you? Double your fare if you can keep up without being seen."

"Yes, sir!" He cracked his whip and we were off.

I knew, of course, that I had no money, but a rough plan had formed even as I was chasing after Willis's cab. I needed to see where he was going. I suspected he was haring off to report to Ralph Bateman, but I had to make sure. I figured that once I discovered his destination I could then direct my cab to take me back to the Lyceum, where I could run inside to borrow money from Bill to pay the fare. That was the plan. I didn't want to examine it too closely in case there was a glaring hole in it.

Chapter Fourteen

As I had half expected, the chase led across town to Clerkenwell and the Sadler's Wells Theatre. My cab pulled in to the side of the road a short distance away from where the growler had stopped, and I watched Herbert Willis disappear into the building. I sat and waited. It wasn't long before Willis reappeared, accompanied by Ralph Bateman, and the two of them went across the road and into the Bag o' Nails tavern. I decided to follow.

I felt in my pockets and located a piece of paper. I borrowed a pencil from the cabdriver and hurriedly scribbled a note that I handed to him.

"Drive to the Lyceum Theatre on Wellington Street," I said. "Give this note to Mr. Abraham Stoker, the theatre manager, and he will see that you are paid." I got out.

The cabdriver was hesitant. I'm sure he'd been told a story like this before only to find that the person to whom he had been sent knew nothing of his fare. But I was in luck in that not only had he heard of Mr. Stoker but he also decided that I looked respectable enough to be trusted. He turned the hansom and trotted off down Rosebery Avenue. I walked along to the Bag o' Nails.

I made my way through the usual gathering of dirty-faced, raggedy children hovering at the doorway, past a crone playing a hurdy-gurdy, and peered into the smoky atmosphere of the tavern. It was a crowded lunchtime with every table full. The place reeked of cooking, wood smoke from the fireplace, tobacco smoke, and sweat. Serving girls moved through the throng, bearing tankards of ale and balancing platters of food. Boys in grubby aprons cleared tables as fast as they were vacated and squeezed patrons onto the benches. It took me a long time to locate Willis and Bateman, who sat some distance from the door and close to the bar. I entered and cautiously made my way toward the pair.

As I drew near I pulled my hat lower on my head—it was really useless trying to hide my mop of red hair—and managed to slide onto a bench, squeezing in at a table immediately behind where they sat. I scooped up an empty tankard left by a previous customer and held it in front of my face, studiously ignoring the serving girl when she came. I leaned back, hoping to catch some of the conversation between Ralph and Herbert. With the clamor of the crowd, it wasn't easy.

"Go for the man at the top," Willis was saying. "Grab 'im and you can make 'em do anything you want."

"I don't think the boss would go along with that," said Bateman. "I think he'd draw the line there."

"But 'e didn't mind poisoning 'im, did 'e?"

"We don't know that. Not for certain, anyway."

"Oh, come on!" Willis sounded annoyed. "'Ere! If'n you won't grab Irving, what about 'is lady?"

"Miss Ellen Terry?"

"'Oo else?"

Again Bateman dithered. I couldn't blame him. If they

were talking of kidnapping, as I'm sure they were, then it would be a difficult move for them to try to snatch either the Guv'nor or Miss Terry.

"I'll have to talk with the boss," Bateman said.

I wondered who this boss could be. I recalled that ten days ago, when I had spotted Bateman on the Embankment with Ogoon and Charlie Vickers, he had referred to a "boss" when talking about paying Vickers for work done. So Ralph Bateman was definitely not the one making the decisions. I thought that Mr. Stoker would find that interesting.

"Can you still get into the Lyceum and move about there?" asked Bateman.

"O' course I can!" Willis sounded confident, if not cocky. "No problem. I'm your man. Don't 'ave no nevermind on that score."

"Hmm." Bateman didn't sound so certain.

"Well, well, well!"

I looked up at the now familiar voice and nearly dropped the tankard I held. The dark face of Mr. Ogoon stared down at me from across the table where I sat.

"Mr. Bateman, I think you should be aware of who is listening to your careless talk!"

"What?" Behind me Ralph Bateman came to his feet.

I jumped up, planning to get out of there. With the number of patrons crowding the Bag o' Nails, I hoped I would be able to get away, but I was trounced before I began. My foot caught on the bench as I attempted to swing over it, so that I could run. I tripped and fell on my back. Herbert Willis took great delight in pouncing on me, grabbing my arms, and twisting them behind my back. He and Bateman dragged me to my feet and, to cheers from the diners, pushed me toward the doorway. I struggled but quickly desisted when I found Ogoon at my side, holding a greasy but sharp serving knife to my ribs.

"Quietly, Mr. Rivers," he hissed. "Let us not make a scene." He nodded to Bateman. "Where to?"

"To my office," Ralph replied, and led the way between the tables toward the exit.

Ten minutes later I found myself standing in a small room at the back of the Sadler's Wells Theatre. Bateman had taken a seat behind the desk in the room, Willis had dropped onto a plain wooden chair alongside it, and I stood at the side of the desk opposite where Bateman sat. Ogoon stood boldly with his back to the door, fixing me with his gimlet gaze. I still had trouble equating the urbane, elegantly dressed man with the apparent lunatic of a couple of nights ago.

"So the great and grand Lyceum Theatre has taken to sending spies to listen to our conversations, has it?" said Bateman.

"I just happened to be in there having lunch," I said.

"You was up in Paddington talking nice and smooth to me," sneered Willis. "You 'ad to 'ave followed me down 'ere."

"Don't flatter yourself," I said.

"Enough!" Ralph slammed the flat of his hand down on the top of the desk. "I don't care where you were before. You were most definitely spying on us just now. That's all I know."

"Yes," I said. "And heard you planning to kidnap Mr. Irving and Miss Terry."

Ralph laughed. "Ha! Did you hear that, Mr. Ogoon? Kidnap people? I think you must have overheard some other patrons, Mr. Rivers. It was quite crowded in the Bag o' Nails, you know? It was someone else you heard. Surely you realize that."

I ignored him.

"'E was the one what got me fired!" snarled Willis. "'E always 'ad it in for me."

"You got yourself fired, Willis, with your drinking," I said. "You know it and I know it."

"This is beside the point, is it not?" observed Ogoon.

"Yes, it is," agreed Bateman.

"So where do we go from here?" I asked.

"*You* don't go anywhere," said Bateman. "Leastwise, nowhere you'd like to go."

That didn't sound good. I wondered what they had in store for me if, indeed, they had thought that far ahead. I wondered if Mrs. Crowe knew what her young brother Ralph was up to. Perhaps she was the "boss"? Somehow I doubted it. In fact, now that I thought about it, that mysterious figure had been referred to as a male.

"Well, I have work to do, Bateman," said Ogoon, turning to the door and taking hold of the handle. "You do what you think fit. You know where to find me."

There came a sudden commotion from outside, with raised voices followed by a banging on the door. Ogoon opened it to reveal George Dale, blinking rapidly through his dirt-smeared spectacles.

"I couldn't keep 'im out, Mr. Bateman . . ." he started to say.

Then I saw a large and welcome figure advancing rapidly toward us. The top hat was slightly askew and the face beneath it was grim.

"Ah! There you are, Harry!" Abraham Stoker's voice had never sounded so welcome.

"Right here, sir!" I cried.

My boss's burly figure filled the doorframe, and even Ogoon stepped back a pace.

"Come on, then. Don't shilly-shally! I need you back at the Lyceum. Now that's a *real* theatre!"

He turned away and I scurried after him. No one made a move to stop me, and Mr. Stoker and I strode out of Sadler's Wells and off along Rosebery Avenue. It didn't take long to hail a cab and for me to leave all the unpleasantness behind me. I couldn't believe that Mr. Stoker had come all this way to rescue me. But then, that's the sort of boss I had.

I sank back in the seat of the hansom and gradually stopped shaking.

"How did you know where to find me, sir?" I asked.

"Straightforward, Harry. I enquired of the cabbie whose fare you had me pay."

M r. Stoker seemed well pleased after I had later reviewed my day's events.

"You might have been a little incautious, Harry," he said, leaning over his desk. "But you've learned some interesting facts. Well done. We shall certainly be on our guard against any possible abduction of the Guv'nor or of Miss Terry."

He sat with a parcel of letters on his desk and one of them open and in his hand. I recognized the pile as being the ones that Jenny had managed to obtain for us.

"Anything worthwhile?" I asked, nodding toward the epistle he held.

"Yes, indeed, Harry," he said. "Our Mr. Richland found a lot to occupy his time, since he was not treading the boards nightly."

"Oh?" I sat on the straight-backed chair facing his desk.

"He was very careful with his wording, I will give him that. No direct threats, but plenty of innuendo. In this particular letter"—he tapped the missive—"he intimates that this Daisy—whoever she may be—is more than willing to divulge to the newspapers the fine details of the Guv'nor's purported philandering with her. I'm sure she cannot substantiate one word of it, but I am equally sure the newspapers would delight in reporting whatever she might tell them. Truth or not, it could severely damage the Guv'nor's reputation and—perhaps more to the point—thereby make a sizable inroad into the Lyceum's profits."

I whistled, a sound that brought a momentary frown to my boss's face. He had, a number of times in the past, requested that I not whistle, but it was something of a reflex action. I tried to look apologetic, but I don't think it registered with him.

"I have seen such scandal—real or imagined—happen before to other actors," he continued. "Some of the most promising lost both their reputations and their employment. Reputation is all-important, Harry. Don't you forget that."

"I won't, sir," I said.

"However, I am sure you are right in what you suggested," Stoker continued. "She got into this probably at the urging of Peter Richland and in hopes of some financial gain."

"Do the letters cover anything else of interest?" I asked. "Anything else that could affect the Lyceum?"

"There was mention in one of them"—he tapped the pile—"of Ralph Bateman, as you had originally reported. Well spotted, Harry."

I nodded, pleased. "What did it say about him?"

"It was rather disquieting. Something of a veiled threat, perhaps? Richland intimated that his 'valued friend,' as he put it, was Mr. Ralph Bateman of Sadler's Wells Theatre and that said Bateman—'newly returned from his travels'— had it within his power to bring forces to bear that might bring down the Lyceum Theatre." He paused. "He did say 'might.'"

"'*Bring down* the Lyceum'? Did he enlarge on that, say just how that might be accomplished?" I found it hard to credit Ralph Bateman with any true ability to harm such an established theatre as the Lyceum.

Mr. Stoker was silent for a long moment. Then he continued: "This was one of the more recent letters, Harry. Most of them were written before the Guv'nor brought Richland into the company. I think he may then have been 'blowing hot air,' as they say. But if nothing else, they do establish that there was a connection between the two men, Richland and Bateman, and now also Ogoon."

I agreed. For the length of time that Peter Richland had been with us, as understudy, I didn't recall him ever speaking of Ralph Bateman or giving any indication that the two knew each other. This admission in the letter was, then, of some interest. And it had now been confirmed by Herbert Willis, during our recent run-in.

"What of the other letters written in recent times?" I asked.

"You mean, while Richland was in our employ?"

"Yes, sir."

"They did eventually taper off, Harry. Yet there was still the odd one or two that Richland sent. No longer outwardly threatening but just enough to let the Guv'nor know that Richland had the upper hand . . . or so he thought."

"I can imagine the Guv'nor's reaction to such threats," I said.

Stoker nodded and sat back in his chair. "All in all, Harry, I don't think there is anything here we need be overly worried about, especially now that Richland is no longer with us." He ran his hand through his thick hair, and I could tell that he *was* worried. "I think we did right to look at them, though. It's good to have a clear picture of what went on."

"And what about this Daisy character?" I asked. "Presumably she is still about and is something of a loose cannon."

"I think it may be in our interests to track down this young lady, Harry, and to have a word or two with her. What do you think?"

Asking me what I thought was tantamount to saying that he'd like me to do the tracking. What could I say?

"Of course, sir. I'll see what I can do to locate her."

Chapter Fifteen

I boarded the horse-drawn omnibus to St. James's and made my way along to a vacant seat. The floor's normal covering of sawdust was well mixed in with layers of dirty snow trudged in by the passengers. As I took my seat, I focused my mind on this young woman Daisy I was to trace. All I had was the single name and the fact that she had come into contact with Henry Irving at the St. James's Theatre fifteen years ago. Not much to go on. She would no longer be a young woman, of course. If she had been in her early twenties then, she would be nearing forty now. Past her prime for playing juvenile leads, if in fact she had ever played leads, of course. It was not far to the St. James's, and I was still pondering whether or not this Daisy might have had nothing more than walk-ons, or even worked in wardrobe or similar, when I realized I was at my destination. I jumped up and squeezed between a corpulent costermonger and a fragrant fishwife to jump off at the corner of Duke Street.

The St. James's Theatre was at the corner of Duke Street

and King Street. Built in 1835, it had an elaborate Louis XIV–style interior that was much admired by the theatre-going public. The theatre had been renovated just two years ago and was beautiful, at least to my eyes. The manager was John Hare and I found him in his office. He was a large, bald-headed man who seemed to sweat a great deal. He had a fire blazing in the fireplace, which I am sure contributed to his condition. His face was red and his unkempt black mustache seemed to overpower his lower face. It was one of those now out-of-fashion mustaches that flowed outward to join with exaggerated sideboards. His chin was hairless, though it was almost hidden in the profuse adornment of this hirsute gentleman.

"What can I do for a member of the esteemed Lyceum Theatre?" he asked, after I had introduced myself. His voice had a North Country ring to it; Yorkshire, I would guess.

"I—we were interested in tracing a young lady whom we believe was a member of the St. James's personnel fifteen years ago," I said. "I have little to go on but I have hopes that your records may divulge her identity."

His eyebrows—equally bushy as the mustache—rose an inch or so. "Intriguing. You are thinking of retaining 'er services?"

"No." I tried to sound nonchalant. "It's purely a case of completing our own records. Mr. Stoker can be very fussy there." I smiled, hoping to indicate that I was merely following a whim of my employer.

"So what information do you 'ave about this lady of mystery, young man?" he asked.

I told him. "First name Daisy. Was here in 1866, when Mr. Irving was first appearing on your stage."

"1866?" His brow wrinkled and he tapped the surface of his desk with his forefinger. "That's a time or two ago, young man. Hmm. That would 'ave been well afore my time. 1866?" He looked up at the ceiling as though for inspiration. "Benjamin Nottingham Webster was the manager in those days, I do believe."

The name sounded vaguely familiar to me. "The production was *The Belle's Stratagem*," I offered.

With a great sigh he got to his feet and made his way over to a set of wooden filing cabinets in the far corner of his office. He pulled open a drawer, then closed it again and opened the one above it. He dug into the files inside and eventually produced a fat folder that he carried back to his desk. Opening it, he revealed a great many old programs and playbills, handwritten notes and printed posters.

"'Ere you go, lad. The years 1865, '66, and '67. There's a table over in yon corner. I 'avena time to plough through this stuff meself, but you're welcome to look all you like."

I thanked him and carried the folder across to the table he indicated, which I had to clear of assorted papers, books, and miscellany. I pushed everything to the far side so that I could open and spread the folder. I pulled up a rickety straight-backed chair, sat down, and got to work. It was almost an hour before the search bore fruit. I lifted an old, faded program and held it in my hands.

"Found something, lad?" asked Hare, seeing me sit back.

I turned to him. "This may be it," I said. "It's the program for *The Belle's Stratagem*. Now to look through it."

I saw that the Guv'nor was billed as playing Doricourt, one of the four lead roles. It was a romantic comedy of manners that had been very successful since it was first introduced a hundred years ago at the Drury Lane Theatre. I looked down the full list of characters. There, at the bottom, in the minor role of Miss Ogle, was a Daisy Middleton.

The day seemed to have flown by, and I had to hurry to get back to the Lyceum to go over various matters before the evening performance. I decided to forgo lunch. I let Mr. Stoker know what I had discovered at the St. James's and then hurried backstage to check on the properties and deal with the one hundred and one problems that seemed to have materialized while I was away that morning. Time seemed to rush on apace. Indeed, as the Bard had Hamlet say, I felt that time was "out of joint."

After a quick early evening meal, I was just about to slip into my office and catch a few brief minutes of comparative quiet before things really got going, when I was surprised to encounter the Guv'nor himself. He was in costume but had not yet applied his makeup. He stood at the foot of the stairs leading up to his dressing room and beckoned to me, then turned and made his way up the steps. I followed, mystified.

"Come along inside, Mr. Rivers," he said, leading the way. "Close the door behind you, if you please."

Thoughts rushed through my head. What had I done wrong? (It's funny how one immediately thinks the worst when summoned by a superior.) Had I forgotten something? Did he simply want me to run an errand? Mr. Irving sat down at his makeup table and began to apply the greasepaint. I stood just inside the doorway.

"Sit down. Sit down, do," he said.

I perched myself on the edge on a large, comfortable chair close to him. Somehow it didn't seem too comfortable to me at that time. "Is—is there something I . . ." My voice trailed off.

"I was passing by Abraham's office earlier," he said, "when I heard mention of a name I have not encountered in many a long year."

My heart sank.

"Miss Daisy Middleton," he continued. He paused in applying his makeup and turned to look at me for a moment. Then he went back to what he was doing. "I was of a mind to enquire of you, Mr. Rivers, just what had prompted you to bring up that name to Mr. Stoker?"

"I . . . we . . ." What was I to say? I could hardly admit that we had stolen his private correspondence and were now digging into his past.

"Or am I to take it that it was in fact Abraham himself who brought up the name?"

Now what? Did I protect my immediate boss and take the blame on myself, or did I shift the blame to Mr. Bram Stoker, rather than face any wrath from the Guv'nor? Henry Irving, a forceful man when necessary, was not one to be trifled with.

I took a deep breath and began trifling.

"What did you tell him?" asked Stoker, when I stuck my head in his office during the first interval and told him of my encounter with the Guv'nor.

"I told him that we—well, actually I said it was your idea— that you wanted to put together a scrapbook of his many appearances and that in doing so we had come across record of his early St. James's Theatre days. I said that I had noticed that particular name because I believe I have a distant cousin named Middleton." I paused, and then added, "I think he bought it."

Stoker fixed me with one piercing gray green eye, the other scrunched up.

"You are a devious devil, Harry . . . Well done! You're sure the Guv'nor harbors no further suspicions?"

"As sure as I can be, sir."

"Good. All right. Then tomorrow—or as soon as you are able—follow up on this Middleton lady and see if you can trace her. I think we need to speak with her about her future plans, especially if they concern Mr. Henry Irving."

I wanted to see Jenny but knew I couldn't until the week-end. Sunday was her one day off. Not that it was a full day off, just a few hours. I would have to get the letters back to her then, but at least we'd be able to spend some time together. I planned to take her out somewhere special . . . although as yet I had no idea where.

I started the day at the Reading Room of the British Museum, perusing the pages of back issues of *Theatre World*. This is the periodical for actors, actresses, stagehands, lighting people . . . in fact anyone and everyone involved with the theatre in any way. It bears a few articles but is mostly made up of advertisements for vacancies, casting calls, agents seeking clients and clients seeking agents, and sales of stage makeup, wigs, properties, scenery painters, and so on. We always have a copy of the latest issue at the Lyceum, but I was interested in *Theatre World* editions from years back. The year 1866, to be precise. I reasoned that when *The Belle's Stratagem* had closed its run at the St. James's Theatre, a number of its cast members would have been out looking for their next position. Miss Daisy Middleton would almost certainly have been among them. It was a long shot, I realized, but I didn't know where else to start looking.

There is a personal column in the paper where actors and actresses list their abilities, experience, references, and other credentials, hoping to be spotted by casting agents. I worked my way through fifteen issues before I found what I was looking for. A small listing that read:

> *Ingénue now available after long run at principal London theatre. Ready to read for any part, large or small. Small bones; delicate features. Some dancing ability; pleasant singing voice. Miss Daisy Middleton, Box 37, Theatre World.*

I was complimenting myself when I realized that I hadn't actually learned anything, other than the fact that Miss Middleton thought herself to have a pleasant singing voice. I needed to know at what theatre she obtained employment, in order to follow along the trail that would eventually lead to her present position. I sighed. This wasn't going to be easy, but I was determined. I gathered up my notebook and set out for the home of *Theatre World*.

I had visited the journal's office on various occasions previously. It was located on Old Compton Street, above the Admiral Duncan public house. The innkeeper of that establishment, William Gordon, greeted me warmly when I decided to stop in for a ploughman's lunch before going up to the periodical's office. He was apparently well pleased with the fact that so many visitors to *Theatre World* invariably stopped below for a drink or a meal. He recognized me from my previous visits, and we exchanged pleasantries before I enjoyed an excellent lunch.

As I approached the frosted-glass-paneled office door two floors above the tavern, I heard the clatter of typewriting machines. When I opened the door I saw one young lady at a keyboard, working with what seemed a delicate touch, while a coatless man in waistcoat and shirtsleeves pounded heavy-handedly on a second such machine. He was rail thin, with gray hair plastered down across his head and a gray face to match. He clutched a cigar between his teeth as he concentrated on what he was doing. Without looking up, he waved me to the only available chair just inside the door. I sat and waited.

With a final thump and a grunt of satisfaction, the man ripped the paper out of the machine and slapped it down in an already overflowing tray of such papers on his desk. He finally turned to face me.

"Yes?"

He was brief and to the point. I noticed his ink-stained fingers and the splash of egg down his shirtfront. He took the cigar from his mouth and knocked off the ash so that it fell close to the ashtray fighting for survival among the many letters, strips of newsprint, and invoices that covered his desk.

"I am Harry Rivers, stage manager at the Lyceum," I said by way of introduction. I held out my hand. He ignored it.

"Hurry along, then. We don't have all day." His voice was dry and brittle and made me want to swallow.

"Yes. Of course." I cleared my throat. "I am trying to trace a young actress who ran a personal a number of years ago," I said. "She used one of your box numbers—number 37. I'm sure you no longer . . ."

"How long ago?" interrupted the man.

"Oh! Er—more than fifteen years. August of 1866."

He looked across at the young lady, still steadily typing. "Judy! The book."

She ignored him. He sat for a moment and then got up and reached across his desk to hers and grabbed a ledger while she continued typewriting. As he pulled the volume toward himself, a number of disturbed papers on his own desk fell to the floor. He took no notice, reseated himself, and started turning pages in the book. Then he stopped and slammed the book closed. Grumbling to himself he got up again and swung about to the filing cabinets behind his desk. After a little digging he dropped another sister ledger on his desk and began looking through that one.

"Ah!" He studied the page and then apparently realized that his cigar was no longer lit. He patted his waistcoat pockets, found nothing, and stabbed the cigar stub down into the ashtray. "Box 37, you say? That would have been a Miss Daisy Middleton. Never heard of her. Another one as didn't become a star." He sniffed.

"I'm trying to locate her present place of employment," I said.

He sniffed again. "You are in luck, though who knows if it's deserved or not? Seems this Miss Middleton retained that box number all the way through to the end of last year."

"She kept advertising?" I asked.

"Off 'n on." He looked across to the young lady. "Judy, you nearly done? We're waiting on that, you know." He sounded irritated. For her part, the young lady continued to ignore him and to work her machine. He muttered and then turned back to me. "What you want to know, then?"

"Do you have an address for the last time she used your services?"

"Of course. We do need to get paid, you know."

I was not sure if he was referring to Daisy having to pay him for the listing or if he was implying that I should pay him for the information. I decided to play it safe and I placed a half sovereign on a small, uncovered section of his desk. He put his hand over it but did not pick it up.

"New Kent Road, at the number one hundred and forty-two." With his free hand he snapped the book closed. It seemed that was all the information I was to get from *Theatre World*.

On the south side of the River Thames, in the county of Surrey, is an area known as the Elephant and Castle. The name comes from an old coaching inn that once stood on that site. The ancient Worshipful Company of Cutlers, who once met there, have a coat of arms featuring an elephant with a howdah—looking somewhat like a miniature castle—on its back. In Shakespeare's *Twelfth Night* Antonio speaks of "the Elephant" lodgings. The present Elephant and Castle tavern was rebuilt sixty-five years ago and is now used as the terminal for several of the omnibuses.

I took one of the light green omnibuses to the Elephant and Castle hostelry, paying the fourpence fare. The vehicle was crowded, so despite the cold weather, I was forced to ride on the top, in one of the garden seats. In the summer that can be a delightful experience, but with snowflakes floating about as though considering ganging together and starting a storm, I had to bundle up, pull my topcoat about me, and tug my bowler hat tightly down over my ears. I was thankful to descend to the street when we reached our destination.

It seemed a long walk along New Kent Road, but it was not unenjoyable after riding the omnibus. I soon reached number 142, which turned out to be a rooming house, where I rapped sharply on the door three times before anyone appeared. Then it was an older woman dressed in a well-worn black frock with a faded brown shawl clutched about her bony shoulders. Her once-white cap was dirty, and scraggly steel gray strings of hair escaped it. Her face was painfully thin with her mouth a small, tight line. World-weary eyes looked at me as she enquired my business.

"Good afternoon to you," I said. "I was led to believe that a Miss Daisy Middleton resides here? Is that correct?"

"'Oo wants to know?"

"My name is Harry Rivers," I replied, not wanting to get into a lengthy explanation with this woman. "Is Miss Middleton at home?"

"Maybe she is and maybe she ain't."

"I see." I held a shilling in my hand though didn't pass it to her. This tracking of Daisy was starting to cost money, I thought. "Would you care to see if she is receiving?"

She unashamedly stuck out her gnarled hand and so I dropped the coin into it.

"Nah! She ain't receivin'," she said. "Fact is, she ain't 'ere no more. You just missed 'er. Left larst week . . . owing me money!"

She went to close the door but I was too quick. I was determined to get my shillingsworth. I stuck my foot in the door.

"Where did she go? It's important I see her."

"She owe you money, too?"

I shook my head. She seemed to think for a moment.

"You might try at the Elephant. They may know."

"The tavern?" I asked.

"Nah!" She sounded disgusted at my ignorance. "The bleedin' theatre, o' course. That's where she played."

I had eased back on my foot and she took advantage of it

to stamp on my toe. I didn't cry out but I did remove my foot just before she slammed the door. Somehow I knew she would not be reopening it.

By the time I got back to the Elephant and Castle omnibus station, I had stopped hobbling and my toes felt almost normal again. I rounded the corner and saw the Elephant and Castle Theatre before me. It was in a poor state of repair and I recalled reading somewhere—probably in *Theatre World*—that it was to be reconstructed. It certainly needed it. It was built on the site of the old Theatre Royal, which had been destroyed by fire. The new theatre was then itself partially damaged by fire just two years ago. Refusing to close, it had struggled on with blackened walls and boarded windows. From a legitimate theatre it had become a home for concert parties and variety shows. I peered at a faded poster on the wall beside the entrance. It advertised:

A NEW AUTUMN PRODUCTION
A drama written for this theatre by
Fredk. Melville
THE BAD GIRL OF THE FAMILY
Featuring Miss Daisy Middleton
and her popular song
"Daisy! Don't Eat the Daisies!"
**REFRESHMENTS
OF THE BEST QUALITY**
Supplied at Tavern Prices
by
J.C. RING
White Hart, Walworth Rd.
**GRAND SMOKING SALOON,
BOX PROMENADE.**
No Re-admission after 9 o'clock.

It took me a while to locate the manager. I found him on a stepladder holding up the end of a batten while another man tied the upper end to a longer batten that stretched across the front of the stage. I introduced myself.

"You got an act, Mr. Rivers?" he asked.

"No. No, I'm here enquiring after your Miss Daisy Middleton."

He gave a short, somewhat bitter laugh. "Oh, she ain't mine, Mr. Rivers. Not by a long chalk. Don't know that she's anyone's . . . nor that anyone would want her."

"Is she still playing here?" I persisted.

He looked up at the man above him. "Bit more to your left, Frank. No, *your* left. That's it." Then back to me. "Yes. We're still bumbling along. Not much in the way of houses, I admit, but enough to keep the curtain going up and down. What you want with her?"

"It's a personal matter," I said.

"Ain't it always? Okay, Frank. That looks good." He turned and slowly climbed down the steps. Dusting his hands, he studied me from under lowered eyebrows.

He was a small man, even shorter than myself. He wore no jacket and had his shirtsleeves tucked up in garters. His waistcoat sported a large regulator watch too large for the pocket. A Freemasonry fob hung from the watch chain. Despite being without a jacket, he wore a bowler hat, I would guess, to give himself extra height.

"Daisy Middleton," he said, thoughtfully. "Now there's a woman to be wary of, and no mistake."

"Oh?"

"You a friend, or a relation?"

"No. Nothing like that," I said. "I just wanted to talk to her. We—the Lyceum management—have some questions regarding her past stage experience."

"You're not looking to cast her in anything?" He looked surprised, and hopeful.

"No," I said quickly. His face relaxed. "Just a few questions. Is she about?"

"I doubt it. Never shows up till just before curtain, and sometimes not even then. Unreliable cow! But you takes what you can get these days. The audiences seem to like her. Leastwise the pit does, and that's what counts. Right?"

"Right," I agreed. The people in the pit at any theatre were the heart of the audience. They've been referred to as the true playgoers. A mix of upper and lower class—though I doubt that the Elephant and Castle, as a transpontine house, saw much of the upper class—they did not hesitate to display their enthusiasm or displeasure during the performance of any play or other entertainment.

"Have you any idea where Miss Middleton might be?" I enquired.

"You could look along Georges Road, if'n she's not in the public bar at the Elephant. That's where she does a lot of her business."

It took me a moment to realize that he was implying that Daisy was supplementing her theatre income by being a dolly-mop, selling her services on the street or in the tavern. Sad as it was as a commentary on the woman's life, it came as a relief to me to know that her word would count as nothing against that of England's premier Shakespearean actor. With a sigh, I thanked the manager and set out back to the Lyceum Theatre.

Chapter Sixteen

Sunday was wet and windy. I attended the small service for Mr. Turnbull, at the Actors' Church. We had been unable to locate any family, so the Guv'nor said a few words declaring that we—the Lyceum Theatre—were all the family he had needed for many years. One or two of the backstage staff took the opportunity to say a few kind words. Mr. Turnbull had been known, if only by sight, to most of us. Mr. Stoker also spoke, relating incidents of thoughtfulness on Mr. Turnbull's part that had seemed to go unnoticed at the time. I saw a few of the ladies brush tears from their eyes. It was a moving ceremony, if brief because of the inclement weather. I admit to leaving the churchyard as soon as I decently could, in order to get over to Mayfair and to Miss Jenny Cartwright.

Jenny was bundled up in a Paramatta waterproof cape, which she confided she had borrowed from Susan, one of the other maids at Mr. Irving's residence. I carried a large umbrella that demanded my full attention in the wind in order to keep it over the two of us. Once again Jenny's bright face and sparkling eyes set my heart aflutter. She looked up at me from under curling dark lashes, driving all thoughts of the weather from my mind. Diamonds of raindrops gave her dark brown hair, peeping out from under her hat, an air of refinement, and I felt proud to be accompanying her, be it in rain, snow, or sleet.

By mutual consent, we hurried off to the ABC tearoom on Regent Street, where we had exchanged confidentialities the week before. We shook off our outer garments and took a table in a corner far from the door, so as not to be disturbed by the comings and goings of other patrons.

"How has the week been for you, Jenny?" I asked, gazing into her eyes and failing to notice the waitress who had appeared at our elbows. "Oh! So sorry," I said, as menus were placed in front of us. "What would you like, Jenny?"

I sensed that Jenny was as distant from our surroundings as was I. She glanced at the menu but seemed unable to focus on the items it advertised.

"May I suggest a pot of tea for two and some petit fours or sandwiches?" asked the waitress, who had obviously encountered such self-absorbed couples before.

"Yes. Yes, please," I said, and Jenny nodded.

"Is that the petit fours or the sandwiches?"

"What? Oh! Some of each, please," I said, feeling my face redden.

With a smile and a nod, the waitress took back the menus and made off toward the kitchen.

"Is the play going well?" Jenny asked.

"Very well, thank you," I said, jogging my chair just a fraction closer to her. "Oh! I just remembered." I turned and dug into the pocket of my mackintosh hanging from the coat-tree close by the table. I pulled out a brown-paper-wrapped package that I handed to her. "Here are the letters you borrowed for us, Jenny. Mr. Stoker sends his most grateful thanks. They were certainly an eye-opener. I know we have all done a great service to Mr. Irving with this. Thank you."

She blushed prettily and slipped the package into her reticule.

When the tea arrived, we busied ourselves with eating and drinking before I brought Jenny up to date with the events of the past week. The time passed quickly as I amazed her with stories of Voudon rituals under the stage of the Lyceum and of bare-knuckle fighting and chasing Herbert Willis across London. I played down the incident of being caught eavesdropping by Ogoon and Bateman, telling myself that I did so simply to avoid making Jenny feel at all distressed.

Her own week had been uneventful, she said. "You lead such an exciting life, Harry. It must be very exhausting."

"I wouldn't change it," I replied, and I meant it.

Every morning, on first getting to the Lyceum, I would take a walk through the theatre just to satisfy myself that all was well. I would cover the stage itself, the wings, backstage, dressing rooms, greenroom, wardrobe, properties, lighting, and Mr. Stoker's office. I'd leave the checking of the front of house to Herbert Gardner. Everything was usually in order—other than the occasional misplacement of objects—and I was always telling myself that I was being overly conscientious. My job, as stage manager, really concerned the actual production itself. However, Mr. Stoker had instilled in me a sense of pride that could not be sloughed off for convenience sake. I made my routine inspection at the start of my every day.

This particular morning, fresh from my excursion to the Elephant and Castle and the investigation of Miss Daisy Middleton, I varied my routine slightly by checking on dressing rooms, backstage, and the wings before looking at

the main stage. The *Hamlet* set was up, of course, and all
seemed prepared for that evening's performance. The play
opens with a scene at a guard platform at the Castle of
Elsinore. Mr. Irving has that take place downstage, with
only that apron section lit, so that for the following scene—
a room of state in the castle—the lighting is brought up to
include the full stage with all of the inner castle scenery and
furnishings. I crossed the downstage area, from one side to
the other, and just happened to glance upstage in passing. I
came to a sudden stop. Something lay center stage; a bundle
of rags or a pile of costumes. As I moved forward to examine
it, my blood ran cold. It was a body.

Sergeant Bellamy stood with his feet apart and a frown on
his brow, scribbling into his notebook. Mr. Stoker and I
stared down at the figure lying on the stage.

"You say you don't know this person?" The policeman
looked up briefly, first at Mr. Stoker and then, more briefly,
at myself.

We both shook our heads.

"He was most certainly not known to me, Sergeant, and
Mr. Rivers has told you he was not conversant with the
man," said my boss. He was a little testy, having been interrupted in the middle of his Indian club exercise regimen.
"Mr. Rivers is more in touch to the point of facial recognition. If and when we establish a name for the man, I can
look through our list of employees. We do have close to four
hundred persons in our employ here at the Lyceum."

Sergeant Bellamy did not appear impressed but main-
tained a steady scribble in his little book.

"I do have to say that there is a certain familiarity to the
man's face," I said, stooping to get a closer look. "Not a stagehand or anything like that, but I'm almost certain I have
seen him before, outside the theatre."

The dead man was short and had a pinched, malnourished look. His hair was thin and dirty brown, with a prominent bald spot. He had an unnaturally black mustache and beard. As I studied the face I gasped. I reached forward and tugged at the beard. It came away, along with the mustache.

"Well I'm . . ." The sergeant nearly dropped his notebook. I hadn't realized that he was watching my actions.

"Charlie Vickers!" said Stoker.

"Of course!" I recalled the figure I had seen, some weeks before, talking to Ralph Bateman and Ogoon on the Embankment. The man my boss had later described to me as a regular scoundrel. More to the point, perhaps, he had been the one asking Bateman to be paid for climbing high above a stage and then complaining when Bateman refused. Had he been climbing above *our* stage and fallen? I wondered what he was doing there, if so.

"I can let you have some details of the man, Sergeant," offered Stoker. "I keep records of such malcontents we have encountered, in my office."

"What do you think he was doing, sir?" I asked. "He was obviously up to no good or he wouldn't have been here at all. I wonder how he came to fall? I understood him to be quite agile and familiar with the flies."

"And why the makeup, the false beard?" said Stoker.

"He hadn't put it on very well," I said, leaning down again. "Somewhat lopsided, I think. He wasn't in any sort of costume and there is no performance until this evening, so what was the point?"

"Hmm. I wonder." Stoker had his thoughtful look, with his finger alongside his nose.

"Broken neck, by the looks of it," volunteered Bellamy. He prodded the corpse with his toe. "Not surprised if he fell from up there." He jerked his thumb in the general direction of the area above the stage.

"Would you like to climb up and have a look from up

there, Sergeant?" I asked, knowing full well the reply I would get.

In fact I didn't get a reply, leastwise not a verbal one. The policeman merely fixed me with his beady brown eyes, squinting at me as though to make a point. He gave a sniff and then turned away. I noticed a slight smile on my boss's face.

"We will have our men take care of this, Mr. Stoker. Just as soon as convenient."

"Convenient to you or to me?" asked my boss.

Bellamy did not reply and Stoker gave me a nod and strode from the stage. I trotted after him.

In his office, Mr. Stoker put away his Indian clubs and then sat down at his desk with a sigh. I took my usual seat on the wooden chair in front of the desk.

"Several questions that need answering, Harry, and I don't think we are going to get the answers from the Metropolitan Police."

"Sir?"

"Number one, of course, what was Mr. Vickers doing here in the Lyceum after hours? I had instigated a search of the theatre after every final curtain, before the last person leaving and locking up for the night, with a team going through above stage and below. Do we have a second secret entry from outside, d'you think?"

"I doubt it, sir," I said. "Though we can't be certain. How long was that opening from the Lyceum Tavern in operation before we happened upon it the other night? But I just don't feel that there's another one."

Stoker grunted. "I agree."

"Vickers must have broken in somehow. Either that or he gained entrance before last night's final curtain and managed to hide until everyone had left."

The big man nodded. "That is my thinking. Yet the question remains, why?"

It was my turn to nod. "I suppose Bateman is still trying

to bring down our production. And I'm still very uneasy about Willis's urging Bateman to kidnap the Guv'nor, or even Miss Terry."

"I can't see Vickers achieving that, and especially not from the flies above the stage. No, Harry, there is more here than meets the eye."

"But you have an idea, sir?" I felt I knew my boss by now.

"Yes, and no," he said. "No to exactly why he was here, but yes to why we found him here."

"I'm not sure I follow you, sir."

"Think, Harry. You said yourself that Vickers was agile in the space above stage. It was almost certainly he who led you on that merry chase across our rooftop. How, then, did he come to fall? . . . If indeed he did fall."

A flash went off inside my head. "You're saying he didn't fall; he was pushed?" I cried.

"Pushed. Dropped. Placed. I suspect his neck may have been broken before his body met our stage. And did you notice the fingernails?"

"Fingernails?" I realized I had dropped into my frequent and annoying—even to myself—habit of repeating what Mr. Stoker said. But then he so often caught me by surprise.

"The fingernails had traces of blood under them. Evidence, perhaps, of the man fighting off his attacker and trying to escape. Just another indication that he may not have fallen accidentally." He paused a moment before continuing. "You had spoken of hearing him complaining to Mr. Ralph Bateman. Perhaps he complained too much?"

"Why the fake beard, sir?"

"That I have not yet resolved. You said it was badly placed so I suspect that, too, was added to the body after it was in situ. Some sort of allusion to this being part of our seemingly ongoing feud with Sadler's Wells, perhaps?"

I had to agree. Bateman—or more probably his boss— must have decided they had no further use for Charlie Vickers. Perhaps because of his complaining or for some other reason. Whatever it was, they must have thought it expedient to drop off his body on our stage, with no real agenda for the action. Hopefully the police would remove it long before curtain time. Stoker interrupted my thoughts.

"I would surmise that the Bateman-Ogoon group is not entirely harmonious. Some sort of rivalry, perhaps, in the ranks?"

"Between Vickers and Willis?" I hazarded.

"What is the name of that scene painter at Sadler's Wells that you know, Harry?"

"You mean Jack Parsons? Yes, I think he may be the only honest man at that theatre. Why do you ask, sir?"

My boss ran a finger around his shirt collar and straightened his cuffs. "I don't think we can safely send you off there again, Harry, even in makeup, excellent as your excursions have been. But it would be nice if we could get some sort of information as to what is truly going on there. Do you think Mr. Parsons might be willing to give us that information? Perhaps you might buy him a lunch, or something of that sort? What do you think, Harry?"

B efore Sergeant Bellamy left the theatre he cornered me. It was unusual for him to speak to me for any length of time, here at the Lyceum. He had, that once, stopped by my rooms and addressed me directly, but other than that, if I was with Mr. Stoker then Bellamy always addressed everything to my boss and virtually ignored me. Now, however, he spoke to me directly.

"A work of caution, young man."

"I beg your pardon?"

"It would seem to us that you are more closely tied in to what goes on here than you are willing to admit, Mr. Rivers."

I shook my head. "What are you talking about? I am the theatre's stage manager so of course I'm tied in, as you put it, to what goes on here. I've never made any pretense otherwise."

"That's not what we are saying, sir. It's all these murders and things. Bodies freshly dead and bodies missing. Severed heads. People being run down by cabs."

"What are you talking about?" I repeated. I couldn't believe what I was hearing. "Are you saying that I'm responsible for Peter Richland being run down? I wasn't even there when it happened. Also, I was not onstage when the head came flying out of the scenery. And now this body of Mr. Charles Vickers . . . why would I be associated with that?"

Sergeant Bellamy tried to look stern. "We are just saying, sir, that things are very suspicious. We have you in our sight, Mr. Rivers, and are keeping a close watch on you."

"Well, enjoy the view, Sergeant!" I sniffed and walked away. But I didn't feel comfortable. Sergeant Bellamy seemed to have an uncanny knack of putting together two and two and coming up with five. I had enough to do without worrying about a suspicious policeman watching my every move.

I t was later that day I found myself at the Silent Woman on Cochran Street, with Jack Parsons, paying for two very mouthwatering pork pies with peas and new potatoes. Since Mr. Stoker had given me the money for this repast, I was happy to add two large porters to wash down everything. The Silent Woman was well-known for its ancient sign outside showing a headless woman, but it was equally well-known for its pork pies. I had sent a message to Jack asking him to meet me there, rather than at the Bag o' Nails, which was frequented by so many of the Sadler's Wells crew.

"So what's this all about then, 'Arry?" Jack asked, after sinking his teeth into his pie and chewing for a while. He spoke with his mouth still full, spewing bits of excellent flaked pastry over the table.

"Just trying to keep up with everything," I said. "I was wondering how things were going at Sadler's."

"'Ow come this sudden interest?"

"Not really sudden, as you well know, Jack," I said. "But we have heard rumors of some sort of disagreement among Ralph Bateman's cronies, and I was wondering if you knew any details?"

He chewed for a while, his brow wrinkled, and then he filled his mouth with porter. Swallowing and then giving a belch, he wiped his mouth with the back of his hand and looked hard at me.

"That's funny," he said. "You're the second fella what's been asking questions like that."

"I am?" I wondered who else could be interested in the affairs of our two theatres.

"Yes. Young fella give me an 'and with torn flats a while back. Bit strange looking 'e was. Just somethin' about 'im; about 'is 'air. Funny color. Anyway, 'e was full of questions."

I broke out in a sweat. Obviously he was talking about me, when under the influence of Mr. Archibald's transformation. I raised my tankard in front of my face and took a long drink.

"You and me, we got a lot in common, 'Arry," Jack said. "You seem to know what's 'appening backstage, as it were, and I seem to 'ave the way of over'earing what ain't exactly none o' my business." He grinned.

"Care to share some of that eavesdropping?" I asked, lowering my drink.

There was another belch. "Seems as 'ow young Mr. Bateman ain't keepin' too firm an 'old on 'is workers. Mind you, 'e ain't exactly one of the theatre crew, so what 'e does with 'is cronies shouldn't be no nevermind to anyone else, if'n you follow me?"

"Oh, I follow you all right, Jack." I nodded to encourage him to continue.

"If'n Mrs. Crowe ain't worried about what 'er brother gets up to, then 'oo am I to question it? Right?"

"Right, Jack."

"Take that little runt Charlie Vickers. 'E's been nothing but an 'eadache as long as e's been around Sadler's. Was a time 'e was up in the flies, all legit like, but 'e couldn't 'old down a job like that for long. Then 'e was doin' God knows what for Mr. Ralph. Then 'e got too big for 'is britches there, too. Next thing I knew they was all 'aving a right old barney."

"Fighting?" I asked.

"Matter o' fact it did come to fisticuffs," said Jack. "Charlie Vickers and that 'Erbert Willis was the worst. They 'ad a right up-and-downer just a couple o' days ago. Left deep scratches all over Willis's face, which didn't improve it."

I smiled. "Thanks, Jack," I said. "Thanks a lot. That seems to follow what we had guessed."

"Care to let me in on it, then, 'Arry?"

I wondered if I should let him know about finding Vickers's body on our stage and decided, why not? He was bound to find out eventually anyway, and it was useful to maintain good terms with him, so I told him.

"So someone finally snuffed 'is candle, did they? Huh! I'm not surprised."

"Any idea who?"

He shrugged. "Could be any of a dozen or more," he said. "'Erbert Willis 'eads the list, from 'ow I sees it, but it could o' been anyone. Willis was only the latest 'e rubbed the wrong way."

"Any idea why Vickers's body was dumped on the Lyceum stage?"

Again he shrugged. "Can't see Willis, or any of them lot, trying to leave any sort of a message for you with summat like that. They'd just as soon leave 'im where 'e dropped. But 'oo knows, eh, 'Arry?" He returned to his porter.

On my way to the theatre on Tuesday morning, I looked in at St. James's Division police station to follow up on Sergeant Bellamy's report regarding the headless body. I was not a little relieved to discover that Sergeant Bellamy was not himself there but "out on a case," according to the sergeant who was apparently in charge. He stood behind the enquiry counter.

"The unidentified torso recovered from Lambeth, sir?"

"Yes, Sergeant."

He went to a large, untidy clipboard and started thumbing through the dog-eared and grubby papers attached to it.

"Sergeant Bellamy?"

"Correct."

"Ah! Here we are, sir. Yes. Yes, it appears there is a report here." He read from the scribbled notes. "Reported by one Arthur York, rag-and-bone man of . . ."

"Yes, yes, Sergeant," I interrupted. "I am somewhat familiar with the rudiments of the case. I was just wondering if it has been ascertained that this torso and the previously discovered head that fell out of the scenery at the Lyceum Theatre were in fact of a pair?"

"Of a pair, sir?"

The sergeant was tall and thin but with a pronounced stoop that diminished his height by a good three or four inches. He was elderly—too elderly to be an active policeman by my estimation—with a bald pate thrusting through nearly pure white hair that ran down the sides of his face and pooled in a ragged, once-trimmed beard and mustache. There were prominent bags under his eyes, and his nose told the story of evenings spent at the nearby Rose and Crown tavern. I learned that his name was Sandler.

"Did the head actually belong to that body? Did they, together, make up the complete corpse?" I never in my wildest dreams would have imagined myself standing here having this conversation.

"I see, sir."

I rather wondered if he did see. Perhaps it would have been better if Bellamy had been there. At least he would know what I was talking about.

"One moment, sir. I will just step down to the morgue and have a word with the officer in charge of that department. I am sure he will be able to answer your questions, sir."

He disappeared through the opening behind his desk and I heard his hobnail boots slowly and laboriously descending to the lower regions. I had no desire, myself, to go back down to that cold, ascetic, white-tiled basement with its sheet-covered corpses, and I took a seat on a hard wooden bench against the wall to await the sergeant's return.

I had a long wait, but eventually he reappeared clutching yet another clipboard, this one folded back to the relevant page.

"It is the opinion of the Metropolitan Police, sir," he said, while trying to recover his breath from the exertion of descending to the basement and returning, "that the headless body discovered by the Lambeth rag-and-bone man did, in all probability, go with the bodiless head that had apparently jumped out of your theatrical scenery."

I was not going to get into an argument as to whether or not the head actually did jump out of the scenery. "You say, 'in all probability,' Sergeant," I said, rising and coming forward to the counter behind which he had installed himself. "Surely it would be very straightforward to determine whether or not the two fit together? I mean, how many possibilities are there? Do you have a number of severed heads on hand?"

He fixed me with what I think was meant to be a steely gaze, but regrettably, his left eye had a habit of twitching and the other eye was inclined to water profusely.

"I merely report what I have on hand, sir, and that is the determination of the coroner, sir. He it is who uses the phrase 'in all probability.'"

Something wasn't right. I had had enough dealings with the police to know when they were evading a straight answer. I took a very deep breath and drew myself up to my full height . . . a good six or more inches shorter that the sergeant.

"I think I would like to have a word with your coroner, Sergeant Sandler."

Chapter Seventeen

My initial visit to the police station morgue had been to identify Peter Richland's body. I had not been over-joyed to be there and nor was I overjoyed at this return visit. The place was cold—understandable with dead bodies litter-ing the area—and still reeked of carbolic soap. I had origi-nally been entertained there by the stoic Sergeant Samuel Charles Bellamy. The coroner himself had not been present on that occasion, but on this visit he was there. Dr. Rufus Entwhistle was a short, stocky man, even shorter than myself, which gave me a little more self-assurance. He was what might be described as mild-mannered, spoke with a soft voice that demanded I lean in toward him the whole time, and had a strong Lancashire accent that equally demanded my full attention to make out what he was saying. His head was completely bald but had any number of red lines across the top of it where he habitually scratched his head as he talked. I suspected some sort of skin infection.

He was clean shaven but wore his sideboards in the old-fashioned muttonchops style. The hair was a brilliant white, though his eyebrows were gray and bushy, casting shadows over his pale blue eyes.

"Sergeant Sandler tells me you 'ave questions, lad?" he said. At least, I think that's what he said.

"Yes, sir." I risked a quick glance around the tiled room. I saw only two sheeted figures in evidence . . . one apparently the headless corpse and the other some obese and nameless man whose feet protruded from the bottom of his sheet. "The sergeant tells me that your report says you feel the severed head that rolled onto the stage of the Lyceum Theatre a while back 'in all probability' belongs to the headless corpse discovered by the rag-and-bone man."

"Aye, lad. That's reet."

"Forgive me, sir," I said, "but I feel my boss would have trouble with the words 'in all probability.' He is inclined to be fastidious and will want to know categorically whether or not the head did indeed go with that body."

He gave a long, sad sigh, shaking his head. "Aye, well . . . we would all like to know that, I'm betting. But truth be told, lad, it cannot be done."

"Why ever not?"

"Because we don't 'ave the 'ead."

"What?"

"Nay, lad. It seems that the 'ead—not appearing to be of any use to anyone anymore—was disposed of. And afore you ask, that means it was in all probability burnt."

I was aghast. "Burnt? But—but now that we have the body as well it should have been put back in the grave from which it was robbed!"

He scratched his head as it nodded up and down. "Aye, lad. 'Indsight is a powerful tool and nay mistake. What we might do if we all could 'ave it at all times."

"But surely you don't get that many severed heads, even

here in the morgue? You must have known that it belonged to someone, somewhere?"

"Aye, well. What's done is done." He gave another long sigh, shook his head, scratched it again, and then seemed to perk up. "Was there anything else, lad?"

"The torso," I said. "When the body was intact, when it was first brought in here, Sergeant Bellamy mentioned that he had determined that the person run down by the growler was an actor because of the stage makeup on the face. Have you found traces of such makeup on the torso?"

"There was no sign of any of that stage makeup grease on the 'ands," the doctor said. "We normally look carefully under fingernails for clues such as that. As you say, we did make mention of the presence of said grease on the face when we first received the complete body after it was trampled."

"Yes," I said. "Are you saying, then, that there was no sign of greasepaint under the nails of the original body? I remember the greasepaint on the face—that was how you came to believe it to be our Peter Richland—but I don't recall you talking about the fingernails at that time."

Doctor Entwhistle looked slightly uncomfortable, or as uncomfortable as he was likely to look. I felt he was a man who believed himself to be in possession of all the facts.

"The grease on the face was—at that time, lad—sufficient for our identification. Further checking, such as under fingernails, was not *then* necessary . . . or so we believed. It was not, at that time, expected nor foreseen that the 'ead would be separated from the rest of the body."

It was my turn to sigh. It was extremely annoying but it seemed there was nothing I could do about it. "So it probably *is* Richland's body but there's no guarantee. I wonder who else could it be?" He did not respond.

I continued, as much to myself as to him. "Mr. Stoker

should see the way this police station is run! Now he is a stickler for order." I spoke petulantly. But then I thought of the "order" of Mr. Stoker's desk. I moved on. "I think I'll take a trip out to Lambeth and Blackfriars and have a word or two with Mr. York . . . just in case there's anything that may have been missed."

The coroner sniffed and once again scratched the top of his head. "You must do as you think fit, lad," he said stiffly. "We do our job to the very best of our abilities, understaffed as we may be."

"I'm sure you do," I said with as much sarcasm as I could muster.

The days seemed to get shorter, with all the running around I was obliged to do. I just wasn't getting all my theatre work done as efficiently as I would have liked. To save some time on Wednesday morning I took a hansom, rather than an omnibus, over Blackfriars Bridge to Webber Street, off Blackfriars Road. This wasn't a prosperous neighborhood by any means. In fact it was very much run-down, to the point where the hansom, as soon as it had dropped me, turned around and made off at a good trot back to the City.

I stayed in place for a moment, studying the line of attached houses. They stood uniformly shoulder to shoulder, with the only distinctions being the amount of dirt on the walls and the number of broken panes of glass at the windows. Rubbish mixed with horse droppings, abandoned trash, and detritus of all kinds filled the gutters and overflowed onto the pavement and roadway. Nearby, grubby, barefoot children in ragged clothing sat on doorsteps and played listlessly in the street. A knife grinder sat pedaling his sharpening stone, sparks shooting from the pair of scissors he was working on. A crippled boy crouched on a crudely made box on wheels and sang as he shook a hat with a couple of coins in it.

On the far corner of the street hung the three brass balls of the pawnbroker, though one of the balls was missing. Next to it was an abandoned stable and then, next to that, I could just barely read the faded letters for the rag-and-bone man's business: *Arthur York & Son—Rags, Bones, and Bottles.* I made my way there, passing around the crippled boy. I dropped a sixpence in his hat. It was immediately grabbed up and disappeared into his pocket. He didn't miss a beat of the tuneless song he sang in his high-pitched voice. I ducked into the dark doorway, stepping over a pile of moldy clothing and worn leather boots.

"Wotcha want?" demanded a young voice as I entered the shop.

I stood inside the doorway surveying the mountains of rags covering all available floor space. Hanging from nails driven into the wooden walls was a huge variety of clothing, men's and women's. Hats stretched out along high shelves and shoes covered lower shelves. A single oil lamp hung suspended in the midst of it all, its light failing to reach all four walls. From somewhere in the murky background a short figure approached. It materialized into that of a young boy, no more than ten years of age by my estimation. He was well covered by a great number of woolen pullovers, the elbows ripped and the hems unraveling. On his head was a brown bowler hat with a rip in the side. He wore it at a rakish angle. Oversize hobnail boots covered his sockless feet, and his knee-length shorts shone, in the light of the lamp, from the grease and dirt they had acquired.

"I'm looking for Mr. York," I said.

"So's a lot o' people," he said, wiping his running nose on his sleeve. "You sellin' or buyin'?"

"Neither," I said. "Where is Mr. York?"

"I'm right 'ere." A raspy voice came from off to one side.

Its owner struggled into the light. He was a man of my own height, though he appeared much shorter due to his pronounced stoop. He moved laboriously, hindered by a clubfoot. His suit—if I can so describe it—was of the same hue as the boy's trousers; it was difficult to tell the color under the accumulation of dirt. He wore a dustman's hat, the long leather peak hanging down his back. Incongruously, he wore a bright red bow tie, probably from a recent ragbag. Uncontrolled whiskers covered his face and chin, the spaces between filled in with grime.

"Mr. Arthur York?" I asked.

"None other. An' 'oo might you be?"

I introduced myself. "I understand that you reported the finding of a headless body?"

"The bluebottles 'ave been 'ere already," said the boy.

"I know," I said. "It was the police who told me. And you are William, I take it?"

"'Ere!" He looked anxiously to the man.

"It's all right," he said.

"Nothing is wrong," I hastened to assure them. "I just have one or two questions."

"You wif the gavvers?" asked William.

"Indirectly," I said. "Sergeant Bellamy directed me here." I turned to the man. "Now, Mr. York, how was the body dressed, when you chanced upon it?"

"'Chanced upon it'? It weren't no chance. It just sat there at the side o' the road in a bag full o' rags."

"It weren't dressed," chipped in William. "Just in 'is unutterables."

"S'right," agreed York. "Looked as though 'e'd been stripped of anyfing worfwhile by someone. Which is wot I'd 'ave done if'n I'd been the first to find it."

"Do you still have the undergarments?" I wondered if there were any clues to be found in them.

"Oh yes! Them was tofficky togs nefer mind bein' unutterables. Should bring a pretty penny in the right quarters, I'm finkin'." He waved at the boy. "Dig 'em out, Will. Show the gent. 'E might even be interested in buyin'." He looked hard at me.

"I very much doubt that," I said, then indicated my height. "I'm probably far too short for the clothes of most gentlemen."

The boy scrambled away over the piles of clothes and rags—the two indistinguishable to my eyes—and soon returned with a bundle wrapped in newspaper and tied with string. He handed it to York, who carefully unwrapped it.

"'Ere you go," he said, holding up a suit of combination underwear.

It was remarkably clean, I thought. I reached out and fingered it.

"Silk," I said, very much surprised.

"Din' I say as it was tofficky?"

"You did indeed. Was this all there was?"

"That's it," cried William. "Just a body wifout an 'ead dressed in them very unutterables. Stank to 'igh 'eaven as well. Cor! Give me a right turn an' no mistake."

"There is no blood on the garments around the neck," I murmured. "Only a little where the chest was caved in from the horses' hooves."

"Why's that, then?" asked York.

"To my understanding it indicates that the head was not removed from the body until after death," I said. "But I'm no expert. I may be wrong."

"Cor!" said William.

"Well, I thank you," I said, and turned to leave.

"What 'appened to the crossin' sweeper?" asked York. "I'd be 'appy to take '*is* clothes since 'e won't be needin' 'em no more."

I paused. "Crossing sweeper?"

"'Im as was run down."

"I'm not sure I follow you," I said. "This is the one who was run down, and he was an actor, not a crossing sweeper. And this happened about a fortnight ago."

William threw up his hands in disgust and stomped off out of the shop.

"Just after we picked up the bag wif the 'eadless body in it," explained York, speaking slowly as though explaining to a child, "an 'ansom come swingin' around the corner, off Gravel Lane Crescent onto Southwark, and sent a kid sweeper flyin'. This was days ago. 'E never did get up. I fink the bobbies took 'im off. I'm surprised they din' tell you. We couldn't 'ang about. We'd got work to do."

I found Stoker deep in conversation with a man unknown to me, when I went to report my findings. I slipped out again for a quick lunch at the Druid's Head and they were still in conference when I returned. I got on with my work, and it was after the matinee before I was able to sit down with my boss.

"Silk undergarments?"

"Yes, sir. That surprised me, too."

I could almost see the wheels going around in Stoker's head. He had a brilliant mind, or so it appeared to one such as myself.

"Tell me, Harry. Did Mr. Richland appear to you to be the sort of man who would affect silk undergarments?"

"It's difficult to say, sir," I said, scratching my head. "One just never knows what a man might be hiding under his outer wear."

"True," he conceded. "But my question was, did he appear to you to be the sort of man who would affect such wear?"

I paused only a moment. "No, sir. He did not."

Stoker nodded. He remained in thought for a while, and

then said, "I was just in conversation with Dr. William Wynn Westcott."

"I thought the Guv'nor was pretty much over the poisoning?"

"He is, Harry. Recovering remarkably well. But then the Guv'nor is a remarkable man. No, Harry, Dr. Westcott was not here as a medical man. He has earned a reputation outside that of his medical practice. He is considered to be one of the leading authorities on the occult, and I was apprising him of our own findings relating to Voudon."

"Sir?" I was not too certain what was meant by the occult, though it gave me an uneasy feeling.

Stoker glanced down at a piece of notepaper where he had apparently been making notes about his visitor. "A decade ago William Westcott became a Freemason. As you know, many prominent men today are of that brotherhood." I nodded. "In fact the Guv'nor is desirous of entering that fraternity at some point. But, from University College Dr. Westcott had gone on to become a partner in his uncle's medical practice in Somerset. Two years ago his uncle died and the good doctor took a suitable retirement at Hendon so that he might devote some serious time to study of the Qabalah, Hermetics, and alchemy."

He was losing me, but I remained with my attention fixed on his face and hoped he wouldn't notice any glazing of my eyes as I tried to follow him.

"He has just completed that study and was kind enough to visit me, at my request, before returning to the West Country."

"I'm sorry, sir," I had to say. "I don't quite see . . ."

"Just bear with me, Harry. Among the many disciplines with which Dr. Westcott is familiar is the West Indian religion of Voudon. I went over my own thinking with him and, in fact, took him below stage to see the inscription on the wall of the secret room there."

"What did he think of it?" I asked.

"He agreed with me, Harry. The fact that the vévé drawn on the wall is that of Guédé would seem to indicate that the rituals performed here are of the black magic variety. Negative, Harry. Of no benefit to the theatre; in fact quite the reverse."

"I think we gathered that, did we not, sir, from witnessing that ritual?"

"Oh, undoubtedly, Harry. And I am still not comfortable with the apparently inexplicable death of our dear Mr. Turnbull, since Dr. Cochran attested to his previous good health. That was just the sort of thing that might—and I do say 'might,' Harry—have been caused magically. There are many examples of such murders in the literature. Dr. Westcott concurs. It is not, however, the sort of conundrum that I believe our Metropolitan Police friends are capable of solving."

I was uncertain what to say. Here was my boss, a university-educated man, talking blithely about magic as though it were an everyday occurrence. Did he really believe in it, or was he letting his Irish superstition get away from him, I wondered?

"So, what does all this mean, sir?" I asked.

He looked at me in his characteristic pose of one eye closed and a forefinger alongside his nose. "What indeed, Harry?" he said enigmatically. "What indeed?"

"There's something you'd like me to do?" I asked, still uncertain of his intentions.

"I don't think there's anything you *can* do, Harry. Not at present. We will have to see where all of this leads us. No. I think that for the moment we will continue to focus our energies—outside the theatre performances, of course—on tracking down our poisoner and determining exactly why Richland's body was removed from its coffin and the head deposited on our stage."

"But you do think there was some connection between that body snatching and any mumbo jumbo performed *under* our stage?" I persisted.

"I do, Harry. But before we can connect all the dots, we need all the facts. Now! You say that there is no absolute answer on whether or not the head and body were a match?" I shook my head. "Very well. We'll just try to keep everything in mind."

He reached for some papers and I felt dismissed.

In fact I didn't have the time to do any more extracurricular activity that day. Someone had managed to step on Yorick's skull and crush it. It was not a real skull but one made of papier-mâché, constructed in our props department. When John Whitby had earlier dropped it onstage— not the first time he had done that—it hadn't helped. It was time to build another fake skull and I got someone busy doing that. Other small crises kept me busy till the evening curtain-up.

The following morning, a Thursday, Mr. Stoker was out of the office on some business of his own and I was able to spend time catching up on my paperwork, plus double-checking the properties list and going through Miss Price's prompt copy.

At lunchtime I took a cab to Little Vine Street and the St. James's Division police station to see if Sergeant Bellamy had any further news. As I had half expected, I found him to have gone around the corner to the Stag's Head to have his lunch. I went there to join him.

"How's the bread today, Sergeant?" I asked, as I slipped down onto the chair opposite him. "Stale again, or is it a fresh batch?"

He didn't look up but answered as though we had been in conversation for some while.

"They've got a good ham they're slicing, if you fancy something other than cheese," he said. "The bread is all right. But then just about anything is all right if you wash it down with enough ale."

"I'll drink to that," I said with a chuckle. I nodded toward his newspaper. "Still checking the horses?"

"The horses are running well enough to pay for this ham sandwich, Mr. Rivers. Now we're sure you didn't come here to chitchat. What can we do for you?"

"I was wondering about the headless corpse," I said, waving down the serving girl and giving her my order. "It has been intimated that there was a possibility of it not being Peter Richland's body, based on the absence of greasepaint under the fingernails."

"'Possibility,' Mr. Rivers. That was the word used. There is the possibility that it is not your Mr. Richland's body, but there is also the possibility that it is."

I sighed and cut in half the thick sandwich the girl placed in front of me.

"If not Richland's, then whose? Do you get a lot of headless corpses, Sergeant?"

"No, sir, we do not. Most unusual, in fact. All the more reason to believe that it probably *is* the late Mr. Richland. We do get a lot of unknown corpses though, we must admit. There are a great number of crimes committed in the East End, with bodies left in alleyways, stuffed into privies, and dumped in the River Thames. But very few of them—in fact we can't think of one other one—that are without the head."

"Your Dr. Entwhistle said that you had disposed of the head?"

"Yes, sir. Possibly we were a mite hasty in that, but you can only sit for so long waiting for a body to turn up."

"I suppose so," I said. I took a bite of my sandwich. Bellamy was right; the ham was excellent. "I went to see the rag-and-bone man," I said. "He showed me the underclothing that the corpse had been wearing. I don't think there's any doubt in my mind that the body had been trampled by horses."

"There you are correct, sir. Yes. It most certainly had that appearance."

"Then surely that would confirm that it was Richland's body?"

"As we said, sir, there is still that possibility."

I took a good drink of the dark ale and then shook my head at the cautiousness of the police. They would admit to nothing and deny everything, if it suited them. But it was a shame that we couldn't match up the head and the body. I'm sure Mrs. Richland would wish for a complete corpse to rebury.

"Do you know anything of Voudon, Sergeant?" I asked, on impulse.

His hand stopped halfway up to his mouth. He looked at me over the edge of his bread.

"Hoodoo and mumbo jumbo?" he asked. He took a bite from the sandwich and chewed thoughtfully for a while. "No, we don't get much call for that. Now the yellow men in Limehouse, they've got their own sort of mumbo jumbo. Very mystical and very ancient, so we've been told. Why do you ask?"

"No reason," I said, not willing to draw the sergeant into everything going on in the Lyceum. "Just wondering."

He fixed me with his police sergeant eye and continued chewing thoughtfully. I turned my attention to my own lunch. Then I was struck by a thought.

"Sergeant, if someone was run down by a hansom, much as our Mr. Richland was by that growler, where would the body be taken?" I was thinking of the crossing sweeper that the rag-and-bone man had mentioned.

"Where did this accident take place, Mr. Rivers?"

"Off Blackfriars Road, just south of the bridge."

"Well, normally the body would go to Lambeth Division—L Division—on Kennington Lane, but we happen to know that they are 'indisposed,' we think the term is, at the present time. Their drains have all backed up. Nasty mess!"

"So where would the body go?" I persisted.

"On to our own excellent premises at Little Vine Street, sir. Why do you ask?"

I thought of the morgue I had recently visited there, with its two corpses. No sign of any other victims. No sign of a young crossing sweeper. Something was not right. I decided not to immediately pursue it with the sergeant.

We exchanged remarks about the weather, the amount of traffic on Oxford Street, and the unreliability of racehorses before the sergeant, with a belch and a sigh, got to his feet and bade me farewell. I finished my own lunch, drained my beer glass, and thought about where I should next direct my feet.

Before I could leave, a well-dressed figure stopped at the table, pulled out the chair recently vacated by Sergeant Bellamy, and sat down. It was Mr. Ogoon, the West Indian friend of Ralph Bateman.

"Mr. Rivers," he said. He removed his top hat and laid it on the table. He ran his hand over his smooth scalp and glanced about him. "My sources tell me that this is a worthwhile eatery. Good food and honest ale, I am told."

I said nothing. What did he want, I wondered?

"One cannot exist for any length of time on nothing but scraps," he said, his dark eyes suddenly boring into me.

Was he referring to the feeding of zombies, I wondered?

"You are strangely silent," he said. "Yet but moments ago you were conversing freely with one of the Metropolitan Police's officers. Why now this reticence?"

"What do you want?" I asked.

"Who said that I wanted anything, Mr. Rivers? No. As a visitor to your fair city I am but enjoying all that it has to offer. I understand that the entertainment here is exceptional. The theatre district is one of the best in the world, I understand."

"That it is."

"Yet theatre-going is not without its risks, I hear?"

What did he mean exactly?

"The Holborn Theatre. The Grecian. Astley's. The Olympic. Covent Garden. The Royal Coburg . . . all destroyed by fire. Your own Lyceum, Mr. Rivers, burned to the ground less than fifty years ago. The Royal Brunswick a few years earlier, with many people killed and injured. The Elephant and Castle just three years ago. Tragic! And how easily these theatre fires start, Mr. Rivers. But you must be well aware of that, are you not?"

"Are you threatening us, Mr. Ogoon?" I asked. I tried to remain calm, but my heart had started to race. Did this man plan on setting fire to the Lyceum? Surely not. Then I had a thought. "Is your magic not powerful enough, then, Mr. Ogoon, that you have to resort to incendiaries?"

He again ran his hand over his head, and he smiled at me. "Magic, Mr. Rivers? Do you believe in magic?"

I didn't know what to say. Suddenly he replaced his hat on his head and stood up.

"I think I was misinformed," he said, looking about him. "I think that this establishment is not as salubrious as it had been made out to be. I fear I must go in search of other means of satisfaction. Good day to you, Mr. Rivers."

He strode away and I was left with an empty feeling in my stomach, despite the meal I had just finished.

Chapter Eighteen

I was greatly disturbed at Ogoon's suggestion that the Lyceum might experience a devastating fire. It was true that a number of English theatres had suffered such a fate. The Lord Chamberlain, the statutory authority over theatres, had never bothered much with such matters as sanitation and fire protection. He was the one who licensed all theatres . . . all except Drury Lane and Covent Garden, which were under royal patents. But just three years ago the new Metropolitan Board of Works had been given authority, by Parliament, over new theatre construction, and they did emphasize fire safety. Gas lighting had been a major factor in several of the fires. Now many theatres, as with the Lyceum, were converting to the new electricity, which was much safer. Indeed, later this year the Savoy Theatre was to open as the first London theatre lit entirely by electricity.

The main objection to this new source of lighting was the noise of the steam engines and dynamos used to create it. Each structure had its own, and these were usually housed outside the theatre rather than inside, though not always. Happily, they were so placed at the Lyceum.

I caught up with Mr. Stoker in the late afternoon, when he returned to his office. I told him of my encounter with Ogoon and my concerns about his implied threat.

"It is indeed a very real threat, Harry," he said. "As you know, these wooden theatres are highly combustible. It's a constant worry, believe me. We must alert the staff and keep our eyes open. But unfortunately, there's nothing more we can do."

I was kept busy for the rest of the time till the evening performance, though the worry about fire never left me. I found myself checking every dark corner.

Friday morning saw me riding the light green–colored horse drawn omnibus from Ludgate Hill over Blackfriars Bridge to the south side of the Thames. I walked along Southwark to the corner of Gravel Lane Crescent and then stood and looked about me. There was not a lot of traffic, and I couldn't imagine a hansom cab, going fast, swinging around the corner and hitting a crossing sweeper, especially in the early hours of the morning. I had a special fondness for crossing sweepers, if only because I had been one myself when I first came to the City. Many newcomers to London start out that way, especially those who, like myself, have no family and little money. I had been but fourteen years of age. Some are as young as ten.

Crossing sweepers are found at all of the main intersections, ready to run out into the road and sweep it clear of dirt, mud, garbage, and horse droppings so that ladies and gentlemen—the ladies especially, with their full skirts—may cross the street in comparative cleanliness. Major crossings, such as at Piccadilly Circus and Trafalgar Square, have gangs of boys and men who stake their claim to the areas, while every large crossing is fought over. On a good day a sweeper can earn a shilling or more in tips. A new broom, which may be needed once a month, costs threepence.

On hotly contested crossings a sweeper may take a chance and dash out between horses in order to stake a claim to the hoped-for tip from the pedestrian. Some boys and girls have been knocked down in that way. But it is almost unheard of for a cab to deliberately run down a sweeper. I felt there was more to this "accident" than met the eye.

A sad-faced girl of about twelve stood leaning on her broom at the curbside. As I approached her, she prepared to run out into the street.

"No! Wait!" I cried. "I'm not crossing. I just want to ask you something."

She looked wary. "You a bluebottle?" she demanded, dark eyes looking up at me from under a man's cap pulled down over her auburn hair. She wore fingerless gloves and a too-large boy's jacket buttoned and pinned over a dirty, checkered dress that hung down to her booted feet.

"No," I said. "I'm just trying to find out about the boy who got run down here the other morning. Do you know anything about him?"

"Billy White. Why ya wanna know for?"

"It's important," I said. I let her see a sixpence in my hand. "What can you tell me about it?"

Her eyes locked onto the coin. "What ya wanna know?"

"How did he come to be run down?"

She shrugged. "'E didn't get out of the way quick enuff, I'm finkin'."

"Was he taking chances? Was he running between cabs?"

She wiped her nose on her sleeve, her eyes still on the sixpence. "Nar! Bleedin' cabbie was a devil. Din' even slow down. Just 'it poor Billy and took off. Bloody magsman!"

"Was Billy killed?" I asked.

She shook her head. "Nar! But 'e ain't goin' nowhere. Busted 'is legs, they says."

"So the police didn't come and pick up Billy?"

"Nah. Ain't never 'ere if'n you needs 'em, is they?"

"Who said that Billy's legs were broken?" I asked.

"The two old dears wot took 'im in."

This was indeed news. So the boy had not been killed and had been taken in by two old ladies. If I could speak to him, perhaps I could find out why he had been run down and by whom. There might well be a connection to the headless body left across the road for the rag-and-bone man.

"Where can I find them?" I asked.

The girl looked up and down the road, as if afraid of losing customers. But there was no one looking to cross the street. She stared hard at the sixpence.

"Don't know!"

I gave her the coin, which she snatched and tucked into a coat pocket.

"There's another tanner if you can remember," I coaxed.

She gave me a quick look. "You sure you ain't no blue?" she asked.

"Certain," I said, and produced the second sixpence, which I held up in front of her.

She wavered just a moment, her loyalty to her neighbors being weighed against the easy money. "The Cooper sisters," she said, with another quick glance about her. "Just up the road, corner o' Lavington Street, 'ouse wif a blue front door." She snatched the coin from me and hared off across the road to take up a post on the far side.

It took me but a minute to find the blue-doored house. The paint was faded and badly flaking but recognizable from its neighbors. I knocked on the door and waited. There was no response and no sound from inside the house. I knocked again with my cane, twice more, but still no response.

"We don' wan' none, whatever it is you're 'awkin'," came a voice from behind me.

I turned to find an old woman approaching, pushing a

battered perambulator, its inside stuffed with sticks, pieces of wood, and a variety of odds and ends apparently gathered up from the local gutters and scrap heaps. The woman herself would have been tall if she had stood upright, but she was stooped with age. Her hair was a yellowish gray and escaped her cap, sticking out in all directions. Her face was lined and dirty, her nose large and hooked. One eye favored her left shoulder while the other eye looked to the right. It was difficult to know which one to focus on.

"Are you one of the persons who took in Billy White?" I asked.

"'Oo's Billy White?" she asked.

"I would like to speak with him," I said.

She mumbled something I didn't catch and busied herself straightening the various items in the pram.

"I don't mean him any harm," I said. "I just want to speak to him." I flashed yet another sixpence. This was getting really expensive, I thought.

She froze, the left eye latching onto the coin.

"I have heard of how he was run down. I would like to hear from him exactly what happened. I want to find out all the details. I am not a policeman, nor am I connected with them." I turned the sixpence in my fingers.

She pressed her mouth into a tight line and twisted her head one way and another before nudging the perambulator closer to me. But however much she wanted the coin, she resisted it. I admired her for that.

"Look, I believe that Billy was run down because of something he saw. Perhaps something to do with a bundle of rags being picked up by a rag-and-bone man. Do you know anything about that?"

Again she mumbled something to herself. Then she pushed the perambulator along to the faded blue door and painfully climbed up onto the doorstep, starting to tug on the pram handle. I moved forward and helped her lift it. She stood with one hand resting against the door for a long moment before starting to tap repeatedly on it with her long, soiled fingernails. I don't know if it was some sort of a signal or just her way of getting the attention of the person in the house, but eventually the blue door was edged open. It revealed another old lady but much shorter and, if possible, skinnier than the first one. Her eyes were firm in her head and immediately locked onto mine. Then she looked back and forth between myself and the taller woman.

The cross-eyed lady pushed the pram to the side and took a loop of string hanging from the handle and dropped it over one of the cast-iron railings, ensuring that the vehicle didn't roll off the step. Then she pushed into the doorway, causing the second woman to withdraw. She disappeared inside, leaving the door open. I took it as a signal and followed her inside.

The hallway was dark and dingy, and I followed her through it and into the front parlor. There, lying on a horsehair-stuffed settee, with tufts of stuffing sticking out, was a white-faced young boy, his legs covered by a filthy, once-colorful tartan blanket. On a small occasional table pulled up beside him sat a cracked bowl of grayish-looking gruel and a spoon. I suspected the liquid was cold.

"Are you Billy White?" I asked.

He looked fearfully at the women, his eyes wide.

"It's all right," I tried to reassure him. I nodded at the women and gave the sixpence to the taller one. She grasped it, but her eyes—both of them—did not leave my face.

The shorter woman seemed to take her cue from the taller one. No words were spoken, but she cleared bits and pieces off the only chair visible in the room and gestured toward it. I pulled it close to the boy and sat down.

"I need your help, Billy," I began. "I was wondering

about the hansom that ran you down. Was there a reason he did so?"

"I dunno."

"But it wasn't just an accident, was it? Did he try to kill you, do you think?"

The boy shrugged.

"What happened immediately before it?" I persisted. "Did you see something? What was going on?"

He shrugged again. "Dunno," he said. "There was these two men what stopped in this 'ansom and pulled out a big bundle of rags."

"Two men? Can you describe them?"

"One was real tall. 'E seemed to be the boss, I guess."

"How was he dressed?" I asked.

Another shrug. "A toff. 'Ad the other one do all the work."

"Then what happened, Billy?"

"They got back in the 'ansom and was about to drive off when the toff saw me lookin' at 'em. Nasty piece of work, I thought. I turned away and started sweepin'."

"Then what?"

"Next fing I knew the 'ansom comes galloping down on me and sends me flyin'. Then it takes orf. Din' 'alf 'urt, I can tell you. I fink he run over me legs, both of 'em. Wot 'e done that for? Mrs. Cooper says 'as 'ow 'e broke me legs! Wot the bleedin' 'ell was 'e up to?"

The boy tried to sit up straighter but the effort hurt his legs. He cried out and his face creased in pain.

"'Ere! Enough!" cried the tall woman, and she moved forward, grasping my arm.

"No! No, it's all right," I protested. I turned back to the boy. "My guess is that the man didn't want any witnesses to him dumping that bag of rags."

"Witnesses?"

"He didn't want anyone able to tell the police what he

looked like," I explained. "One more thing, Billy. Was this tall man black? Was he dark skinned?"

"Nar!" He shook his head. "I told you, 'e was a toff."

I felt excited. Could Billy have caught sight of the mastermind behind all the plots against the Guv'nor and the Lyceum?

Chapter Nineteen

Saturday turned out to be one of those bright, sunny days that can leap out at you in the middle of a long, dark winter. There was little warmth in the sun, but its very existence was enough. I noticed that people smiled more than usual and walked with a spring in their step. We all knew that it was only a temporary respite from the general harshness we had experienced in February, but we were determined to make the most of it.

Saturday is a matinee day at the Lyceum, so I knew I would be kept busy with the extra performance. That was good, I thought. Tomorrow, Sunday, I would be seeing Jenny, so this would keep my mind busy and I wouldn't be counting the minutes. Or would I? I smiled to myself as I walked briskly along Wych Street, swinging my cane and admiring the wood-fronted and gabled Elizabethan buildings. Wych Street was the ancient way leading from the north side of the Strand to Broad Street, St. Giles. Its purlieus to the north consisted of filthy and fetid slums displaying the accumulated dirt and squalor of centuries. But, for now at least, Wych Street and its neighboring Holywell Street were places of fascination and interest. In the centre of Wych Street lies the New Inn. A narrow alleyway leads back from it into the dark and dismal Clare Market.

As I drew level with the New Inn, a four-wheeler rumbled up behind me, its width a tight squeeze between the overhanging buildings. I was surprised to see such a vehicle there. I glanced at it, and as I did so, two ruffians came leaping out of the narrow court from Clare Market and grasped both my arms. My stick and my bowler hat went flying as they ran me toward the growler. A third man had stepped out of the carriage and now held the door open while the two pushed me inside. Then all three jumped in, and with a great lurch, the horses leapt forward and all of us were borne along Wych Street and out onto Broad Street. As we passed St. Clement Danes church, a bag of some coarse material was roughly pulled over my head and a rope or cord was tied about my neck to hold it there. I shouted and demanded to know what was going on, but not a word was spoken by any of the men. I tried to struggle, but the hands holding mine were strong and unyielding.

I soon stopped attempting to break free and instead tried to determine where the carriage was going; with the bag over my head I was quite blind. I was aware of the first two or three turns, but with the lurching of the vehicle and the unevenness of the cobbled streets, I soon lost my bearings. As I relaxed and stopped struggling, so did the tightness of the hands restraining me, though they remained about my wrists. At some point I sensed that the carriage was crossing a bridge, most likely over the Thames, though I couldn't be certain. The drive was a very long one; it seemed to go on for hours.

In my mind I ran over the possibilities. I discounted a casual kidnapping. Far more likely that this was tied in to the threats of Mr. Ogoon and, presumably, Ralph Bateman. But why were they snatching me away? What use could I be to them? Surely if they were solely interested in harming the Lyceum, they would have taken Mr. Stoker or even—had they dared—the Guv'nor himself. My one regret was that, should they detain me for any length of time, I would miss my assignation with Jenny, something I had been looking forward to all week long. And then it struck me that if I failed to meet with her, she would have no way of knowing what had happened to me and might well think that I had abandoned her. I almost redoubled my efforts to struggle but realized it would be fruitless. I sat and seethed.

It was a very long time later that the carriage slowed. I had been nodding in my seat, the restraining hands no longer grasping mine. As the growler came to a halt, the hands once again clamped onto my arms and I was manhandled out of the carriage to stand on the pavement. I heard a gate creaking as it was being opened, and I was urged forward. Under my feet it felt like paving stones, and then, almost immediately, I was onto grass. The ground was frozen and I was almost thankful for the steadying hands, though I knew my arms would shortly be exhibiting bruises.

There was another creaking, this time I guessed from a door of some kind. I realized I was being pushed into a building. I sensed it to be small and I smelled rotting wood . . . perhaps an old shed? I was roughly pushed down onto a wooden bench, and coarse rope was used to tie me there.

"All right!" I cried. "You have got me here. I'm your prisoner. Now what is it you want? Would somebody please answer me?"

But nobody did. The men went away and I heard the door close and what sounded like a bolt slide across it. All grew quiet and still. I sat for a while gathering my wits about me, and then I began straining at the bindings. They did not give. Whoever had tied me was no stranger to ropes and knots. As my wrists became sore, I desisted. It was very cold in the shed, if shed it was. With the brightness of the day, that morning I had eschewed my heavy topcoat and worn but a light one. Now I was sorry. I wondered how long I would be left there.

It was the matinee day at the theatre so I knew that I would be missed by noon. What time was it now, I wondered? With the long drive out to wherever we were, I guessed it to be close to midday. That meant that my absence would be noted. Surely Mr. Stoker, if no one else, would guess that something had happened to me? But then, I often got involved in matters that took me away from the theatre, even up to curtain time. The matinee performance started at two of the clock, so I might not yet be missed.

I sat and shivered. If I could only rid my head of the sack or bag or whatever it was, I might glean some sort of clue as to my whereabouts. I tilted my head and rubbed it against my shoulder, hoping to dislodge the bag. It remained firm. I wondered if I could chew my way out, but then almost laughed at the ridiculousness of the thought.

Or was it ridiculous? Not so much to eat through the fabric but at least to dislodge it. I again leaned my head into my shoulder, the better to force the material against my mouth. I got a good mouthful—it tasted vile—and then tried to tug at it. By rotating my head against the pressure of my shoulder, and holding firmly with my teeth, I was eventually rewarded with something giving way. It must have been the cord that had been tied about my neck to hold the bag in place, I realized. Yes, after some more shrugging and tugging, the bottom of the bag was pulled away from whatever encircled it and I found that I could look directly down and see, in a very restricted way, the lower part of my body tied to the wooden bench. I tugged and shrugged some more and was rewarded with a slightly wider view.

Working at it for the next many minutes I was eventually able to shrug and tug and bite to the point where I managed to shrug the bag up and off my head. It fluttered to the ground at my feet. I breathed a great sigh of relief.

It was murky in the shed. There were two windows but both had been boarded up. A little light came in through holes and chinks in the boarding of the side walls. In a couple of places whole planks had slipped down out of place, allowing shafts of low light to filter in. It seemed that the early morning bright sunshine had greatly diminished, probably from encroaching clouds.

I studied my surroundings. I saw a pile of canoe paddles and a pair of oars. Rope lines were piled in a corner and there was the seat from a rowboat. I surmised that I was in an old boathouse. No wonder it was cold . . . It must be on the riverbank. At this time of year I knew that the river was frozen solid, so I was, in effect, sitting on top of a huge block of ice. I shivered again.

I didn't know how long I might be left there, so I needed to free myself just as soon as possible, so that I didn't freeze to death. Perhaps that was the plan? I shivered for a different reason.

The bench to which I was tied was an old rustic affair, probably once set out on the lawn beside the boathouse, overlooking the river. I tried rocking it and after a few tries was pleased to find that if I really put energy into it, the seat was ancient enough to sway slightly. If I could rock it long enough and vigorously enough, I thought, it would surely fall apart. But then I might find myself worse off, sitting in a pile of wood and tree limbs, perhaps in an extremely uncomfortable position. I quickly decided it was worth the risk . . . What choice did I have? I just might be able to break free of the bench even if I could not rid myself of the ropes binding me. I set to, rocking first one way and then the other. The bench creaked and groaned but refused to die.

I had to rest from time to time but I persisted. Slowly the old bench moved farther and farther to each side as I threw my weight back and forth. Suddenly, with a loud cracking, it slid off to one side, collapsing on its legs and dropping me unceremoniously to the ground. I was still tied to the seat part of the bench, but I found that the ropes securing me were now considerably looser.

I took time to recover my breath. As I sat there on the floor, in the shambles of the rustic bench, I reassessed the situation. If I should be able to free myself from my bonds, I would then have to break out of the boathouse itself. I remembered hearing the sliding closure of a bolt, when my abductors left, but studying the decaying nature of the structure, I didn't think that would be a major problem. I just hoped that I could effect my complete escape before the kidnappers returned.

I rolled onto my knees and attempted to stand up. The length and thickness of the bench seat prevented me from doing so. I saw that the ropes around me had been secured to the various intertwined limbs making up the decorative nature of the bench. I started working at sliding individual tree limbs out from the ropes. It took a long time, but one by one I managed to wriggle and push—sometimes grasping limbs between my knees—and extricate enough branches to allow me to pull free of the structure. With the ropes now loose about my body, I was able to then concentrate on loosing the knots tying my wrists and ankles. Since my hands had not been tied together but had been lashed to the original chair arms, I was able to get to the separate knots and finally stood up, free and clear of the jumble that had once been the rustic bench.

I breathed deeply to slow my racing heart and then moved to the largest of the holes in the wall and squinted through it. As I had guessed, the structure was on the bank of a river, stretching out over the solid ice. I couldn't see enough, nor was I familiar enough with all parts of the river, to be able to locate exactly where I was. I moved away from the chink of daylight and went to the door. It was solid, despite the decaying nature of much of the boathouse. It did not budge at all when I applied my shoulder to it. I moved over to where the largest of the broken planking had dropped on the inside of the wall. Raising my foot, I gave a hard kick to the wood. Again, no sign of weakness.

I looked about me and then took up a short oar. I wedged the blade into the crack between two of the wall planks and grasped the handle of the oar. Hoping it would work like a lever, I tugged on the handle. There was a loud cracking followed by a snapping sound. I staggered back, still clutching the oar while the broken blade remained wedged into the wall.

I was not to be beaten. I jammed the thicker broken end of the blade into the crack, alongside the thinner section wedged there. I grabbed up a piece of the broken bench and pounded the oar firmly into the crack. Then I again took hold of the handle and started pulling on it. I was at last rewarded with the creaking and cracking of the plank. A larger band of daylight began to grow as the wood was pried apart. I was just about to give a final heave when the door behind me opened and two of the kidnappers appeared.

The men were understandably surprised to see me standing there, and both of them uttered curses. The larger of the two—they were both of them taller than me, of course—moved forward and swung his fist at me. I may be small, but I can move quickly when there is good reason to. That swinging fist was the incentive. I ducked under it and tried to run for the door. The second man, though larger than me, was also quick. He threw out a leg and tripped me.

"Damn your eyes!" cried the big man. He grabbed up a stout branch from the garden seat debris and swung that at me. It caught my shoulder as I was struggling to my feet, and I went down again.

"'Old 'im, yer bloody fool!" snarled the second man. "'E's a quick 'un, an' no mistake."

There ensued what might have been viewed as a comedy routine were it performed on the pantomime stage. I dodged mighty blows thrown by hands and by makeshift weapons: boat parts and bits of the broken seat. I ran around one man to be cornered by the second. This odd dance was repeated several times. At one point I did manage to grasp a length of sturdy wood. A cursory glance suggested it to be the broken half of a punt pole. I had no time to study it; a slap on the side of the head with a canoe paddle got my attention.

What saved me was the fact that the two men were so intent on either grabbing me or hitting me that they forgot all about the door through which they had entered. It hung, sagging on its rusty hinges, half open. I ducked under a pair of outstretched hands and was quickly through the door and running from the boat shed. They wasted no time and, with loud yells, pounded after me.

I darted to my left, which I immediately realized was not the best choice. That way led to the river. However, all was not lost. After a long and typical English winter, the river was frozen so solid that a wagon and horses could drive across it. My boots gripped well enough that I had no trouble keeping my feet as I ran from the frozen grass of the riverbank and aimed over the ice toward the far-off Surrey shore.

My pursuers came after me. The larger of the two men swung slightly to one side, probably hoping to cut me off, while the second man came more directly. I thought I could outrun them. I was lighter and possibly fitter.

"Aagh! Bert! 'Elp me!"

I wondered what was wrong. It was the larger man who had cried out. The other one slowed but did not stop. He and I briefly glanced back as we ran. It seemed that to one side of where the boathouse protruded onto the river, someone had been cutting blocks of ice. I glimpsed an icehouse toward the rear of the boathouse. It was common practice for householders to have ice cut from the frozen river. The cutting must have taken place only a few days ago since the surface water had frozen over again, yet not to any great thickness, it seemed. The larger man had broken the surface and crashed through the hole. He was now frantically beating at the icy water around him. I realized that, in all probability, the man could not swim.

"Bert! Christ, Bert! 'Elp me!"

But Bert dithered. Whoever had paid these men to capture me obviously had a strong hold on them. Bert would let his companion drown so long as he was able to recapture me.

I could not be so callous. At the back of my mind I had some sort of crazy notion that I could help save the man and then still make off, but I knew there were no guarantees.

"Come on, Bert, or whatever your name is," I cried, swinging around and making back to the floundering man. "We've got to get your friend out of there before he either drowns or freezes to death. Come on!"

With very poor grace, it seemed to me, Bert joined me in retracing our footsteps to the hole in the ice. Since the ice blocks had been cut from the surface, the edges were strong and sound, with no fear of them breaking off when we stood at the very edge. I managed to persuade Bert to get some of the rope from inside the shed while I held on to his companion to keep him afloat. We got a loop of it under the drowning man's arms and together started hauling him from his icy snare. Eventually we had him out and lying, gasping and shivering, on the solid surface.

I thought it time to leave. But Bert was ahead of the game. As I straightened up from the whalelike figure before me, I caught just the briefest glimpse of what must have been a solid chunk of wood brought from the shed by Bert, along with the rope. Everything went black.

When I came to my senses, all was dark. Not just dark, but pitch-black. My head ached and pounded. I lay on my back trying to piece together the events that had so recently taken place. I recalled that I had finally succeeded in breaking out of that odious boathouse. Or had I? I remembered at some point grabbing up a canoe paddle and lashing out as the two toughs came at me. They were seasoned fighters. Whoever had hired them to abduct me had chosen well. Bits and pieces of the skirmish came back to me like broken images of a dream. One of the men had wrenched the paddle out of my hands as though taking a stick from a two-year-old. The other had punched me full in the face. Ridiculous as it now seemed, I remember wondering if Jenny would mind if I had a broken nose. But then things got blurred. Had I somehow got out of the boathouse and made off across the frozen river? Then there was something about beaching a whale . . . or a drowning man? I shook my head but immediately stopped as stars filled my vision. I could not recall everything—or anything—at all clearly.

I was lying on something hard. I did find that I was not bound up, which seemed a blessing. I tentatively reached out my hand, but it encountered something solid. A wall? I moved my arm about and also raised the other hand. There were rough, and what felt like wooden, walls close on either side of me. I was in the narrow gap between the two. I felt above me. It was there as well! Heavens! I was in some sort of box, closed on all sides. No wonder the complete darkness.

Suddenly a paralyzing thought struck me . . . I was in a coffin! I panicked and tried to sit upright but hit my head on the low surface above and reactivated the stars. *Calm yourself*, I said. I tried to breathe slowly and deeply. How much air was in this space? I changed to shallow breaths. Trying hard not to panic, I slowly and deliberately moved my hands, as well as I was able, to discern the limits of my containment. It did not bring me any satisfaction. With my feet, I was able to verify the end of the structure. Everything seemed to point to my being confined in a coffin. My thoughts flew to Bram Stoker's stories. Was I about to be turned into a zombie?

Chapter Twenty

It is strange what thoughts pass through one's mind when under stress. As I lay in the coffin I thought of a recent book I had seen, dealing with premature burial. It was a subject that had been frequently broached in the newspapers for many years. It dealt with a fear that a lot of people seemed to have. This particular book, as I recall, had a number of illustrations showing various devices designed to rescue anyone unfortunate enough to be interred in error. A small lever inside the coffin would raise a flag on the surface of the grave. A bell could be rung. A breathing tube was patented to ensure there would be no suffocation of a living "corpse." The newspapers had recently reported that all possible devices had been combined and patented by a Russian chamberlain to the czar. Any detected movement in a coffin would cause an air supply to open, a flag to be raised, and a bell to be rung. I realized it was fruitless to contemplate such inventions since none of them was available to me. Yet I could not simply lie there inert.

I wondered if the coffin had yet been lowered into a grave and covered with earth. Escaping from the confines of the casket was one thing, but to have to dig one's way out of the ground was quite another. I once again felt all about me, running my hands over the surfaces of the walls and lid. There was no lining, I noticed. That seemed strange, until I thought about the origins of zombies, as detailed by Stoker. In Haiti, or wherever in the Caribbean Islands they were created, there would be no such finery. Bodies, he had said, were placed in wooden boxes and dropped into graves just as soon after apparent death as possible.

But we were not in Haiti. We were—I presumed—still in London, in England. However, if this operation was being directed by Ralph Bateman's Caribbean friend, the Haitian customs would probably prevail.

I had to do something! I couldn't just lie there and wait either to die or to be removed by an evil boko. I put up my hands and pressed up on the lid above me. It seemed to be tightly fastened. But with screws or with nails, I wondered? It struck me that if the lid was screwed down, then I was doomed. Yet if, in fact, this Boko was to have his minions remove the lid so that he might command me to rise, then it would almost certainly be a temporary fastening, such as light nailing that could be easily pried open. I prayed that I was right.

I managed to bring my knees up to my chest. I prayed that I would not cramp in that confined position. I pressed my knees against the lid, pushing and straining as I have never strained before. I had my hands up also, pushing along with them. I turned my head and sniffed at the surface. Pine. Good, I thought. Pine is a soft wood and does not grip nails anywhere nearly as tightly as does oak or other hard woods. I pushed harder, my heart thumping in my chest. After what seemed like many long minutes, I heard a creaking and cracking sound . . . the sound of nails being forced out of wood.

I had to rest for a while. I struggled and again got my legs down and straight before any signs of cramping came upon me. I breathed deeply—heedless now of the air capacity in that confined space—before a second attempt. Then I again struggled to ease my legs up till my knees were once more on my chest. I started pushing upward again, knees and hands forcing against the unpliant wood. I would press, hold it as long as I could, and then relax for a moment before more straining. Each time I applied the pressure, I heard more screeching, as the fasteners were drawn out.

I quickly became aware of dim light seeping in through the tiny opening I had created about the top of the coffin. At least, I thought, I can now get air. I pressed, pushed, and strained. Suddenly the top came free. One end of it popped off and the balance swung away, bending the nails fastening it. I sat up and pushed the lid out of the way. It came fully free and clattered to the floor. I hoped no one was about to hear it.

The first thing I noticed was that it was not a coffin per se in which I sat. It was a large packing crate. There were two others nearby, one partly filled with straw, so I may have simply been stuffed into it just because it was available. No real coffin; no graveyard burial; ergo, no Haitian Boko. Or so it seemed. I was relieved and hoped that I was right.

I climbed out of the crate and looked about me. The light was very dim and I guessed that I was perhaps in a basement. Yet on inspection I saw that the floor was made up of rough wooden planks. I revised my thinking to the top of a building. It could be that I was in an attic. I looked upward. In the dim light I made out rafters and crossbeams. Yes, it must be an attic.

I felt for my watch chain but it wasn't there. My watch had either been torn off at some point or one of the miscreants had removed it. I wondered what the time might be. How long had I been there? Was it still Saturday or had I been unconscious for far longer than I thought? Was this, perhaps, Sunday morning light that I saw filtering through? I felt a pang at the thought of abandoning Jenny, but I comforted myself with the knowledge that at least I would by now have been missed. Mr. Stoker would surely be on the trail to find me.

I felt hunger pangs. I had not eaten since breakfast, though whether today or yesterday I didn't know. Perhaps more than one day had passed. But hunger was the least of my worries. The first thing was to remove myself from my immediate surroundings before the kidnappers once again came back and caught me. There was a door at the far end of the long attic room. I moved swiftly to it, trying not to tread too heavily on the floorboards. I didn't know where the abductors might be and didn't want to alert them if they were immediately below me. I tried the door and found that it was not locked. They must have felt confident that the packing crate would hold me.

With a last glance around, I eased open the door. I found myself at the top of a flight of wooden stairs leading down into what I presumed was the main part of the house. There was little spare space where I stood, and I saw two other doors besides the attic one I was exiting. Probably servants' quarters, I thought. I had no choice but to go down. Halfway down, one of the stairs creaked. It sounded very loud to me and I froze in place, holding my breath. After a long time there came no sounds from below, so I cautiously continued downward to the bottom of the stairs.

I found myself on a small landing with a back staircase and a front one, the back one presumably leading farther down, eventually, to the kitchen. There was a short corridor with doors on either side, which I surmised to be bedrooms. I went to the closest of these and tried the door. It opened easily and I peered in on a small room that seemed not to be currently in use. There was a narrow, iron-framed bed bearing a thin, faded mattress. It was not made up with any bed linen. The second door was to another bedroom but much more interesting. The first thing I noticed was a clock on the mantelpiece. It showed a time of six thirty, which accounted for the dim light that still filtered in through the window, though whether this was six thirty in the evening or the morning, I still had no idea. However, that was good in that it meant that no one was likely to come up to the bedrooms for a while if the house was inhabited, something I did not know for certain. Presumably, however, the three abductors were somewhere in the building.

The room was obviously that of a male, and a fastidious male at that. The wardrobe doors were partially open, and three suits, along with some nondescript trousers and coats, were in evidence hanging therein. On the shelves I found neatly folded shirts and underwear. The bottom drawer contained an assortment of socks, all carefully paired. Well-polished shoes and boots were set in the base of the wardrobe.

There was a small drop-front writing desk by the window, and I moved across to that. I was surprised when I opened it to find letters and invoices addressed to none other than Peter Richland. Was I in Richland's home? If this was the house I had visited out at Twickenham, then his mother had obviously kept his room much like a shrine to her departed son. It appeared as though nothing had been moved since his untimely death. I ran a finger along the top of the desk. The maid still kept the room clean.

I peered out of the window and tried to recognize whether or not it was the Twickenham house, but the light was insufficient and there were no immediate street gas lamps to illuminate the area and cut through the mist that came off the river. I could not afford to linger; I needed to get out of the house and away.

It seemed to me that my best bet would be to use the back stairs, where I would only meet servants, if anyone. I listened at the top of the stairs and then cautiously made my way down. When I arrived at the kitchen door I became aware of the murmur of voices within. I could make out several male voices plus two female ones. I presumed the latter to belong to the maid and the cook. I had no idea if there were other servants. The male voices could have been the kidnappers or they could have been male servants, but judging from what I had seen when I had visited Mrs. Richland—if this was indeed the same house—I didn't think she had more than a maid and a cook.

I saw the pantry off to my right and made my way to that. Supplies were sparse, it seemed, but what caught my eye was a small window high up in the outside wall. It wasn't large, but then neither was I. If I could get up to it, I thought there was a good chance I might be able to climb through it and get away.

I heard the chink of crockery coming from the kitchen. I carefully dragged a tea chest over underneath the window and balanced a wooden crate on top of that. I clambered up and reached across to the window. It was stiff and obviously had not been opened in a while. As I pushed to move it, it made a screeching sound. I stopped and stood balanced, not daring to move. From behind me the sounds from the kitchen stopped. I hardly dared breathe. Then the conversation started again, and the sounds of plates and teacups continued. I could almost swear that I heard one of the ladies say the word "cat," but it may have been wishful thinking. As I clawed my way up, a bag of flour tumbled to the tile floor and burst open. It didn't make much noise, and this time I didn't stop to see if anyone had heard anything. But as I reached across to get my head and shoulders through the window, behind me the pantry door opened.

I swung around, ready to throw whatever might be at

hand so that I might make my escape. Standing staring at me was the larger of the two men with whom I had fought in the boathouse. He clutched a blanket about him, and his hair, although now dry, was still plastered about his head. He stood stock still for a long moment, just staring at me.

I could almost see the images passing through his head, like a miniature play being performed. The scene of his falling through the ice, the panic that must have ensued, the rescue from certain death by myself when his own partner ignored his cries for help. He stood and studied me, and then he turned away and returned to the kitchen, closing its door firmly behind him.

I sent a quick prayer of thanks up to whatever deity watched over me, then spun around and dragged and pushed to get my head and shoulders through the window opening. With some wriggling and kicking—I heard other items fall—I eventually slid out into the open, dropping a few feet onto my head and shoulders into a privet hedge. I wasted no time. I rolled out of that and got to my feet. I thought I saw the light of a lantern being carried into the pantry behind me, but I ran off across the frozen lawn and along the iron railing to a gate that opened onto the road.

By the time I got back to the Lyceum it was nearly noon. It was indeed Sunday; I had missed the Saturday performances and, more to my chagrin, had missed my meeting with Jenny.

Despite it being the Sabbath morning, I found Bram Stoker standing by the stage door, fiercely looking up and down the street. I descended from the growler I had procured in Twickenham and asked him if he could pay the driver, since my wallet and all of my money seemed to have disappeared. He did so—with some muttered comment about this becoming a habit—and then, to my immense surprise, he threw his arms about me and hugged me to him. Such was the warmth of his embrace I was afraid that, after surviving the many trials of my abduction, I would be suffocated by my boss.

"Come inside, Harry," he said, his voice strangely husky. "Come along in and get warm. I'll send out one of the lads to get you a good meal. Come and tell me all about it."

I was touched. I knew Bram Stoker to be an emotional man. At one of his earliest meetings with Henry Irving, in Ireland, he had been invited to dinner with the Guv'nor in response to writing an exceptionally favorable review of *Hamlet* at Dublin's Theatre Royal. At the dinner, Irving recited Thomas Hood's popular and extremely poignant poem *The Dream of Eugene Aram*, giving a histrionic performance. At the end of it Irving affected a theatrical swoon, but Stoker joined him in a very real swoon, being so overcome by the recital. He was never one to hide his emotions.

I related to my boss all that had transpired, pausing only briefly to start eating a late breakfast of eggs, bacon, kidneys, sausage, fried potatoes, and tomatoes. I downed several mugs of tea, all brought in from a nearby restaurant by the attentive Bill Thomas, who dawdled long enough to listen to the end of my story.

"So you did not recognize any of these men?" Stoker asked.

"No, sir. I had a good look at them before they put the bag over my head, but I'm sure I had never seen any one of them before."

"Rogues hired by that young Bateman, no doubt," muttered Bill as he gathered up the empty plate and utensils. Bill went out and Stoker sat with a deep frown on his face.

"This is not good, Harry. Who knows what their intention was? I spent the day awaiting perhaps the arrival of a blackmailing note, but they made no contact."

"Perhaps they were waiting a day or more to make sure my being missing was really noticed?" I offered.

"Hmm. Maybe. I did let your Sergeant Bellamy know, however."

I looked up, surprised. "You did? Well, thank you, sir. What did the good sergeant have to say?"

Stoker sighed. "He said to wait a day or so, since you just might turn up." He sighed again. "And so you have."

"No thanks to the Metropolitan Police," I murmured. I finished off the last of the mug of tea.

"What did you determine of the house where you were kept? You mentioned that you thought it was the home of Mr. Peter Richland and his mother."

"Yes, sir, I did. In fact I am certain it was. I do remember that, on my original visit there, I noticed an old boathouse out in the garden. That must have been the one where they first placed me."

"But you saw no sign of Mrs. Richland?"

"No, sir." Memory came flooding back. "But I did find what used to be Peter Richland's room. Upstairs in the house. She keeps it as it was when he was alive. No surprise, I suppose, considering that our queen keeps whole palaces as they were when Prince Albert was alive. Oh, and when I looked in some of the drawers there, I saw no sign of silk undergarments, just plain cotton ones."

"Interesting."

"I wonder if Mrs. Richland even knew that her house and boathouse were being used," I said, after a few moments' thought. "I suppose that it's possible she was away from home and Ralph Bateman—being an old friend of Peter Richland—had his men make use of that facility."

"As a convenience?" asked Stoker. I nodded. "I don't know, Harry. But it should be easy enough to find out whether or not Mrs. Richland was in residence this weekend."

I yawned. I couldn't help myself. I was tired and my head was still sore.

"Take yourself off home, Harry. You look a mess. Get some rest. It's Sunday so I don't want to see you here again until late tomorrow morning."

"Thank you, sir. Yes." I got to my feet. *Sunday*, I thought! What about Jenny? I had to get to her and explain my absence. I think Stoker read my thoughts.

"Oh, and I sent a message around to Jenny for you, Harry. Told her that you had been delayed."

I was both surprised and delighted. "You did? Oh, I cannot thank you enough . . ."

He pooh-poohed my thanks, flapping a hand at me. "Get yourself cleaned up and see her when you can, Harry. Now, off with you! Oh, and one more thing, Harry."

"Yes, sir?"

"Get yourself another cane—a good stout one—and be ever vigilant. We don't want you snatched away again."

I had thoughts of bathing and getting into some clean clothes. It wasn't Friday—the traditional "bath night"—so I couldn't count on Mrs. Bell heating water for me. I decided to visit the public baths, and there I soon felt refreshed and able to look life squarely in the face again. I went back to my rooms, put on clean clothes, and left the house. Still feeling hungry, I felt that I could not face one of Mrs. Bell's culinary disasters but made my way to the King's Arms on Carey Street. There I lunched on a platter of roast beef, Yorkshire pudding, Brussels sprouts, and roast potatoes, together with a tankard of porter. I dug into a freshly baked loaf of bread laden with recently churned butter. By the time I had finished, I felt considerably better, if not overindulged. I had persuaded Mrs. Bell to let me have one of her precious supply of Dr. Clark's Pills for Nervous

Headache. I don't know that my headache was especially "nervous," but it was most certainly a headache. I washed down the pill with a healthy swallow of porter.

It was exactly two of the clock when I finally arrived outside 15a Grafton Street. I had stopped briefly at Mortimer's on Regent Street and, as Mr. Stoker had suggested, purchased a new cane. Jenny must have been watching for me from the upper windows. She emerged from the gleaming black-painted front door wearing the same ensemble she had worn on the previous Sunday. I'm sure it was her only good outfit, but she looked wonderful in it. Her eyes were bright and gleaming, her mouth in a delightful smile.

"Mrs. Cooke was kind enough to let me change the hour of my time off," she said.

We set out to enjoy a few short hours together. She clung to my arm and urged me to tell her all of my adventures.

"All in good time. Let us enjoy the day for a while first," I said, a smile on my face. I looked about me, feeling both happy and lucky. How easily things could have gone wrong and I might never have seen my dear Jenny again. I beamed at her, feeling blessed. Her eyes sparkled as she returned my smile.

The weather continued to be relatively fine for the time of year. The sun peeked intermittently through the clouds and there was no wind to speak of. We made our way over to Green Park, on the far side of St. James's Park. Piccadilly was on its north side, and we stopped briefly to listen to an old man playing a hurdy-gurdy at the end of Queen's Walk.

"Has the Lyceum been busy?" asked Jenny, her hand in the crook of my arm. There was no snow and I carried no umbrella, so there was really no necessity for her to hold on to me, but I squeezed my arm to draw her tight against my side. She smiled up at me and my heart beat loudly enough that I was sure she would hear it.

"*Hamlet* is doing very well," I said. "The Guv'nor keeps

them in their seats. Mr. Stoker said that people do not come to the Lyceum to see *Hamlet*, they come to see Henry Irving playing Hamlet."

"I wish I could see it," said Jenny wistfully.

"Oh, you will, if I can manage it," I said, mindful of my promise to her.

We had just turned from Queen's Walk to go up Constitution Hill when I saw a man striding purposefully toward us. He had come out of the trees along the wide walk leading up to the Palace, and with a start I recognized him as one of the men who had held me captive the previous day: the third one in the carriage, not one of the two who had been at the boathouse. Before I knew what was happening he had reached out and grasped Jenny's arm. She screamed.

I had gone a step farther when following Mr. Stoker's advice. The newly purchased cane I now carried was in fact a sword-cane. With a quick pull, I drew the blade and lunged at the man.

Jenny had given a cry when he took her arm, but it was his turn to cry when I stabbed him just above the wrist. Blood spurted and he leapt back, releasing Jenny. I may be small, but I was fencing champion at the Hounslow Institution for Boys; it was the only sport at which I did excel. This ruffian was tussling with a fiery redhead and my blood was up! I stepped forward in front of Jenny and jabbed again with the blade. It pierced the man's forearm. He pulled back, turned, and ran. I was tempted to run after him but was mindful of my companion.

"Jenny! Are you all right?" I asked.

"Oh, Harry!" she cried. "My hero!" She threw her arms about my neck and kissed me full on the lips. I almost dropped the sword-cane but had the presence of mind to wrap my arm, still holding the weapon, about her slim waist and draw her to me. It might not have been the gentlemanly thing to do, but I felt very much the knight in shining armor.

The kiss was all too brief and Jenny stepped back, her face flaming red and her eyes cast down.

"Who—who was that, Harry?" she gasped. "Where did he come from? What did he want?"

I had sheathed the blade and now, straightening my bowler hat, I took a firm grip on Jenny's arm and started us in the direction of St. James's Park.

"First things first, Jenny. I think we need to find somewhere to sit down and have a cup of tea. There is a small refreshment stand in the park, I believe. Let us repair to that and I will tell you a story . . . a story of my adventures yesterday."

Chapter Twenty-one

Ellen Terry, the darling of the Shakespearean theatre and leading lady to the Guv'nor, has been on the stage since the age of eight, when she first appeared with Charles Kean at the Princess's Theatre. Bram Stoker had many times related to me her brilliant career. I think the fact that Miss Terry's father was of Irish descent made her special in his eyes. She had been married three times and had caused some scandal along the way. It was just at the beginning of the present year that she had separated from her third husband, Charles Kelly. Yet such was her acting and stage presence that she was forgiven much that others would not have been. Her second husband was the architect-designer Edward William Godwin . . . though in fact they never actually married since she was separated but still married to her first husband, the eminent artist George Frederick Watts. But with Godwin she had two children, a daughter, Edith, and a son, Edward.

Edward was now nine years of age and Edith was twelve.

Edward usually accompanied Miss Terry to the theatre and had taken on the role of callboy, he who alerts the actors as to when they need be in the wings, ready to go on. Edward took the job very seriously and was much loved and appreciated by all.

On Monday, after my so pleasurable Sunday sojourn with Jenny, I had reported the attempted attack in the park to Mr. Stoker but then got on with theatre work. It was early evening that the day started to unravel.

Sam Green came to me two hours or so before curtain-up. Actors were drifting in and backstage staff was checking and double-checking scenery, lighting, and props. I had just started on my rounds when Sam accosted me.

"Mr. Rivers! 'Arry! Any idea why the scenery bay doors should be unlocked?"

I was surprised. The big doors were only opened when newly built flats were being brought into the theatre or, at the end of a run, when old flats were being taken out. Some of the scenery could be quite tall, and appropriate doors are necessary. Throughout the entire run of a production there is no necessity for them to be opened.

"What do you mean, Sam?"

"Jus' what I says, 'Arry. Them doors is unlocked. I found one of 'em swingin' in the breeze, as it were . . . wondered where the cold draught was coming from! It's a rum do an' no mistake."

That was his favorite expression. I hurried off in the direction of the scenery bay, Sam stretching his long legs to keep up with me. I found the doors shut but not locked.

"I shut 'em," volunteered Sam. "Keep the bleedin' cold out. But I ain't locked 'em cos I didn't know what was goin' on."

"Quite right," I said. I scratched my head. "Who has a key to these doors?" I asked, though I knew the answer. I was just playing for time while I considered the possibilities.

"As you know, 'Arry," Sam said, well aware of my tactic,

"you, me, Mr. Stoker, and Fred Summer, the electrician. 'E's somewhere up in the flies, if'n you wants 'im."

I bent over and examined the locks. It looked as though someone had used a betty on the lock, or otherwise forced it. A betty was a skeleton key and the tool of a burglar. I was no police detective, but I could make out scratches all around the keyhole of the one door.

"All right, Sam," I said. "Get some of your lads and make a run through the theatre. Look everywhere. Someone either got in, got out, or both. I want to know if anything is missing. Keep your eyes open for any stranger. My guess is that whoever it was couldn't get past our Bill, up by the stage door, so they decided to get in from here."

"Right, 'Arry!" He went running off and I headed for Stoker's office.

Nearly an hour later Sam came to find me and to report. I was still with my boss.

"No sign of anythin' missin', 'Arry; Mr. Stoker, sir. No sign of anyone wot don't belong 'ere. O' course, it could be someone's been and gorn by now."

"Very true, Sam," said Stoker. "Thank you. You can get on about your work." He turned to me as Sam departed. "My guess is that this is a follow-on from your abduction on Saturday, Harry. They may have been simply preparing the door for future use and the wind blew it open, or they may have come in and realized that whatever they had in mind was not feasible. This is most decidedly an ongoing battle we have been thrust into, and we need to keep alert at all times."

"Yes, sir," I said. "Do you think it's Bateman behind it?"

"Almost certainly. Though just what he has planned and how he hopes to implement it, I don't know."

"I'm still worried about that threat from Ogoon about a theatre fire," I said. "And there seems to be so much that has not been explained."

"What do you mean?"

"Well, sir, we still haven't found out who tried to poison the Guv'nor, and we don't know if Peter Richland was killed accidentally or if, perhaps, he was pushed in front of that growler. We have no explanation for Mr. Turnbull's death; even Dr. Cochran couldn't explain that. We don't know—although we suspect Ralph Bateman—who was behind dropping weights on both me and the American gentleman. And then there was my kidnapping. Now it looks as though the theatre has been entered. What can that be leading up to?"

Stoker nodded. "It is worrying," he agreed. "But let's not become overly concerned without concrete evidence." He looked at me sternly. "I don't want you getting superstitious on me, Harry!"

I almost laughed.

He continued, "I've been having two men make continual sweeps of the entire building, keeping an eye open for any suspicious piles of rags or paper, or anything that could be ignited. Theatre fires in the past have shown what death pits these places can be. We must remain constantly vigilant . . ."

He broke off as the door swung open. I turned to find the Guv'nor himself framed in the doorway. His face was strained. His complexion never looked especially ruddy without makeup, but now it looked positively ashen. For a brief moment I thought he had been poisoned again. But he stood straight and tall, his hand on the doorknob.

"Ellen cannot find Edward," he said. "He came to the theatre with her, and we assumed he would attend to his duties as callboy, but he has disappeared."

Stoker was on his feet in a flash. For a big man, he could move surprisingly quickly when necessary.

"You've started searching?" he said.

Mr. Irving had turned to go back to the stage area, and we were right behind him.

"Oh yes. As soon as she said she couldn't find him, I had

stagehands start looking. Ellen is most upset, Abraham, and from what you have told me of our Mr. Rivers's recent experience, I must admit that I am not at ease myself."

I was momentarily surprised to learn that Stoker had discussed my abduction with the Guv'nor but, on reflection, realized he would have done so. I felt a lump in my throat. Was this what I had been expecting? Or was I acquiring Stoker's old granny's "second sight," or something?

If young Edward was missing, it might be explained by the open scenery bay door. The young boy would not have gone out by himself; he was far too well behaved and extremely conscious of his job here at the Lyceum. No. Edward could even now be sitting in a fast-moving carriage with a bag over his head and be scared out of his wits.

"I must go to comfort Ellen," said the Guv'nor, making for the stairs up to the star dressing rooms.

"Tonight's performance?" queried Stoker.

Irving's voice came back from above. "The show must go on, of course! The show must go on!"

I t was snowing when we left the theatre. The lamplighters had long since made their rounds. I followed behind the large figure of Bram Stoker, feeling a little like the Page following in the footsteps of Good King Wenceslas. We went around to the far side of the Lyceum to where the scenery bay doors gave access. Once there, Stoker examined the ground immediately outside the door.

"It has been snowing for too long, I fear," he said.

"You were hoping for footprints?"

He nodded. "I thought it too much to hope for, but it would have been nice to have gleaned some sort of clue from them."

"We could have followed them all the way to wherever they went, and rescued Edward."

"Hardly," he said. "At most they would have led to the curb and the perpetrators would have got into a carriage. But at least we might have discovered how many people were involved. Ah, well! Let us press on, Harry."

"Where are we going, sir?" I asked.

In answer he led me to the closest crossing sweeper, a young boy who swept a clear passage among the horse droppings with great vigor, obviously as much to keep himself warm as to garner tips from those seeking to cross the street unsullied.

"Ho, boy! Tell me, have you been here all day?"

"Yessir." The lad, who was little more than Edward's age, paused and, resting the handle of his broom on his shoulder, closed his fists and blew into his hands to warm them. I noticed that his fingerless gloves were old and worn and probably gave little warmth. He had a similarly worn and frayed muffler wrapped about his neck, but his head was bare and already covered with snowflakes.

"Did you notice anybody at those big doors recently?" Stoker indicated the theatre bay doors. "Anyone going in or coming out? Anyone with a boy, such as yourself?"

"Lemme see." The boy screwed up his face as though thinking hard. "'Tain't easy 'membrin' fings in this 'ere snow, mister. Kinda gets in yer eyes, yer know?"

Stoker produced a shilling and held it up.

"'Course, fings does come back to me on occasion, yer know?"

Stoker gave him the coin. "Well? What comes back to you now?"

The coin disappeared into a pocket and the boy went back to blowing on his fingers. "Come to fink on it, yeh. Yeh, there was some brown-polish bruiser wif a kid. He'd got the kiddy tight agin 'im, wif an 'and across 'is north an' south. I s'pose 'e di'n want the kid shoutin' out."

"Where did they go?" snapped Stoker.

"Beats me. They got into a growler wot pulls 'round the corner. Was waitin' for 'em, is my guess."

"Damnation!" It was the first time I'd heard my boss swear. Well, the first time in a long while, to be more accurate. "Which way did they go?" he demanded of the boy.

"Well, now . . . let me see . . ." He once again screwed up his face. Stoker produced another coin—a sixpence this time. The boy grabbed it. "Off up Bow Street, would be my guess," he said.

"Come, Harry!" cried Stoker, and strode off in that direction. I broke into a run to keep up with him.

There was little traffic about at that time, so by dint of questioning crossing sweepers, itinerant musicians, a hot-potato seller, a roast-chestnut purveyor, and various street peddlers, we determined—at least to Bram Stoker's satisfaction—that the four-wheeler taking Edward had gone east on Long Acre. But where it might have gone from there, we had no idea.

I spotted a pie shop and pointed to it.

"Don't you think we should stop and fortify ourselves, sir?" I said. "Review what we've got so far and plan where we're going?" I tried to sound convincing though, truth be told, I did feel we needed some plan other than running off in all directions at once. Perhaps that was the Irish way, but I gave Mr. Stoker more credit than that. He stopped and studied the shop as though he'd never seen one before.

"You are right, Harry. Yes. A cup of hot cocoa would be good."

"And a pork pie," I added.

We seated ourselves by the window where we could look out at the now fast-falling snow and the passing traffic.

"What did the sweeper mean by 'a brown-polish bruiser'?" I asked. "I haven't heard that expression before."

"It must have been your Mr. Ogoon," Stoker replied, warming his hands around the steaming mug of cocoa.

"Brown polish is street language for someone with darker skin."

I don't know what made the Caribbean gentleman in question *my* Mr. Ogoon, but I was too tired to argue. "So where do we look now, sir?" I asked, turning my attention to the pork pie I had insisted upon.

"They could be anywhere, though it would seem they are heading north or perhaps also east. We must start counting our credits, Harry." He removed his hands from the cocoa and began indicating on his fingers. "One, we now definitely know that Edward was taken from the theatre against his will. Two, we know who took him—Ogoon, almost certainly at the instigation of Ralph Bateman. Three, as we've said, we know that they are heading into the East End."

"A really unsavory area," I said. "Full of thieves and scoundrels."

"That's as may be. But yes, Harry, we must acknowledge that it's a far cry from the West End. Now then, do we have a 'four' in our favor?" He held up his fourth digit.

"What about we know they are in a growler and so there's probably more than Mr. Ogoon involved?" I suggested. "If it was just the two of them, they'd be more likely to take a hansom."

"All right. Very good, Harry." He closed his hand and then drank deeply from his mug, despite that I found mine still too hot to savor. "We must apply some logic, I think," he continued. "Since they have made off with Edward, then there is a good chance that they have plans for him. If they were thinking of killing him, they would almost certainly have made for the river: the favored place, it seems, for casting off bodies. This means that they may be considering making kidnap demands."

"Like what?" I asked.

"My first guess would be demanding that we close *Hamlet* and let Sadler's Wells benefit from the playgoers."

"The Guv'nor would never agree to that, would he, sir?"

Stoker frowned and then shook his head. "It's a hard one, Harry; a hard one. That boy is the apple of Miss Terry's eye, and the Guv'nor will do almost anything for Miss Terry."

"Anything?" I asked.

"I did say *almost* anything," he replied. "It will remain to be seen whether or not closing the production is on the cards."

"Are such battles between theatres common, sir?" I asked.

"I wouldn't go so far as to say 'common,' Harry. But they are far from unknown. When every penny counts, it's surprising what some theatre managements will do to keep drawing an audience. But it is unusual in the larger theatres such as the Lyceum and Sadler's Wells. More to be expected in the penny gaffs and the pantomime and melodrama houses." He drained his mug of cocoa.

"Perhaps Sergeant Bellamy can help," I suggested.

"Perhaps," he replied. He didn't sound very confident. "Come on, Harry. Drink up. We need to keep on the trail while it's hot."

Looking out at the snow didn't make me think of anything hot other than the cocoa before me. I sipped at it. "I really doubt we can do much more tonight, sir," I said. "I feel really badly for young Edward; he must be scared to death. But what are the chances we'll catch up with them when we have no idea in which direction they went? Perhaps we'd have better luck starting fresh in the morning? Should we get back to the theatre and confer with the Guv'nor and Miss Terry? It's going to be a hard night for her, I'm sure."

"So it is, Harry. All the more reason for us to press on. Find something positive we can take back to her."

I finished my pork pie and made headway on the cocoa, determined to fortify myself before having to once more venture out into the March weather. "I'm sure you're right, sir. So where do we go?" I asked.

Stoker stared out of the window at the thickening flakes.

He spoke as though running thoughts through his head and uttering them out loud. "They didn't head west, as I expected," he said. "Twickenham is west, so they are not planning on taking Edward to where they held you, Harry, at Mrs. Richland's. No, they are going in the opposite direction." He suddenly turned to face me. "What lies that way, Harry?"

"What? Why—er—of course! Sadler's Wells. The theatre is almost into Islington. Of course they'd go there!" I took a deep gulp of cocoa, burning my throat in the process.

Stoker came to his feet. "I am going to hurry back to the Lyceum and advise the Guv'nor and Miss Terry what is afoot, Harry. She will be relieved, to an extent at least, to know that we have discovered that Edward was abducted and that we know who was responsible. I think she may be doubly relieved to know that we are on the trail. I want you to take a cab along to Sadler's Wells and I will join you there immediately." He moved to the door and finished speaking as he prepared to step outside. "Do not attempt to enter that theatre, Harry. Stay in your cab and keep watch. I will be with you before you know it."

He disappeared into the night. I drained my cup and came to my feet. Wrapping my muffler more firmly about my throat, I buttoned my coat and followed my boss into the falling snow to look for a cab.

We sat in a hansom across the road from the stage door of Sadler's Wells Theatre. It was late and all was quiet, with no lights on other than the single gas flame over the stage door. The audience had long since gone home, as they must have done from the Lyceum by now. I wondered how the *Hamlet* performance had gone. Had Miss Terry's Ophelia suffered because of her worries about her son? I was sure it had not. She was too much the seasoned trooper.

Even a dire family crisis would not keep her from giving her best on the boards.

At the far corner of the road sat a four-wheeler with its lanterns still alight. We were certain it was the one that had been used to transport Ogoon and Edward. The fact that it was parked there—the driver in all probability sitting snoozing within—was a good indication that the abductors had not finished with it. We had instructed our hansom driver to wait until it moved . . . if it did. He was then to follow at a discreet distance. Stoker had paid him a number of sovereigns in advance to ensure that he would follow instructions.

"You don't think we should simply force our way in and rescue Edward, sir?" I asked.

Stoker snorted. He was good at giving impressive snorts when necessary. They somehow always seemed to fit the mood and to convey his meaning. "On what grounds, Harry? We are presuming that Ogoon has taken him in there. We are presuming that that is the same four-wheeler used to whisk him away from the Lyceum. But we don't actually know these things for a fact. No. Better, I think, to wait and see what their next move might be and to strike at the very best opportunity, catching them red-handed."

I conceded the point. I knew, deep within me, that they had Edward right there in the theatre, just as I'm sure Stoker knew it. Yet he was correct that we must exercise patience. We sat there another half hour. The cabdriver tapped on the trapdoor and, opening it, peered down at us.

"You gents sure 'bout this?"

Stoker didn't even look up but kept his eyes on the doorway across the road. "We are."

The driver continued studying us for a minute or two and then, with a grunt, closed the trap. I thought how wonderfully cabdrivers can be controlled with gold coin.

Ten minutes later—just as I was wondering if we would

all freeze to death sitting there—a light showed as the stage door opened.

"Here we go," murmured Stoker.

A figure emerged, turned back and extinguished the light inside, and then locked the stage door. Whoever he was, the man started along the road in the opposite direction from where the growler still stood.

"What?" I sat forward on the seat, puzzled.

"Quickly, Harry!" cried Stoker and jumped to the pavement. He started across the road toward the figure. I leaped out and followed him.

"You there! Stop!" cried Stoker. The figure did so and turned to face us.

"Good Lord! George Dale!" I said. It was indeed the stage door keeper closing up for the night.

"Quickly!" snapped Stoker. "Who else is still in the theatre?"

George looked bewildered. "Why, no one, sir. I'm always last out. Just locked up, I did. Ain't no one in there now. Leastwise, there ain't better be."

Chapter Twenty-two

Stoker swung around and ran toward the parked growler. He wrenched open the door to reveal the driver, bleary-eyed, sitting back on the passenger seat and looking very surprised.

"Who are you waiting for? How long have you been here?" asked my boss.

The driver picked up his bowler hat from the seat and settled it on his head. He tugged his coat about him as he struggled out of the door and down onto the pavement. "I ain't waitin' for no one. Not now, anyway. Looks like I done my time. I can take off now."

"What do you mean? Explain yourself."

I had never seen my boss so irate. The driver clambered up onto his box and took up his whip. "I was paid to sit here a spell afore takin' off," he said. "Gent I brought 'ere paid me to just sit, so that's what I did."

"Damnation!"

"What's it mean, sir?" I asked. "Have we lost Edward and Ogoon?"

Stoker took a number of deep breaths and seemed to calm a little as the growler pulled away and trotted off back in the direction of the city.

"They were one step ahead of us, Harry. Smarter than I gave them credit for. They knew we would come here after them and they left the growler here as a decoy. They guessed we would sit and watch it for a while, thinking they were inside the theatre. That gave them extra time to get away."

"So we've lost them?" I felt devastated. It had all been too easy, it seemed. Now where were we to go?

"Not if I can help it." Stoker strode over to where George Dale still stood scratching his head and looking about him, not knowing what to expect.

"Mr. Dale. We need your assistance. I am Mr. Abraham Stoker of the Lyceum Theatre . . ."

"Oh yes, sir. I knows you. I know young 'Arry, 'ere. We been mates for many years."

I would not have put it quite like that, but this was not the time for niceties. I quickly explained to George what was happening and asked if he could help.

"They took the young 'un? Miss Terry's boy?" His eyes opened wide. I nodded. "You sure about that . . . ? Not that I'm doubting your word, sir," he said to Stoker, "but takin' a young boy from 'is mother, right out of the theatre . . . now that ain't right."

"Not at all right," agreed my boss. "Now, time is of the essence. We need to find where they have taken the child. How can you help us?"

George lifted his well-worn bowler and again scratched his head. "I'm your man, if'n I can be," he assured us. "'Oo did you say was involved?"

"Mr. Ogoon, Ralph Bateman's foreign friend," I said. "And Ralph himself, of course. We don't know who else. Tell me, George, who has been hanging around with Ralph and Ogoon recently?"

"Only one as I know of would be that 'Erbert Willis."

"Willis? Of course!" muttered Stoker. "We should have guessed."

"Was he with them tonight?" I asked.

"No. Monday night is 'appy night for Mr. Willis. Never misses."

"Happy night? Whatever do you mean, George?" I was intrigued.

"In Whitechapel, as I 'ave it. There's a 'ticular one as our Mr. Willis goes to. Never misses."

I looked at Stoker for an explanation. "Opium, Harry. There are lots of dens in Chinatown. Used mostly by seamen, but quite a few so-called gentlemen from the West End go out to Limehouse on a lark. Some for more than just a lark, too. I didn't realize they were also in Whitechapel."

"Ho, yes!" said George. "There's ones in Whitechapel a bit more posh than them Chinatown ones, they say. It appears our Mr. 'Erbert Willis is somewhat addicted to the stuff, as I 'ear it."

"You know where this particular den of iniquity is, Mr. Dale? There's a sovereign in it if you do. We have to find out from Willis where Messrs. Bateman and Ogoon may have taken young Edward. Time is of the essence."

"'Ave no fear, Mr. Stoker, sir." George Dale pulled himself up as straight as he ever could. "I don't 'old with the doings of Ralph Bateman and I most certainly don't 'old with takin' a young man like that, especially one belonging to Miss Terry. You don't 'ave to pay me no sovereign, Mr. Stoker. I'll tell you all I know. No problem."

The hansom made good time to the Whitechapel area, just north of the Commercial Road. I was worried about the passing hours and said so to Mr. Stoker.

"I don't think we need be too concerned, Harry," he said. "Time is certainly of the essence, as I have observed, but I don't think they mean young Edward any immediate harm. I'm presuming they have in mind some sort of ransom demand. If so, then they can do nothing until tomorrow morning at the earliest, so they will be holding the boy in some safe place. The location of that place is what we need to learn from Mr. Willis. Now, the inestimable Mr. Dale said we should find him just off New Road, Whitechapel, at the end of Green Street. Ah! We seem to be arriving at our destination."

He banged on the trap with his cane and the driver pulled in to the curbside and stopped. We alighted.

"Wait for us here," Stoker said to the man, and then led the way along to the top of the well-worn stone steps descending to a cul-de-sac. There was one solitary street gas lamp at the top of the stairs, its light greatly diminished by the fog drifting off the river. I took hold of the rickety handrail and followed the bulk of my boss as he moved slowly downward. At the bottom of the steps we paused and looked about us.

"Over there," said Stoker, swinging his cane to point in the direction of a small cluster of shops alongside the solid blackness that was one of a set of warehouses.

As we drew near the group I was able to make out a low-flamed gas jet protruding, globeless, alongside the front entrance of the shop. It was the only illumination in that area. The shop doorway itself seemed tightly closed.

"I don't think there's anyone here," I muttered. It didn't seem right to speak loudly, for some reason.

"Nonsense," said Stoker, his voice booming and echoing across the water lapping the wharf. "This has to be the place."

He raised his cane and rapped on the door. There was no

response. He rapped again, a dozen times at least. A small grid in the door, which I had not noticed before, slid to one side and a pair of eyes looked out and studied us. No words were spoken. Stoker himself said nothing but held up a half sovereign, turning it in his fingers so that it might catch the glimmer of light issuing from the gas jet. The grid slid closed again.

"Now what?" I asked.

"Shh! Patience, Harry,"

We must have stood there for two or three minutes before we heard a lock turn and the door inched open. An ancient Chinese face filled the narrow gap. I couldn't tell whether it was a man or a woman. The figure held a candle, which sputtered in the slight breeze.

"You want?"

"We want entrance," stated Stoker. "Kindly step aside."

But the figure remained firmly blocking the doorway. "Name?"

"*My* name?" responded Stoker. "I don't think . . ."

The person tut-tutted and shook his head. I had pretty much decided that it was a man, though some slight doubt still remained. "Herbert Willis," I said.

The face turned to look at me, raising the candle higher. Then he held out a skeletal, clawlike hand with long, dirty fingernails. "*Crown*," he said.

"How did you know he needed Willis's name?"

"I guessed that we required some sort of introduction, sir," I said. "I remembered that Willis is a regular here so assumed his name would give us passage."

"Well done, Harry."

As soon as Mr. Stoker had paid the crown we were allowed in, with the door being closed firmly behind us. The man led the way back into the darkness, his long, loose-flowing robe dragging on the floor. He opened a second very low door and we followed into a long room with dim light coming from two or three lanterns hanging along the length of the room.

The room was filled with a sweet-smelling smoke that I found attractive yet repulsive at the same time. The floor of the room was covered with pallets in low wooden frames, side by side and end to end, stretching away into the far reaches of the establishment. Two young Chinese boys, dressed in soiled blue canvas jackets and ragged short trousers, wearing the rope-soled shoes favored by the Chinese, scampered back and forth over bodies stretched out on the pallets. The pair brought long-stemmed pipes and glowing charcoal to the variety of men lying in various stages of stupor. Some were sitting up drawing on the pipes, while others lay flat, the ends of the pipes still held between their lips, their eyes glazed, closed, or half hooded. One or two of the imbibers muttered to themselves, a few laughing quietly at something imagined.

I looked to Mr. Stoker. I had heard of these opium dens but never seen one before. My boss did not seem at all affected by his surroundings. He looked about him and even rolled a couple of men over onto their backs the better to see them.

"Ah! Here we are!" he cried.

"Shh! No talk!" hissed the man who had led us in. He waved his hands to silence us.

Stoker ignored him and dragged Willis into a more or less upright sitting position.

"Here, Harry. We're going to have to get him out of this idiocy if we are to get any sense out of him."

"Shh! No talk! No talk!"

We ignored the man until I became aware of another figure who had advanced from the dim, smoky, far end of the room. It was the largest man I had ever seen. He was stripped to the waist and stood with massive arms folded across a huge barrel of a chest. His jet-black hair was pulled back in a queue, and his equally black eyebrows met together in a frown that did more to quiet us than did any number of "No talk!" orders.

The man reached across two other semicomatose figures to pluck Willis off of his pallet. Slinging Herbert over his shoulder, the giant pushed past us and made for the door through which we had entered. Reaching it, he flung it open and pitched Willis out into the night. As he then turned to us, Stoker and I squeezed around him and dashed out of the building. I heard the door slam behind.

"Fank you for wasting my 'alf crown!"

Willis's dirty blond hair looked dirtier than usual. It stuck out at different angles, making him look like a scarecrow.

"Let us have the information we seek and I shall be happy to reimburse you," said Stoker. "Now, where would Mr. Bateman have taken the boy you kidnapped?"

"Kidnapped? Boy? I'm sure I don't know what the 'ell you're goin' on about." The nervous tick in his right eye started working overtime.

"You know perfectly well. I will be more than happy to hand you over to Sergeant Bellamy if I don't get some sense out of you. Some of his men can be none too fussy about how they extract information when it is needed." Bram Stoker is a big man and he can look fearsome when he wants to. He wanted to now. He drew his brows together and glared at Willis, his face only inches away.

I pulled out my new half hunter and looked at it. I was surprised to see it was almost two of the clock in the morning. Stoker glanced at the dial and then turned back to Willis.

"Two minutes, Mr. Willis. That is all the time we can

give you. Two minutes in which to tell us where your con-federates are hiding the boy."

"I don't know."

"Of course you do."

"I don't, I tell you. They wouldn't tell me."

"Where *could* they be hiding him?" I said.

"They wouldn't hold him at the theatre," said Stoker. "And I doubt very much they'd be foolish enough to try to secrete him at the home of any one of you. Where else is there, that would be secure?"

I had an idea. "Willis, when Mrs. Crowe took over Sadler's Wells Theatre, she had to clear out a great deal of stuff she didn't need, did she not?"

"Good, Harry!" cried my boss. "Yes. I remember when the Guv'nor took over the Lyceum, the same thing. He threw out a vast quantity of material and a tremendous amount was put into storage, just in case it should be needed for some future production. I particularly remember several thousand peacock feathers, for example."

"You can't keep everything backstage," I agreed. I turned back to Willis. "So where is the storage for Sadler's?"

Willis looked somewhat surprised. I honestly think he hadn't known where Ralph had taken the boy, but I think he now saw that I was probably right. It would be a good place to hide someone, and not at all obvious.

"Ralph did say somefink just a few days ago about the old warehouse," he muttered grudgingly. "I asked 'im what he was goin' on about but 'e just told me to shut up!"

"Good." Stoker nodded. "Now all you have to do is to tell us where it is located."

"All I know is that it's off the Mile End Road."

"South of the gas works?"

He nodded, his brow furrowed. I could see him trying to picture the route. I imagine he had not traveled it any great number of times, the last time probably far in the past.

"Not far from the Docks," he said. "London Docks. Off Old Manor Road. I fink it was Salmon Lane, on the left as you gets toward the river."

"Salmon Lane?" said Stoker.

"I fink so." The tick was at work again.

"Hmm. And where exactly on that road might we find it?"

"It's a bleedin' big ware'ouse on the left. I fink it's the first one you come to. Fact I never went no farther down the road so it may be the only one, for all I know."

"How far would that be from here, sir?" I asked my boss.

"Not too far," he said, cryptically. "But whatever the distance, we must be on our way. Mr. Willis, if you should be misleading us . . . we will meet again; have no fear."

Willis seemed to shrink back and looked down at his feet. "Don't you worry none," he mumbled.

Stoker gave a final *hrmph* and turned away, leading us back to the still-waiting hansom and leaving Willis to fend for himself.

The weather had worsened and the snow fell heavily. Our two-wheeler turned onto Whitechapel Road and then, from there, to Mile End Road. There we turned south. Through the driving snow I barely made out the Commercial Gas Works on our left, under their many flickering gaslights, though the "bad-egg smell" was inescapable. The gas was produced by fueling with coal. I envied the men in there working in the heat, no matter how suffocating it might have seemed.

Then we were on past that, down Old Manor Road. It was difficult seeing through the driving snow, and I think our cabbie earned every penny of his fare. Many times he slowed as he came to a side road, presumably to make out the name of the road. Eventually we came to Salmon Lane and made the turn. The cab stopped and the trapdoor opened.

"You sure you know where you're going, mate?"

"I most certainly do, cabbie," said Stoker. "Now, you have been paid and paid well. Pray continue."

The cabdriver grunted and said something under his breath that I'm sure was not polite. We eventually came to a high fence, behind which we could just make out what looked like a warehouse. We were not far from the Limehouse Basin and the London Docks. Many such warehouses are scattered along the roads about that section, on the north bank of the river. My boss had our driver stop, and Stoker and I disembarked. I was stiff and took some time stretching, while Stoker negotiated with the cabdriver to wait for us, not knowing just how long we would be. The man was very reluctant, after all this time, but there was no chance of him finding a return fare in that area, so he climbed into his own cab to sleep until such time as we returned.

"Softly, Harry. Softly," said Stoker as we started walking toward the warehouse gates.

There was a single street lamp alight close to the warehouse, but the light was dim in the swirling snow that still descended. One bonus of the snow was that our footsteps were muffled in the growing accumulation.

"What now, sir?" I asked.

"If this is the correct place, then they have almost certainly secured the boy inside. In all probability they will have left a guard with him."

As we stood there, growing colder by the minute, we were startled to observe our hansom cab suddenly go rattling past us at a good pace. It seemed that the driver had decided it wasn't worth the discomfort to wait on our pleasure. Besides, he had been paid in advance. Stoker cursed . . . not for the first time that night. My boss and I were left alone in the blackness of the night, shivering in the falling snow. Without a word we both moved forward to the warehouse gates. They were wrought iron, high, and securely chained. Behind them the windowless building was only faintly discernible through the snow.

"We must presume that Edward is in there," said Stoker. "They would not have driven all the way out here with him only to take him back again to the theatre."

"Unless this was just one stop, for some reason," I said, "and they are going on to some other destination to actually leave him."

Stoker looked at me and I could feel his eyes boring into me. "Don't be foolish, Harry," was all he said.

He was right; or more correctly, we had to believe that he was right. We had no way of continuing a chase and had now lost our prey. Edward *had* to be in the warehouse.

"Can you climb these gates?" he asked.

I studied them. They were old and rusted but still solid. If I could get a good grip, I thought I could scale them. Getting over them looked a little trickier, since there were some decorative spikes across the top, but I thought I could do it. I told Stoker so.

"But what about you, sir? Do you want me to go in alone?" I didn't mean for it to sound plaintive but it seemed to come out that way.

"Fear not, Harry. We go together. I'm hoping there is some item or items on the inside of these gates that you can commandeer to assist me in following you over the top. For instance"—he pointed—"I think I can make out some planks of wood over in the corner, leaning against the wall. We may be able to make use of them."

I took off my topcoat and bowler hat and threw them

over the top of the gate. Then Stoker had me climb up onto his back and, with a knee on his shoulders, I was able to stand upright and then reach the ornate gate tops. I eventually clawed my way over. I hung for a moment on the far side before dropping to the ground. I had hoped there was now enough snow to give me an easy landing, but it jarred my leg and I yelped like a puppy.

"Are you all right, Harry?"

"Yes, sir. I'll be fine. It was just a bit more of a drop than I anticipated. Not to worry." I put on my hat and coat again as quickly as I could and then limped off toward the planks he had indicated. I found that my ankle was extremely painful.

"Just start with one, Harry," my boss called. "We'll see how that goes. Get it over here to begin with."

I dragged a long wooden plank from the side of the warehouse over to the gate. Following Stoker's instructions, I turned it on edge and slid it out through the rails of the gate. Stoker then lifted the end, turned it flat again, and wedged it in and onto an iron fleur-de-lis partway up. This formed a long ramp. After tossing his own overcoat over the gate to me he stepped back a short distance and then ran at the sloping surface.

The first time his foot slipped on the frosty surface as he tried to run up it. He slid sideways and rolled off and to the side.

"Are you all right, sir?"

He got up and dusted himself off without a word. He went back and began his run again. Planting his feet firmly on the wooden plank, he got far enough up the incline to be able to jump and grasp the top crossrail of the gate. Without a pause he kicked and pulled and, gasping, rolled over the top, ripping a large hole in his expensive jacket as he did so. He landed in a crumpled heap on my side of the gate.

I now didn't feel so badly about my own performance, and for a large man, I couldn't help but admire his agility.

"We'll worry about getting out again later," he said, struggling back into his coat. After catching his breath, he led the way toward the dark building.

Chapter Twenty-three

There were large loading doors at the front of the warehouse, but they were securely fastened. It wasn't until we had moved around to the end of the building that we discovered a regular door. It was closed and locked, but the upper half of it included four small glass panes. A brief search uncovered a good size rock, and Stoker smashed out two of the panes. Reaching through, he unlocked the door, and moments later we were both inside the building.

It was a relief to be out of the snow and away from the raw wind that had grown up.

"Let us waste no time, Harry. We don't know whether or not the men intend to return. We must search the place and find Edward."

"Yes, sir."

"Proceed cautiously. We don't know whether or not they have left a guard here. I'll go this way and you go that. If no luck, we'll meet back here. Off you go."

Trying not to make any noise, I hurried as much as I

could with my sore ankle. There seemed to be no light in the building. I found myself in a corridor. A ghostly sort of glimmer came through the windows, from the snow out-side, but not enough to give any real light. I checked a num-ber of rooms that seemed to be offices. I eventually rounded a corner and was surprised to see a low light coming from one of the glass-fronted office doors ahead of me. I advanced just as softly as I possibly could.

Peering through the door's window, my heart skipped a beat when I saw a small figure seated in a chair. It only took a moment to recognize Edward and to see that he was tied to his seat, in much the same way that I had been tied in the boathouse in Twickenham. The boy's head was slumped for-ward on his chest, and I imagined he was asleep. Hopefully that and not drugged, I thought.

There was no other sign of life in the room. I supposed that he had been left there and the kidnappers would return for him in the morning. I carefully tried the door handle. To my surprise, and delight, it was not locked. Since the outside door had been locked, I presumed the abductors had not wor-ried about this inner one. I eased it open and stepped inside.

"Shh! Edward!" I hissed. "Edward. It's Mr. Rivers. I've come to . . ."

"Well, come on in, then, Mr. Rivers," said a voice.

What seemed at that moment to be an abnormally large man emerged from out of the shadows and grabbed my arm. He locked onto it and then wrapped his other arm around my neck. I tried to gasp but found I couldn't.

"Help!" The young boy in the chair came alive and started struggling against his bonds. "Help!" he cried.

Dragging me across the room, the big man aimed a kick at the chair and sent Edward crashing over onto the floor, bouncing off the corner of a desk on the way.

"Shut up, you!" snarled the man. "Ain't no one as is comin' to 'elp you, so shut yer mouth!"

"Hey!" I managed to get out. "Leave the boy alone. Ouch!"

He gave a squeeze with the arm around my neck. It wasn't pleasant.

"They said as 'ow someone just might come lookin' for the kid. Seems as 'ow they was right."

Suddenly the grip on my arm loosened and the arm about my neck came away. I almost fell as my burly captive staggered back a pace or two and then collapsed in a crumpled heap. Behind him I saw the equally burly figure of Bram Stoker, holding a cricket bat.

"I found this in one of the rooms back there," said Stoker, looking at the bat. "It's signed by W. G. Grace, no less."

Dr. W. G. Grace was shaping up to be England's finest cricketer. Last year he had scored England's first ever Test century in his debut Test match against Australia. I could understand Mr. Stoker's excitement, even if it seemed a little misplaced at this moment.

"That's wonderful, sir," I said, rubbing my neck. "Let's look to Edward."

The boy had started shouting and using a few phrases that I am sure he had not learned from his mother. *Perhaps they are from Shakespeare*, I thought. I hurried to his side and with Stoker's help we righted the chair. I applied myself to untying the knots.

"Easy, Edward," said Stoker. "You're all right now. We're going to get you out of here."

"Thank you, sir," the boy was grateful enough to say. "I knew you'd come! Mother always said you were someone I could trust."

"Yes. Well, never mind. Let's get on," growled Stoker, obviously embarrassed at the praise. I thought a small sign of gratitude for myself might not be amiss, but I'm sure there was time yet for that. We still had to get out and safely back to the Lyceum.

Stoker picked up the lamp from where it sat on a bench top and led the way back along the corridor. As we turned the corner and headed for the exit I saw lights outside the window. We stopped and looked out.

A four-wheeler had drawn up outside the gate. It looked as though the other men had returned. Perhaps they had merely gone for refreshments or for some other reason. Whatever it was, it boded ill for us.

"What now, sir?" I asked.

"We need to hide. Quickly, Harry and Edward. I had found the main warehouse space in my searching. Through that door there, down the passage to the next door, and in! Fast as you can!"

While the men outside were unlocking and removing the chains from around the front gates, we moved along and into the warehouse proper. It was mostly bare with no obvious place to hide. Stoker held up the lamp he had taken from Edward's room and we surveyed the area.

"I had no light before," he said. "I rather hoped that we might find something here we could utilize."

We moved into the middle of the bare space. There was one large packing case off to one side, a couple of very small wooden boxes, and a light handcart; there was nothing that looked as though it would be of the slightest use. We heard the men come into the building; they commented on the broken windowpanes. It sounded as though there were three of them. We heard two of them hurrying off in the direction of the room where we had found Edward. They must have decided to break up as Stoker and I had done on first entering, for the door into where we were began to open.

Once again displaying his ability to move fast despite his size, Stoker thrust the lantern into my hand, leapt across to the opening door, and swung the cricket bat he still carried. There was a dull thud and Ralph Bateman rolled into the area and lay still. In the distance we heard the others give a shout, apparently discovering that Edward was gone.

"Quickly!" cried Stoker. "We don't have any choice. There's no time to get outside. Harry, lift up that grating."

In the middle of the floor there was a circular grating over an opening, which was obviously for draining off any water that accumulated in the warehouse. It was a large opening, much like a manhole. I gave Stoker back the lantern and then ran across to the hole, ignoring my still aching ankle, and with great effort managed to lift the cover. I looked down into blackness, what I believe the poets refer to as "Stygian darkness."

"Hop on down, Harry," said Stoker.

"I beg your pardon?"

"Quickly now," he said. "Here, I'll go first and then you can pass Edward down to me."

"I can get down by myself," protested Edward.

As I watched, Stoker lowered himself into the hole and disappeared. Edward was right behind him. I couldn't be left, so I advanced to the gaping opening and again looked down. I saw that there were horseshoe-shaped steps hammered into the side of the rough-hewn shaft. I could see the glimmer of Stoker's lantern at the bottom.

"Hurry up, Harry. And pull the cover back over," came his voice.

Despite my newfound fear of closed spaces, I lost no more time and, balancing on the top step, dragged the metal cover up to the lip of the hole. I eased myself down and pulled the cover all the way across. With my heart thumping in my chest and sweat starting out all over my body, I climbed slowly downward. Above, I heard shouts and the stamping of feet.

"What are they doing?" asked Stoker from below me. "Can you make out anything?"

There came the sound of something being dragged across

the floor and then a thump as all the light that had been seeping down through the grating disappeared. I knew instinctively what had happened. I climbed back up and tried to open the grate again. It wouldn't budge.

"I think they realized where we had gone," I called down the shaft. "They've dragged that big packing case over on top of the manhole cover. We're trapped! We can't get out again!"

"So this is what a sewer is like."

Edward sounded calm and captivated. For myself, I was a nervous wreck. Prior to my run-in with that packing crate, I had never before realized that I had a fear of being enclosed. The darkness didn't help. Stoker held the small lamp in front of him as we advanced along the channel of the sewer. His great bulk in effect cut off any illumination from reaching where I brought up the rear. I found myself sweating profusely.

"The water is warm," continued Edward.

It was. I had expected to descend into cold if not freezing liquid, but as the boy had remarked, it was tepid if not verging on hot.

"Why is that, sir?" I called ahead. "How is it that it's heated?"

His voice came back, echoing off the close walls. "It's runoff from the Commercial Gas Works, Harry. They produce the coal gas with coke-fired furnaces, taking in water from the Regents Canal, which is next to the works. I believe the water is then pumped through what they call a hydraulic main. Something to do with ridding the gas of tar. It then runs off and comes down here."

"Stinks like rotten eggs," said Edward. "Pheoo!"

It did indeed have an abominable odor. I tried holding my hand over my mouth and nose, but it didn't help, so I abandoned the idea.

"Where are we going, Mr. Stoker?" asked Edward.

"Out!" came back the curt reply.

"There's a way out?" I said. "How do you know which way to go?"

"Look at the flow of the water," said Stoker. "These sewers take the water and refuse out to the river. If we follow the way it's flowing, we will eventually come to where it opens into the Thames."

"How far is that, sir?" asked Edward, putting into words the question I had been about to ask. Stoker did not reply, which I did not take as a good sign.

We continued for some time.

"Are there rats here?" asked Edward, again putting my thoughts into words. "Mama says that the sewers of London are alive with verm . . . verm . . . with rats."

I was not a little disturbed and expected to hear and feel the scampering of creatures over my feet. I had read of filthy rats that grew to enormous size, living off the swill that swept through London's sewers. I shuddered. I was not a rat lover.

"Fear not, Edward," said Stoker. "This sewer is carrying waste water from the gas works so probably attracts far fewer rats than the lines transporting human waste and excrement."

Probably? I thought.

Suddenly all was darkness and Stoker halted and muttered, "Damnation!"

"What is it, sir?"

"The lamp. It must have run dry of oil. Now we have only our instincts to guide us." He moved forward again, at a much slower pace.

"How far is it, sir?" asked Edward again.

"I don't know, I'm afraid. Not far, I hope. We were south of the gas works, somewhere in Limehouse. My guess is that this sewer line runs underneath the Commercial Road and empties into the river somewhere close to Eagle Wharf. I seem to recall once noticing pipes projecting into the river at that point, just west of where the canal itself empties."

"I—I don't like the dark, Mr. Stoker." Edward was obviously trying to be brave and not show fear.

"Put out your hand and feel the side of the tunnel," said Stoker. "That will keep you in the center and help you avoid bumping into the walls."

"It's slimy!" wailed the boy.

"Disgusting!" I added.

We shuffled ahead in silence for a long while.

After several minutes I noticed that the sloshing noise we made as we shuffled through the swill seemed to be coming from off to my left. I stopped.

"Sir?"

"What is it, Harry?"

Yes, his voice was no longer directly ahead of me. "Sir! Where are you? You seem to have moved."

"Moved? What are you talking about?"

I tried to orient myself and to explain my concern. "You don't seem to be directly ahead of me anymore, sir, and your voice sounds farther away."

There was a silence and then, "Put out your hands, Harry, just as we talked about a short time ago. Both hands. Now, can you feel the wall on either side of you?"

I did as he instructed. "No, sir. Only on my right."

"And, now that I do the same, I can only feel a wall on my left."

"What's happening, Mr. Stoker?" Edward's voice had a quaver to it.

"Nothing too terrible," came the big man's reassuring growl. "It would seem that the sewer has forked and that you are starting to move off down the right-hand tunnel, Harry, while Edward and I are going to the left. Hmm! Good thing you noticed it when you did. Just put out your left hand, Harry, and move over to your left as you come forward again."

I did as instructed.

"Ouch!"

"Sorry, Edward," I said. "I must have caught up with you now."

"Good."

"Just one more thing though, sir."

He sighed. "And that is?"

"If the tunnel has now divided and we are going off along the left-hand branch . . . how do we know that this is the correct way? What if it's the right-hand tunnel that will lead us to the river?"

Mr. Stoker was my boss and, as such, was a brilliant man who—it seemed to me—had all the answers. But every once in a while he admitted that I came up with a problem that he had not foreseen. This was apparently one such occasion. We stood in water up to our knees for a very long while.

"You raise a very pertinent point, Harry. One to which there would appear to be no immediate solution. I suggest we continue forward on our present path—the left-hand tunnel—and see where it leads. Hopefully it will shortly open out into the river. If, however, it does not, then I'm afraid we will have no choice but to retrace our steps and then take the other tunnel, hoping that, in turn, will take us where we wish to go."

"And if there are other tunnel divisions, sir?" I asked. "If this left-hand tunnel later divides into two?"

Edward picked up my thoughts. "And then, later, if the one we choose from there divides again . . . ?"

There came no reply from Mr. Stoker, while my wild imaginings saw us wandering for days through the catacombs that were the sewer web beneath the City of London.

We continued for what seemed a very long distance.

"Mr. Stoker, sir?" I eventually called.

He grunted.

"I don't know what this means, but have you noticed that the water is rising? It was around my ankles when we first descended but it's now well over my knees."

We halted again.

"You are right, Harry. My mind was on other things and I had not noticed."

"Are we going to drown?" asked Edward, in a surprisingly bright voice. Despite the dark—or perhaps because of it—I think he was finding the whole thing a big adventure. For myself, I would rather have been safely tucked into bed off Chancery Lane.

"It is probably that the outflowing from the gas works fluctuates," said Stoker eventually. I thought he sounded uncertain. His voice lacked its usual conviction. "Come! Let us press on. The sooner we get to the end of this tunnel the better."

We moved forward at a slightly faster pace but could not keep it up in the darkness. Meanwhile, as we progressed, I noticed that the water level, slowly yet consistently, continued to rise. Stoker halted.

"It makes no sense," he offered, "but it may be that there is some change of depth to the sewer that we have encountered. Much as I hate to say it, I do believe we need to turn around and go back to that division of the sewer tunnel. We must take the other branch and hope that that maintains its level."

With groaning and grumbling from Edward, who had actually been holding up well, I thought, we did reverse ourselves, Mr. Stoker moving to the lead with myself bringing up the rear. With a great deal of sighing and not a little yawning—it must have been well into the early hours of Tuesday morning—we dragged ourselves back through the tepid water in the total blackness that was the inner depths of the London sewers.

With outstretched hands sliding along the walls, we finally found the original division of the ways and started anew along the second sewer line.

"It's getting colder, Mr. Stoker," said Edward. "And it's getting deeper. The water's up to my chest."

"It *is* cold," I agreed. "What's happening?"

Stoker, uncharacteristically, smacked the side of the wall. "Of course! How could I not have foreseen this!"

"Sir?"

"The tide, Harry. The tide."

Edward and I remained silent, neither of us understanding. Stoker gave one of his long sighs.

"From the mouth of the Thames all the way up to Richmond, the river is tidal. The level rises and falls with the turn of the tide, even in the winter. At this time of year high tide is very high; much more so than in the summer and autumn. It must be high tide now, or is approaching it. The water has risen high enough *to flow into the end of the pipe* and is now flowing inward and upward, from the river, and filling the pipe!"

"And the iciness of the river water is overcoming the heat that was flowing down from the gas works," I murmured, finally fully comprehending.

Edward, despite himself, let out a sob.

"Here, Edward." I heard splashing as the big man moved around. "Climb up on my back. Help him, Harry. I'll carry you pickaback. You won't drown."

Thoughts ran through my head. I was only five feet and six inches; quite a bit shorter than my boss. What would happen if the water rose to the top of the sewer?

"It is a whole lot colder," I said.

"As you say, Harry, the water from the icy river is overpowering the heated water from the gas works. Let us just pray that we get out of here both before it grows too cold and before it covers our heads."

Wonderful! I thought. *We can either drown or freeze to death!*

Chapter Twenty-four

The cold water was up to my chin as I struggled on after my boss. He seemed not to be affected by Edward on his back, and the boy had fallen silent. I wondered if he was asleep; it was growing further into the early hours, after all, probably almost dawn. My neck was beginning to ache from holding my head back to keep out any influx of water.

"Sir!" I called out.

"Yes, Harry?" Stoker sounded very weary.

"Sir, here on my right. There's something sticking out of the wall."

As he turned back to me, he created a small wave that splashed into my mouth. I coughed and spat.

"Let me feel, Harry. Where's your hand. Ah!"

I felt his big hand on mine and tried to guide it to the object I had encountered.

"*Dá fhaid é an lá tiocfaidh an tráthnóna*, as my old granny used to say," he cried.

"Excuse me?" I said. "Is that good or is that some kind of Irish swearing?"

"It's good, Harry. It's very good. It means something like 'no matter how long the day, the evening will surely arrive.' I don't have the exact English of it, but that's close enough."

"So, what is this on the wall?"

"Not *on* the wall, Harry. *In* the wall. It's a step. It's like those iron rungs we climbed down back at the warehouse. Feel up above it, Harry. There should be another. It's a way out, Harry! There must be a manhole cover up above us somewhere."

Edward stirred. Now the boy was awake and wanted to know what all the noise was about.

"Reach up, Edward," I said. "I can't reach any higher myself, but you can probably feel higher up the wall from where you are. See if you can find one of those iron steps built into the wall."

"I've found one!" he cried. "Shall I climb up?"

"Best let Harry go first," said Stoker. "There will be a cover to move at the top and I don't think you'll have the strength for that."

I just hope that I have the strength for it, I thought. I took hold of the iron step and first of all felt around below it. I found another and, getting my foot on that, was able to start the climb upward. I couldn't believe how weak I felt, but I forced myself to climb. It seemed like an age, with Stoker and Edward shouting encouragement from below, but eventually I came up against the roof and felt the shape of a metal cover. I got my feet as firmly on the last step as I could and pressed my shoulder up against the lid. I pushed and pushed but nothing happened.

"Take a breath, Harry," called Stoker.

I did, and then tried again. Still no movement from the cover.

"I'm coming up," said Stoker. "Edward, you hold on firmly to the steps behind me but let me go up first."

He clambered up. I could sense that he, too, was exhausted. But soon he was on the step below the one I was on and was reaching up around me to the cover.

"On the count of three, Harry. We'll both push together. One . . . two . . . three!"

The manhole cover came loose and popped off, rolling back with a clang.

I don't know what I expected, but there was no sudden glare of light. It seemed as black outside as it had been in the sewer. There was no moon or, if there was, thick cloud must have hidden it. One thing that did strike me—the tang of the salt air coming off the river; such a relief after breathing that putrid bad-egg smell.

Thankfully it had stopped snowing. From the glimmer that came from the snow on the ground all about us, it looked as though we had come up at the side of a road. I climbed out, followed by Stoker, who reached back to pull out Edward. We rolled the manhole cover over and set it back in place. There was a street lamp burning not far from us, and we sent Edward to see if he could see a street name anywhere near it. He came trotting back apparently somewhat renewed in energy, if still shivering, at our escape from the sewer.

"It's the corner of Brook Street and Butcher Row."

"Close to the river," said Stoker. "I know Brook Street. Come. We need to find transportation and get out of these wet clothes before we freeze to death."

"Down to the river or away from it?" I asked.

"If memory serves me right, we follow Brook Street and it will lead us into Commercial Road. That will certainly have traffic, even at this hour. Going down to the river wouldn't help. The wharfs hold nothing but warehouses that, as we know, are not inhabited."

"There might be an occasional night watchman," I said, "but I agree that Commercial Road will be better."

We were all three of us shivering by the time we reached the main thoroughfare. Stoker had insisted that we walk briskly and even run for short bursts, to keep warm, but we were all on our last legs. I was amazed that Edward was still standing. He was a brave boy.

We eventually saw a hansom and all of us shouted as we hailed it. The driver pulled up beside us and took in our bedraggled appearance.

"'Ere! Wot's wif you, then? You looks as if you bin swimmin' in the river an' no mistake! Bit on the cold side for that, innit?"

"It was something like that," said Stoker. "An accident. I am very concerned about this young lad. Is there anywhere close by that you can take us, where we can get warm and perhaps dry our clothes? I don't think the boy will last on a drive all the way back to the City."

"Lord love ya! You get inside my cab an' I'll 'ave you right in no time!"

We all three of us squeezed in, and he set off at a fast trot.

"You gents is lucky you caught me," he said, opening the trap and talking to us through it as he drove. "I was just on my way 'ome; done for the day. Bin a long 'un, believe me."

"We are extremely grateful," said Stoker. "Where are you taking us?"

"My sister lives close by 'ere, on Bromley Street. Troof be told, I was finkin' of stoppin' by there myself anyway, for a cuppa Rosie."

"Will she up at this hour?" Stoker asked.

"She will be when I bangs on 'er door, won't she?" He laughed uproariously and cracked his whip. The horse moved faster as though realizing the urgency.

In short order we arrived at a small house on a street off

Commercial Road East. I got out and Stoker handed me Edward, who seemed to have fallen asleep again. The cabdriver climbed down off his box and led the way up to the front door.

"I'll take care of Lady Jane after I've got you lot fixed up," he said, nodding toward his horse.

It took a number of thumps on the door by the cabbie, together with him bending down and shouting through the letter box, before there came any sign of life from inside. Eventually the door was pulled back by a tiny little lady, shorter even than myself, clutching a gingham wrapper about her and with her hair bound up in a scarf of some type. She wore overlarge slippers and greeted us with a yawn. I got the feeling that this was not the first time our savior had come calling on his sister in the early hours of a morning.

"Come on, come on, sis! This 'ere's a matter of life and death. Poor kid is like to turn to an icicle at the rate you're movin'! Get the kettle on and I'll bring 'im through."

She dutifully turned back into the house without even giving us a second glance. The cabbie took Edward from me and strode after her. Mr. Stoker and I followed on, unbidden.

Half an hour later we were all sitting around a warm fire that had been coaxed back into life and banked up with coal. Each of us, including my boss, clutched a mug of hot cocoa. Edward was now fully awake, gazing around the room with his eyes wide. He was wrapped in a thick blanket, only his head and hands protruding.

We had learned that the cabbie's name was Percy. His sister insisted we simply call her "Sis," as did her brother. We never did learn her true name.

"We cannot thank you enough, Percy," Stoker was saying. "You have, without doubt, been the instigator of a new lease on life for young Edward here, not to mention Harry and myself. I would like to extend—along with the thanks of the entire Lyceum company—an invitation to your good sister and yourself to attend any and all performances of our productions that you might wish. Do you attend the theatre a lot, Sis?" He turned to the diminutive figure beside him and beamed at her.

"Just the occasional pantomime, and I do like the music hall. I sometimes goes to the Pavilion, up on Mile End Road. They has some right gigs, I can tell you. And o' course there's the penny gaffs once in a while."

"Ah! Yes." Mr. Stoker glanced at me but said no more on the subject.

"I'm not above the occasional drama myself, sir," said Percy. "I seen Mr. Beerbohm Tree a year or more past. 'E was good, as I recall."

"And what play was that, Percy?" I enquired.

"Hoh! I don't know what its name was, bless you. Can't quite keep them fings in my 'ead, you know?"

"No, of course not," I said. I pulled out my half hunter and looked at it. "Upon my word! Do you see the time, sir?" I addressed Mr. Stoker, who I saw had now finished his cocoa and was beginning to look more than ready to depart.

"Yes, Harry. Time moves on apace." He stood up and stretched. "Mr. Percy, Miss—er—Sis. Thank you once again for your wonderful hospitality. Without you I don't quite know what might have become of us. Percy, might I prevail upon you just a little more? This time directly in your line of work. The boy's mother must, of course, be worried more than we can know. Would you be available to drive us home to the Lyceum Theatre . . . at your full rates, of course?"

Edward's clothes had been set to dry in front of the fire. He now put them on as we prepared to leave. Mine and my boss's clothes were still damp but a far cry from the soaking state in which we had been found. Sis insisted that we take the big blanket to cover us on our journey. Percy assured her he would bring it back. We were soon outside and trotting toward the City, under a clear but still dark sky. The snow had stopped falling and the stars seemed to me to be especially bright, but perhaps that was my imagination.

Chapter Twenty-five

"I think enough is enough," said Stoker. "It's time we went to meet the enemy face-to-face and to have it out with him."

Edward had been delivered to his mother, to her relief and undying gratitude. The Guv'nor himself had shaken both our hands and expressed his delight. Both Stoker and I had managed a few hours sleep . . . We had not got to bed until a little after daybreak. Now we were once again in the theatre manager's office reviewing events.

"Face-to-face?" I repeated. "You mean, you think we should go to Sadler's Wells and confront them?"

"Most decidedly! It's something I should have done long ago, and it would have saved young Edward and his mother much discomfort."

I couldn't help smiling. "I don't know, sir. I rather think that Edward considered it a first-class adventure. I understand that he ate an extra-large breakfast this morning and claims he may just forgo being an actor and become an explorer instead."

"Yes, well, his mother will soon change his mind on that!" Stoker stood up and moved to get his topcoat, recently hung on the stand by the door. "Come, Harry! Let us suit action to words. Get your own overcoat and we will hie us to Sadler's."

"Yes, sir." I could tell when his mind was made up.

We took a hansom to Clerkenwell. It was a fine morning, with a weak sun reflecting off the recently fallen snow. The virgin whiteness was rapidly giving way to a dirty gray because of the morning traffic, but the roofs and gardens we passed still glittered and shone.

Alighting at the theatre, we lost no time in entering the stage door. There, George Dale blinked at us as we moved past him in the direction of the front office.

"Mrs. Crowe, George," I called to him as we passed.

It took him a moment, but he finally understood what was happening.

"Just let me tell 'er . . ." he started, but we were past him and on to the lady's door.

Stoker tapped on it with the head of his cane and then, without waiting for an answer, flung it open.

The lady was in conversation with a man wearing a green eyeshade and with his sleeves held up with black garters. When she saw us, she dismissed him.

"Leave us, Wilson. We'll take this up again later."

He left the room, eyeing us suspiciously.

"Come in, gentlemen. To what do I owe this pleasure?"

Mrs. Crowe was a small woman with her prematurely graying hair up on top of her head in a bun-chignon. Her face looked pinched, and her mouth was set in a tight line. Her gray eyes matched her hair, and they glinted at us over the top rims of the pince-nez spectacles she had clipped to her nose. She wore a nondescript black dress and no jewelry. When we entered she had been standing, but now she deliberately sat down. She did not invite us to do the same.

Unperturbed, Stoker crossed and sat in one of the two chairs in front of her desk. I joined him in the other.

"Madam. We are here to throw our cards on the table and to bring to an end your juvenile and, in many respects, pusillanimous attempts at destroying the good name of the Lyceum Theatre."

"What, pray, are you talking about, Mr. Stoker?"

"To take them numerically," he said, "there is first the attempt to poison Mr. Irving. A diabolical plot that merited police action . . . a course that may yet be followed. Had it been successful the person responsible would have been facing a charge of murder and the English stage would have lost its finest actor."

Mrs. Crowe sniffed, unimpressed. "Our Mr. Pheebes-Watson might take issue with your last statement, Mr. Stoker, but to your point . . . there has been no attempt on the part of anyone at Sadler's Wells to interfere with your theatre's well-being, least of all to try to poison anyone, whether or not a competent actor."

"Are you denying that you knew of the poisoning before it was reported in the newspapers?"

"Of course not. You know as well as I do, Mr. Stoker, that there is a network of gossip, and cast and management innuendo, throughout the London theatre scene. I believe everyone knew of the unfortunate incident long before the evening papers."

"Do you then deny any active participation in this occurrence?"

"I most certainly do." She turned to a ledger lying on the desk and started turning pages in it, as if to dismiss us. "Now, I have work to do even if you do not, Mr. Stoker. *My* theatre does not run itself!"

"We are not done, madam!" Stoker roared, banging his fist on her desk. "There is much to discuss, not the least of which concerns your brother, Ralph."

At that she sat up straight again and had the grace to look slightly embarrassed. "My brother? What, pray, does my brother have to do with anything?"

"With *everything*, I am believing," responded Stoker.

I was relieved that he was doing all the talking, for I would have withered under Mrs. Crowe's formidable gaze.

"There are a number of incidents where *someone* has gained unauthorized entrance to the Lyceum in order to do mischief," he continued.

"Mischief?" she echoed.

"Causing scenery sandbags and lighting units to fall and injure, or nearly injure, persons on the stage below."

"Oh dear!"

"Oh dear, indeed, madam! And we have good reason to believe that your brother is at the root of this. If it is not he, in person, who is making this mischief, then he is most certainly directing it. Again, madam, actionable if I should call upon the Metropolitan Police Force."

"The head, sir," I murmured, wanting to use all of our ammunition.

"Ah yes!" He picked up on that immediately. "And an incident that has already, of necessity, passed from myself to the constabulary . . . the interference with a buried corpse and the transportation of that corpse's head to our theatre."

"What!" Mrs. Crowe came to her feet, her hand going to cover her heart. "What are you saying? You are accusing my brother of grave robbing?"

"Indeed I am. One of our actors had the misfortune to die in a traffic accident—an occurrence of which I am sure you are aware—and subsequent to his burial his coffin was violated and robbed of its corpse. The head of that corpse then appeared on the Lyceum stage in the midst of a public performance."

Mrs. Crowe sat down again, seemingly calmer. "And what makes you think that my brother had anything to do with that, might I ask?"

"All indications are that he was the instigator, madam. He and his cronies."

"Cronies? I must warn you to watch your language, sir, or it is you who will face the members of the police force."

"You have knowledge of an 'associate' of your brother's who is from the Caribbean Islands?" Stoker persisted.

"If you refer to Mr. Ogoon, yes. He is our houseguest. When Ralph returned from his visit abroad, Mr. Ogoon came with him. He is an esteemed resident of the Republic of Haiti, to my understanding. They have become good friends. What, Mr. Stoker, are you implying about this gentleman?"

"He and your brother, as recently as yesterday, kidnapped the son of Miss Ellen Terry."

"I don't believe it."

"Have you seen your brother this morning, Mrs. Crowe?"

"Just briefly, yes. Though what concern that is of yours I do not know."

"Was he well?" asked Stoker.

"Well? What mean you, sir?"

"How was his head?"

There was a long pause. Mrs. Crowe pursed her thin lips to the point where they seemed to disappear. She moved uneasily in her chair, less confidant than she had been a moment before.

"His—his head? Why, as it happens he does have some injury, a swelling. He accidentally walked into a wall, he says. What do you know of this, Mr. Stoker?"

"He would have to have been walking backward into a wall to raise a swelling on the back of his head. It *is* on the back of his head, is it not, Mrs. Crowe?"

She said nothing. Stoker continued.

"In rescuing the kidnapped child I had to hit your brother over the head. It was necessary in order to effect the rescue. I am not surprised that he has a swelling this morning, and it does indeed confirm that he was the instigator of the abduction. He was accompanied by your Mr. Ogoon and others."

There followed a very long silence. I noticed that her head sank down toward her chest. She gave a long sigh before, finally, looking up again at my boss.

"I must face facts, Mr. Stoker. Ralph has always been a difficult boy. Yes, I admit that I have long been aware of his, what I tell myself are 'misadventures.' He is no longer a child. He must start taking responsibility for his actions. He is very easily led, though I know that is no excuse. Recently, it would seem he has been heavily influenced by someone; someone other than Mr. Ogoon. But kidnapping— if indeed he was responsible, and it would seem from what you say that it is indisputable—is inexcusable. I will admit that he may have been waging some sort of war against your theatre. As you well know, since my mother left the Lyceum and Mr. Irving took over, there has been no love lost between our two venues. Ralph has seen himself as 'avenging his mother's honor,' or some such; though how he feels about mine, I am uncertain. But professional rivalry is one thing; this is something else and I find it inexcusable." She got wearily to her feet. "I do not expect you to understand, let alone sympathize with, the feelings of a mother for her son nor an older sister for her younger brother. If you would be kind enough to leave this matter with me, I will attend to it."

"Regrettably, madam," said Stoker, "before coming here we were obliged to apprise the police of the kidnapping. This was at Mr. Irving's urging, since it was a most heinous crime."

She once more was silent for a space, before again sighing and nodding her head.

"I understand, Mr. Stoker. I understand."

Stoker stood up. "Is your brother available?" he asked.

She shook her head. "He and Mr. Ogoon left home about an hour ago or more, shortly after I first spoke to him this morning and before I came to the theatre."

"Do you know where they have gone?"

"I believe he mentioned having to go out to Twickenham, though I'm sure I don't know what business he has there."

"Thank you for your candor, Mrs. Crowe," said Stoker, coming to his feet. He turned to me. "Come, Harry! We must hurry. There is work to be done at Twickenham!"

We stopped at St. James's Division police station and picked up Sergeant Bellamy. I swiftly found myself squeezed in the middle of the cab, between him and Stoker. A hansom is built for two passengers, though it can take three in a pinch. I gave silent thanks that I am so slight of build, since Stoker is large and Bellamy no rake. A second hansom, containing two obese constables equally squeezed together, fell into line behind ours. As we headed west out of the city, we discussed everything we knew and believed concerning Ralph Bateman, Ogoon, and the past events at the Lyceum. Bellamy listened in silence. I could imagine him having a mental notebook open with its pencil busily scribbling.

"You realize, I hope, sir, that we have no jurisdiction out at Twickenham," he finally said.

"I surmised as much," said Stoker. "We did, however, want to bring you up to date, since so much of this has taken place in or around the theatre. What would you advise, Sergeant?"

"Well, sir." I could sense his satisfaction at having been brought into our confidence and at being asked for his advice. "When we get to Twickenham, we can make contact with the Thames Valley Police and request that they accompany us to wherever it is we are bound, and effect whatever actions are necessary."

"Excellent," said Stoker. "Excellent, Sergeant."

The Twickenham police station was in a tiny building on Church Street, perhaps conveniently situated next door to the Fox and Grapes, which sat on the very bank of the Thames. Indeed we were directed to the tavern to speak with Inspector Maurice Gulley, an old-school policeman who seemed not to feel the pressures of his duties, such was the bucolic setting of his post. He wiped the froth from the white walrus mustache that overhung his full lips and allowed a soft belch to escape his mouth before setting down his tankard and looking us up and down. He addressed himself to Sergeant Bellamy.

"'Tis a grand morning for the time o' year, is it not, Sergeant?" He stretched out his legs under the rustic table at which he sat, on the back lawn of the tavern.

The water of the river gently lapped not far from our feet, and an enthusiastic young student, well wrapped against the still chill weather, glided past in a punt. The sun had deemed to grace us with its presence, though there was little warmth coming from it.

Mr. Stoker tapped his foot impatiently. Bellamy, very conscious of my boss's actions, nodded to the officer.

"A fine morning indeed, Inspector," he said. "And I am sorry to have to intrude upon it, but there is important, and very immediate, action to be taken."

"Oh? Explain yourself, Sergeant." He again raised the tankard to his lips and allowed his mustache to disturb the head of the ale.

"Yes, sir. We have to request your assistance in apprehending a group of miscreants who have driven down here from London."

"And their alleged crime?"

"Their crime, sir," snapped Mr. Stoker, whose patience had come to an end, "is that of kidnapping. Kidnapping a small child and, further, of placing said child together with two adults in grave danger. There are possibly further charges that might be brought should we be successful in breaking through this lethargy of the Thames Valley Police and actually apprehending them."

The inspector carefully and deliberately set down his ale and came to his feet, attempting to fix my boss with a steely gaze. Unfortunately the inspector was a good head shorter than Mr. Stoker and, if I was to make a judgment, a trifle unsteady on his feet.

"And you, sir, are . . . ?"

Bellamy had the good sense to intervene. "This is Mr. Abraham Stoker, manager of the Lyceum Theatre in London, Inspector. We really do need to be about our business as promptly as possible. I have a carriage full of my own men out front and we simply look for a few of your good men to join us."

When the inspector still hesitated, Stoker added, "We would, of course, Inspector, deem it an honor if you yourself would join us and help lead the exercise."

We approached Mrs. Richland's home cautiously. Behind our hansom came a four-wheeler carrying Inspector Gulley and three of the Thames Valley Police's finest constables . . . their *only* constables, as it turned out. We stopped at the end of a road opposite the line of houses that stretched along the riverbank. From there we advanced on foot.

At the head of the Richland driveway I looked toward the river and could see the boathouse that had held me several days before. Its door still hung sadly sagging on its rusty hinges. There was no sign of life either at the boat-house or at the main house.

Bram Stoker led the way up the driveway and banged loudly on the front door. When the elderly maid I had encountered on my first visit responded, he asked to see Mrs. Richland.

"I am sorry, sir, but Mrs. Richland is not at home," she said, her eyes cast down.

"Are you sure?" snapped Sergeant Bellamy.

"Oh yes, sir. Mrs. Richland is not at home."

"I see," he said. "We would like to come in and check for ourselves."

Inspector Gulley pushed forward. "We don't have a search warrant," he muttered to Bellamy and Stoker.

"No, sir, we don't," agreed Bellamy. "But we're thinking this lady may not question that. Is that right?" he demanded of the maid.

She looked up, obviously terrified to find so many policemen at her door.

"I—I—I'll have to go and ask," she said, turning tail and fleeing into the house.

"Ask whom, one wonders?" said Stoker. "If the mistress of the house is truly not home, then whom is she questioning?"

"Let's find out!" snapped Bellamy.

He pushed forward into the entrance hall. With the briefest of pauses, Gulley followed, Stoker, myself, and the five policemen right behind him. We moved quickly up the staircase to the living room, which was empty. Above us we heard the sound of voices—that of the maid and more than one male voice.

"Come on!" cried Stoker.

We turned away from the living room and continued on up the staircase, coming to a stop partway up the next flight as a figure appeared at the top of the stairs. I blinked my eyes and then rubbed them.

"Damnation but I knew it!" cried Stoker.

There, looking down on us, his face distorted in fury, was the supposedly dead Peter Richland. Behind him stood Ralph Bateman, Ogoon, and Herbert Willis.

"Well! The late Mr. Richland," said Stoker. "Might I say how well you are looking?"

"Damn you!"

Richland bent and swiftly picked up a potted palm tree that stood at the top of the staircase. He flung it down to strike Stoker. The big man fell back a couple of steps, and the rest of us, bumping into one another, also fell back, some of the police constables literally losing their balance, falling to the stairs, and rolling back down them. Richland and his followers turned and disappeared.

"They're making for the back stairs!" I shouted. "We must get down and around to the kitchen."

What followed was chaotic. Constables tried to pick themselves up while those on the upper stairs tried to get past them to lead the way down. Valuable time was lost getting back to the ground floor and then around and down to the kitchen. We arrived to find the outer door open and the miscreants gone.

"Jackson, Ingram, and Rogers! Go through this house with a fine-tooth comb. Any person or persons you find you will apprehend and hold until my return. The rest of you, come with me," cried the inspector.

The other two constables, Sergeant Bellamy, Stoker, and I followed the inspector out to the back garden. We had a quick look in the boathouse and another constable was left there. The five of us then hurried back up to the roadway.

"Over there!" cried Stoker, pointing to a house two doors along.

There was a man working in the front of the house, clearing snow from the path. Stoker advanced on him.

"You, sir! Did you see some men—at least three of them—hurry from this house a short time ago? One of them was tall, almost as tall as myself. Possibly they would have been without overcoats."

The man, who was elderly, stuck his finger in one ear and wiggled it as though to stir up his memory. He knit his brow and squinted his eyes. It seemed obvious he was making a great effort to report, with accuracy, anything he had seen.

"Well now, young man," he said, speaking slowly and distinctly. "You say at least three men?"

"Yes. Yes," said Stoker.

"And without topcoats, even in this inclement weather?"

"Did you see them?" snapped Inspector Gulley. "Speak up, man. This is urgent police business."

"Don't fluster him," urged Stoker quietly.

"Three men in a hurry?" He scratched the top of his head. "You know I do believe I did, don't you know. Though in point of fact there were four of them. I wondered why they were running."

I heard the inspector growling.

"Yes," continued our witness. "I did not observe the lack of outer attire initially, though it did eventually strike me. I remember thinking to myself, 'Why would any man, no matter his station, pursue his business in such inclement weather as we have seen of late—although one must acknowledge that the day is a fine one for the season—why would any man exit his house thus sparsely clad . . . ?"

"Oh, get on with it, man!" cried Bellamy.

The older gentleman gave the sergeant a brief hard look and then continued undaunted. "They ran out from the back of the house, continued around to the front, and then hailed a four-wheeler that was passing," he said.

"They got a growler?"

"Not many of them along here at this time of day," continued the old man. "They were lucky there."

"Tell me, sir," Stoker spoke quietly but firmly. "Were you close enough? Did you happen to hear where they asked the driver to go?"

We all hung on his words.

"Oh yes." He nodded his head several times. "That was not difficult." He chuckled. "The old driver must have been a mite deaf, don't you know! They had to shout it out more than once."

"*What did they say!*" screamed the inspector.

"Teddington," said the man. "Yes, Teddington. Just down the road, don't you know. Only about a mile . . ."

We didn't wait for him to finish but ran across to where we had left the police growler. A constable climbed up onto the box and the rest of us bundled into the carriage. The hansom had long since departed. With a lurch, the four-wheeler rolled out of the side road and turned westward toward the neighboring town of Teddington.

"Why would they be going there, sir?" I asked.

"I'm not certain," said Stoker.

"The lock, I wouldn't mind betting," said Inspector Gulley. "They can cross the river over the lock gate and then they'll be in Surrey . . . and out of my jurisdiction."

"Not if we catch up with them first," said Bellamy, through clenched teeth.

We all clung on tightly as the policeman in the driver's seat whipped up the horses to a gallop.

"I still can't get over the fact that Richland is alive," I said. "How can that be? There were witnesses that saw him run down and killed—why, I even went and identified the body—and then we all went to his funeral."

"Except that the coffin was empty," said Stoker. "I have to admit that I began to have my doubts when you reported that his mother was keeping his room in situ, Harry. Not unknown when a mother loses a son, certainly, but enough to draw out my suspicions in this instance."

"So why did he fake his death?" asked the inspector.

"And whose body was it that we were chasing after?" said Bellamy. "There certainly *was* a body, as we all know. Sometimes with a head and sometimes without, but a body nonetheless."

"Oh yes. There was a body," replied Stoker.

Gulley stuck his head out the side of the carriage and shouted up to the driver, "Turn left along here, Constable. Ferry Road, right off Manor Road." He drew back in and turned to Mr. Stoker. "Pray continue, sir."

Stoker did so. "Don't forget that Richland was in the company of another man at the Druid's Head. They both left the tavern, apparently very much the worse for drink, or so it appeared. I have a feeling that Richland was actually quite sober. And I am pretty certain that the body we took to be Richland—and that he wanted us to think was him—was in fact the body of the stranger he had befriended at the public house. A visitor to the city who would not be easily missed."

"But how could that be?" I asked. "The police—Sergeant Bellamy here—said that they knew the victim was one of our actors because of the traces of makeup on his face."

Bellamy nodded. "That's correct, sir."

"Oh, our Mr. Richland planned it all carefully, Harry, I'm sure. Someone observed that at the scene of the accident one man dragged the victim over to the far side of the road and then down an alley."

"That's right!" acknowledged Bellamy.

"In case there was any chance of identification," continued Stoker, "our man put makeup on the other's face, shaved his mustache, if he had one, and then smashed his face so there could be no absolute recognition."

"I have to admit," I said, "when I was at the police station to identify the man, I was not able to really study him . . . my stomach wouldn't allow it."

The four-wheeler skidded to a halt and the inspector flung open the door. "Here we are. Let's get after the blighters!"

We all tumbled out and ran toward the water.

"There they go!" shouted Bellamy.

I could make out four men ahead of us. We watched them climbing up onto the footbridge that stretched across to the narrow island, at the end of which were the locks and the weir.

As I understood it, the footbridge extended to the island, but in order to complete the river crossing it was necessary to turn and proceed to the lock. There it was then possible to walk across on the tops of the lock gates, a common practice. At this time of the year the river on the Teddington side was frozen, with the exception of around the weir, but on the far side of the island ice had been broken up leading to the lock, to allow passage of boats. The men ahead of us split up, two of them running to the left, to the lock, and the other two to the right, to the weir.

"With me, Harry!" shouted Stoker, swinging to the left in order to pursue what we saw to be Richland and Ogoon.

It was Bateman and Willis, then, who had gone the other way, I realized. What they hoped to accomplish at the weir I had no idea, though in the summer months it might be possible to pick one's way across protruding rocks. I could hear Bellamy panting behind me. Inspector Gulley and his constable went the other way, after the second couple.

Bram Stoker's powerful legs drew him away from me and my skinny ones. I saw him gaining on the two we pursued, but I didn't think he could catch them in time. As I watched, Peter Richland swung himself up onto the top of the lock gates and started across. When Richland got to the middle, where the two gates met, he paused momentarily to look back. Ogoon was close behind him. Perhaps too close, for he slid on the icy wood trying to avoid Richland. The two bumped into each and Peter Richland pitched over the side, crying out as he fell.

Ogoon jumped over where his companion had been standing and, without a word and not looking back, ran on to gain a footing on the Surrey bank. He still didn't look back but disappeared behind the lock house. I hoped I would never see him again.

I ran up to where Stoker now stood on the top of the lock gate, looking down into the icy water. I had a brief glimpse of Peter Richland, floundering as he tried to stay afloat. No one could survive for more than a few minutes in that icy pit. I eased carefully around Stoker and ran to where the life belt hung on its hook, in case of such emergencies. But with the cold and the icy winds that had blown there for some time, the ring of cork was frozen solid to its base. I tugged and tugged until I heard Stoker's voice.

"Never mind, Harry. Never mind."

Chapter Twenty-six

Intermittently since 1705 there had been a so-called Beef-steak Club in London. The first of these had been started by an actor, Richard Estcourt, championing beef. In 1735 the scenery painter George Lambert, together with actor John Rich, formed the Sublime Society of Beefsteaks, who met at Covent Garden. After the Covent Garden fire of 1808, they started meeting at the Lyceum Theatre, in a back room. This had gradually developed into a very private club where the members—mainly actors plus a few politicians—wore a uniform of blue coat and buff waistcoat with brass buttons. The buttons bore the symbol of the club, a gridiron motif, which was also found on their cuff links. The original gridiron, on which the steaks had been cooked, had been rescued from the ashes of the Covent Garden fire.

The steaks were served on hot pewter plates, together with baked potatoes and onions. Porter and port were served, as was toasted cheese. Nothing else was offered. After eating, the table—one long table at which all guests sat—was cleared and the evening given over to revelry. After a checkered existence this early Beefsteak Club had finally disbanded in 1867, but the Guv'nor, Mr. Henry Irving, had decided to revive it just a year or so ago. It now met sporadically, usually very late in the evening after a Lyceum performance. Mr. Stoker was an enthusiastic member, and on occasion he had even been instrumental in inviting myself as a guest. As such, it meant that I did not have to wear the blue jacket uniform as all the regular members did. I did, however, always enjoy the excellent steaks served, not to mention the porter.

The day following our adventures in Twickenham, my boss informed me that there was to be a Beefsteak Club that very evening and that he would take me along as his guest. The room was one that had been used for such club meetings for many years, when the original Beefsteak Club was still in existence. It was part of the Lyceum Theatre, though tucked away at the back where it had some privacy. It had its own kitchen, of course, and Mr. Irving's personal cook prepared the meal. A number of close friends of the Guv'nor were there, though I knew few of them. I did recognize—how could I not?—the prime minister, Mr. Gladstone, a close friend and admirer of Mr. Irving's. The Beefsteak Club was an all-male preserve, so Miss Terry did not join us.

After a most enjoyable meal, well lubricated with both porter and an excellent port, I sat back to see what might be the occasion of this gathering. The Guv'nor was there, of course, as was Mr. Stoker. Also present were Mr. Edwin Booth and Colonel Cornell, Sergeant Bellamy and even Inspector Gulley from the Thames Valley Police. I recognized one or two of the theatre critics, including Mr. Matthew Burgundy of the *Times* and Mr. Horatio Fitzwilliams of the *Era*.

"Perhaps you would be kind enough, Abraham, to run over the events of the past few days, for the benefit of those of us who have not yet been privy to all of the details?" The

Guv'nor sat back and blew smoke from his cigar toward the ceiling, as he smiled at Mr. Stoker.

"Of course, Henry, of course." My boss did not get to his feet, such was the relaxed atmosphere after the repast, and blew his own cigar smoke to the rafters. "And there I think it might be beneficial to go all the way back to the days following your poisoning?"

There was a murmur around the table, from those who were not conversant with all the many little incidents of which I had been a part. Mr. Stoker then started the history, from the apparent death of Peter Richland through to our discovery of the abduction of young Edward. I noticed that he omitted reference to some few details, such as our digging up the Richland coffin and also the Voudon ceremony beneath the Lyceum stage. In the course of the relating, he did have me fill in many of the details and recapitulate on my own abduction and consequent escape from the house in Twickenham.

"So you were able to return the young boy to his mother," said Booth, raising his wineglass to Mr. Stoker as my boss finished the story. "My congratulations."

Stoker waved away the praise.

"And all this led to your rushing out to Middlesex County and the unmasking of the villain," said the Guv'nor. "How did it go from there?"

"The death of Mr. Richland was unfortunate," said my boss. "As was the escape of Mr. Ogoon." He took a long, ruminative draw on his cigar. "I would have liked to have seen both of them brought to justice."

"But you did bring back one of the main instigators, as I understand it?" said the colonel.

"Yes. In fact our good friend Inspector Gulley, of the Thames Valley Police Force, was instrumental in that." Stoker turned to the man. "Would you like to take up the tale there, Inspector?"

Inspector Gulley's face turned red. He was obviously unused to speaking in front of such dignitaries as he saw about him. I think the presence of the prime minister especially unnerved him.

"I—er—well, that is to say . . ." He looked desperately to Sergeant Bellamy, who seemed to me to be totally oblivious to any embarrassment.

"The inspector and his constables did manage to catch and arrest Mr. Ralph Bateman," Bellamy said. "It seems that he and Mr. Herbert Willis were trapped, teetering on the edge of the weir . . . which we must say can be treacherous at this time of year, with ice covering the rocks. Mr. Willis in point of fact did slip and fall into the freezing water, and we were unable to rescue him. He succumbed to the elements, you might say."

"Good Lord," murmured Mr. Gladstone.

I was myself ambivalent about Willis's death. He was a nasty, scheming character, yet I didn't feel that he was as close to pure evil as was Mr. Ogoon. Willis had possessed some redeeming qualities, I thought, though I couldn't for the moment think what they were.

"What became of this Ogoon?" asked Mr. Booth.

My boss answered, "It is my belief that he is now already on board a ship steaming for his island home. And good riddance to him."

"What exactly was his part in all of this?" asked the prime minister.

"Ah!" Mr. Stoker paused long enough to pour himself another glass of port. I suspected that he was playing for time to decide just how much of Ogoon's involvement he should share.

"We do not know the exact involvement of that individual," he said, eventually. "He was close to Mr. Bateman, who had been instrumental in bringing him to these shores from his native Republic of Haiti."

"But you don't know exactly why he was here?" The colonel looked darkly through his cigar smoke at my boss. His monocle gleamed, catching the light from the fireplace where a comfortable fire blazed.

"Exactly? No."

I felt uneasy when I remembered Ogoon's probable involvement in the death of old Mr. Turnbull, though I had to admit that we never had any hard evidence that was the case. And I had a strange feeling that in fact we had not seen the last of Mr. Ogoon. I hoped that I was wrong.

"What will Mr. Bateman be charged with?" asked the Guv'nor.

"We think we can come up with a number of things," replied Bellamy. "Accomplice to murder for starters, attempted murder for another, kidnapping, attempted poisoning, and so on and so forth, sir."

"It seems obvious, looking back, that it was Richland who was responsible for the attempt on your life, Henry," said my boss. "He bamboozled our dear departed Mr. Turnbull at a time when he was most vulnerable, balancing a tray as he entered your dressing room. Almost certainly he introduced the poison into your hot lemonade at that time."

"Of course, Bateman pleads that he was only following the orders of your Mr. Richland." Inspector Gulley had found his voice at last. "Richland, by Mr. Bateman's account, was the ringleader all along."

"Peter Richland seemed such a quiet man," I said. "Unhappy, I grant you. Dissatisfied with his lot, but I would never have thought him capable of violence. And certainly not infamy of such magnitude."

"You can't tell a book by its cover," said Stoker, waving his cigar in the air. "And as for Ralph Bateman, as my old granny used to say, *An té a luíonn le gagharaibh éireoidh le dearnaithibh.*"

Bellamy almost dropped his cigar. "Lor', sir, but that sounds almost heathen, begging your pardon, sir."

"Far from it," responded Stoker. "My old granny was more Catholic than the pope. It simply means 'if you lie down with dogs, you'll rise with fleas.' Most apt for our Mr. Bateman, I think."

"So Richland was the mastermind, as it were," I said. "Then Ralph Bateman recruited people like Charlie Vickers and Herbert Willis to carry out their various plots against the Lyceum."

"Mr. Richland must have been very bitter," observed Mr. Gladstone.

"It seems he saw himself as an outstanding actor held back only by myself," said the Guv'nor. "If I had only had the decency to be sick, or literally break a leg, thus allowing my understudy to tread the boards, then the public would have acknowledged Mr. Peter Richland as the new star in the firmament. Richland would have gone on to fame and fortune . . . at least in his own eyes."

"And those of his mother, I do believe," I said.

Stoker nodded. "Indeed. One can but wonder just what part she may have played in all of this. Mothers can be surprisingly forceful, especially concerning their offspring treading the boards in front of the footlights."

"She claims ignorance of everything," said Inspector Gulley. "I questioned her myself."

"As did I her neighbors and the local tradespeople," said Stoker. "It would seem she had a reputation among the latter as a tough person to deal with, not easy to get her to pay her bills."

"Was she in financial difficulties?" asked Mr. Booth.

"She should not have been," said the prime minister. "I knew something of her late husband Henry Richland. He died two years ago, apparently of a heart attack. He was far from poor."

"He was the lady's second husband," said the inspector,

who now seemed to have overcome his earlier reticence. "Interestingly, her first husband died in a boating accident. He, incidentally, was Peter's real father and died when the child was only ten. Both men were quite wealthy."

"So Richland was not Peter's real name," I said. "His stage name, I presume?"

"Yes," agreed Stoker. "His actual father was Timothy Bottomley, but Peter took his mother's second husband's name for the stage."

"Hmm," mused Inspector Gulley. "Two husbands who died in, shall we say, unusual circumstances? I wonder if we—my department, that is—should look more closely at those deaths?"

"We wonder what she's done with the money if they both were, as you say, well-to-do," pondered Sergeant Bellamy. "The Twickenham house looks rather seedy and neglected."

The answer to this last question—at least in part—did not come until two days later, when we joined Sergeant Bellamy at the C Division station house. Stoker and I were greeted by the sour-faced policeman.

"What is it?" asked Stoker.

"There is no prisoner to be questioned at this time."

"What do you mean?"

Bellamy shrugged. "It would seem that Mrs. Richland still has influence, or money to buy it. Your Mr. Ralph Bateman has been granted bail through the actions of none other than Sir Mortimer Dugdale, Q.C."

"Dugdale?" cried Stoker. "She must indeed have money. He does not come cheaply."

"So does this mean we can't question him about his actions and those of Richland?" I asked, annoyed and angry at this turn of events.

"I'm afraid so. At least not until his trial," said Stoker.

"No date has yet been fixed for that," added Bellamy, gloomily.

"Damnation!"

I had lost count of the number of times recently that my boss had sworn.

"But why would Mrs. Richland pay for Ralph's defense?" I asked.

"Good question, Harry. My guess is that there was far more to the Peter Richland and Ralph Bateman relationship than is obvious on the surface. Either that or she feels she somehow owes something to Bateman."

We once again went over all that we knew, and then my boss and I returned to the theatre.

"When we first encountered Richland, at the top of the stairs in the Twickenham house, you didn't seem too surprised," I said. "In fact you said, 'I knew it.' Might I ask what you meant by that, sir?"

"It was the undergarments, Harry."

"I beg your pardon?"

"The undergarments. The headless body that turned up at the rag-and-bone merchant's, and that we now know belonged to the unknown gentleman sacrificed by Richland, wore silk undergarments. Richland himself, as you found when you searched his room, wore linen. I had the feeling that we might have been dealing with two different people."

"Ah!" I nodded. I thought for a moment. "Who do you think this 'unknown gentleman' was? Has nobody missed him?"

"Another good question." The big man rubbed his eyes. He looked tired, I thought. "It seems that Sergeant Bellamy is onto that, enquiring as to any missing persons. It's possible, if not probable, that the man was visiting London from out of town. It could take quite a while to identify him."

"Another thing." I felt that this was a good time to pick my boss's brains on everything to do with the events of the past few weeks. He was a wealth of knowledge and most adept at putting two and two together. The benefits of a college education, I presumed. "Why separate the head from the body?" I asked.

Stoker gave one of his sighs. "My guess is that, having made use of the corpse to make us think that Richland really had died, he simply decided to make further use of it to undermine the Lyceum production he could never be a part of. I'm sure he hoped that by having a severed head pop out of the scenery, he would frighten the audience into leaving the theatre."

"Ah yes. Well, happily, the Lyceum audience is hardier and more loyal than that," I said.

My boss gave another of his long sighs. "Take the opportunity to get some rest, Harry. It won't be long now before we are deep into rehearsing for *Othello* and working our perhaps dubious charm on the two Americans, Mr. Edwin Booth and the redoubtable Colonel Wilberforce Cornell."

"I really look forward to that!" I muttered.

It seemed that the trial of Mr. Ralph Bateman would not take place in the immediate future. Sir Mortimer Dugdale was a very formidable lawyer, yet our Sergeant Bellamy could be equally tenacious. He was determined to see justice done, yet the Queen's Counsel definitely had the upper hand. We all needed to be patient. I was far more concerned over the fate of Mr. Ogoon. Had he indeed fled the British Isles? Was he truly en route to his native Haiti? Mr. Stoker assured me that he believed that to be the case, and I tried to accept it, yet I still had nightmares in which I was the principle participant in a Voudon ritual!

It was in the morning, two days later, that my boss suggested I go home and change into my best clothes. He was mysterious about why I should do this, but I dutifully complied and returned to the theatre. There he further suggested that I instruct Sam Green to take over my stage manager duties for the afternoon matinee. This I also did. Then Mr. Stoker broke the news that Mr. Irving had agreed to invite his household staff to a theatre performance at the Lyceum. I was thrilled.

Mr. and Mrs. Cooke, young Timmy, Jenny, Susan, and Betsy arrived in a four-wheeler, all dressed in their Sunday best. Jenny, to my eyes, stood out from both of the other maids. Mr. Stoker was already familiar with everyone, since he was a frequent visitor to Mr. Irving's residence, but I made a point of introducing Jenny to him.

"Mr. Stoker, permit me to present to you Miss Jenny Cartwright."

"Delighted, Miss Cartwright," said my boss. "I understand that we are beholden to you in the matter of certain correspondence."

Jenny looked at me, her eyes wide.

"The letters," I muttered.

"Oh yes. Yes, sir. Of course. It was my pleasure, sir," she said, bobbing a curtsey.

"Nonetheless, our thanks. And if I may be so bold, I believe young Harry here to be extremely fortunate to have made the acquaintance of a young lady such as yourself."

Jenny's face turned red and she looked down at her feet. For myself, I was brimming over with happiness. I offered my arm, which Jenny quickly took, and we all moved off into the theatre.

Shortly thereafter we were all seated in the Royal Box, on the gilt chairs with velvet upholstery on seat and back. I was at one end. Beside me, her eyes wide as she looked all about her, sat Jenny. We awaited the start of *Hamlet*. Mr. and Mrs. Henry Cooke sat in the center of the box with the other two maids and young Timmy on their far side. I looked over the front of the box, down at the pit and the stalls below me and then up at the tiers rising above. It was another full house. The Lyceum was back to normal.

As the house lights dimmed and the curtain rose on the scene "A Platform before Elsinore Castle," Jenny leaned across and kissed me on the cheek. I was very happy.